Winds of Amicita

Winds of Amicita

By

J.E. Klimov

HOLLISTON, MASSACHUSETTS

Cover Art by Jeni Hudson.

First printing November 2022
10 9 8 7 6 5 4 3 2 1

ISBN (Trade Paperback) # 978-1-60975-305-4
ISBN (eBook) # 978-1-60975-306-1
LCCN # 2022948170

Silver Leaf Books, LLC
P.O. Box 6460
Holliston, MA 01746

Visit our web site at www.SilverLeafBooks.com

Acknowledgements

I would like to thank Silver Leaf Books for continued support with my writing. I also would like to thank Ursuline Academy, a place that provided me with a positive environment where most of my creative ideas were born.

For all aspiring content creators,
including my son, Nikolai.
Never give up.

Winds of Amicita

Prologue

Sand and flecks of rust swirled together in the tepid breeze, threatening to dispel the boy's new form. He glanced down at his hands, warped by shadow. Anxiety pooled deep within his chest as he inhaled deeply. Although he had harnessed his powers before, the boy always wondered if there'd be a day he couldn't return to his corporeal form. It had happened once before to an ancestor of his. So he was told. The boy could never tell whether his uncle was joking or not.

What then?

The pressure to execute his mission weighed on his shoulders like an anchor. The boy weaved between the skeletal remains of buildings, ignoring the bolts and screws that rolled around the ground as he sped into a jog. He knew that if any of the towering giants collapsed, he wouldn't get hurt. The boy was, indeed, a shadow.

But it didn't make him feel any less invincible.

It was a hollow sensation, like he could vanish into the wind at any moment's notice. Swallowing his fear, the boy approached a two-story temple comprised of granite. He stepped onto the veranda and surveyed his surroundings. Toppled chairs, shattered windows, and a door hanging from its last hinge. Nothing out of the ordinary.

The boy told himself it *had* to be here. He spent hours either skipping a good night's sleep or hiding himself from the others during the day in order to transition the shadow plane and search the island. It was a near impossible task, but he had to succeed.

Placing a hand on the doorframe, the boy poured his focus into altering his shape to slide indoors in one fluid motion. He melded into its shadow, ignoring the uncomfortable tingling that swarmed his body, and rose from the floor. The boy stilled, taking a moment to steady his haggard breath. Each time he flexed his powers, it exacted a sizeable piece of his energy.

Clay pots and candlewax covered the room like a splatter painting. Everything was laden in an inch-long coat of dust, except for the ground. The boy knelt, studying footprints that led toward the back. Cursing loudly, he stretched his body to connect to the altar's shadow. After springing toward the end of the room, the boy circled the altar and felt around beneath the moth-eaten cloth.

Nothing.

The boy clenched his jaw. He climbed the stairs, picking up the pace. If he ran out of energy, he'd awaken back into his body—and there was no time for a failed search attempt. No one knew where the emerald sliver was kept. There was a possibility of multiple fragments, but the boy was only aware of two: the one he was looking for, and the other… well, he didn't care to think about it.

Of course, it had to be this way.

As he arrived on the second floor, the boy noticed a hole in the ceiling. The rounded edges of the twin moons, Adin and Deva, were defined—at least halfway through completing their eclipse. Time was running out. Desperation screamed in the back of his mind. The people he chose to fight this battle weren't ready yet, and perhaps, never will be ready, so he had to find the other emerald fragment. It could be the key to end the threat quickly.

Tearing his gaze from Adin and Deva, the boy continued his search, knocking over crates and vases filled with scrolls. He scoured every corner until he reached a vacant pedestal. Static energy pricked his fingertips. The boy slinked around the pedestal and discovered a shattered glass box on the floor. As he ran his hand over the fragments, the boy sensed a fading energy. His breath hitched, and his mouth ran dry. Despite detecting its presence, the emerald fragment was gone.

CHAPTER

1

14 days until The Luce
Landree

There's nothing quite like the sensation of flight— from the weightlessness that nourishes the body with a taste of freedom to the wind rushing through each strand of hair. Those were the feelings Landree had been chasing for the last five years in her hide-out in the forest, far from her parent's prying eyes. Once she learned to climb trees, Landree secured ropes on the highest boughs and zipped between them with an iron rod meant for stoking fires. That was what she craved.

While she had built her little training camp to prepare for the expedition of a lifetime, she often visited it to escape from the boring dregs of reality as well.

Landree closed her eyes and inhaled deeply. Dust and the scent of leather-bound books filled her lungs, but she pretended she was outdoors, defying gravity once more.

A gong snapped her from her reverie. Its guttural cry reverberated beyond the classroom's tall, narrow windows, sending the seniors of Goldenrod's secondary school into a cascade of enthusiastic chatter. They shoved their parchment scrolls and quills into their backpacks and bottlenecked at the double-doors. Everyone wanted a good spot to watch Mayor Erebus announce the list of students selected for the fifth Luce expedition to Amicita. In the center of the mass of sweat and angst stood Landree. Her chest tightened, emotions ricocheting internally in tandem with the chaos before her. Undoing the ribbon in her chestnut hair, she shook her head to dispel the tension that gripped her skull.

"It's finally growing back. I need to cut it again."

Jane-Marie hooked her arm around Landree's. "Your mother would *love* that."

Landree shot her best friend a sly grin. "It won't matter if I'm selected for the expedition," she replied, successfully masking the quiver in her voice. Although she maintained a relatively cool exterior about this topic, her nerves kept her awake every night for the last few months.

"I can't believe The Luce will appear in a couple weeks. It's like some fantasy tale," Jane-Marie squealed.

Classmates jostled them left and right, moving mindlessly like a herd of cattle. Jane-Marie glared at a blonde whose hair was tied in a bun, squeezing between the two.

Landree tapped a finger against her lips. "That's Amelia, right?" she whispered into her friend's ear.

Nodding, Jane-Marie crossed her arms. Her cerulean

eyes flashed as she studied the blonde from head to toe. "I think so. How does she know where she's going?"

Amelia shuffled amongst the crowd, buried nose-first in a book. Even though her eyes were glued to the pages, she side-stepped students with impressive finesse.

"I envy that." Raising her voice, Landree called out to Amelia. "Hey! What are you reading?"

"Myths and Legends Across the World," she replied, monotone, before vanishing into the crowd.

"Wait, did Ms. Clio assign us a chapter to read?" Jane-Marie asked, color draining from her face.

Landree shook her head and chuckled. "No. Although this wouldn't be the first time you forgot an assignment."

They continued past the classroom exits and through the corridor. Footsteps echoed off the walls. Landree refocused her efforts into passing by a teen boy who was twice her height and weight yet walked at half the speed. The scent of hay filled her nostrils. She wrinkled her nose.

About a quarter of Goldenrod's families owned cattle farms, while Landree's parents managed an inn for travelers. As a child, Landree often complained about the smell that wafted through the streets, but her mother, Rose, would pull her aside and chastise her in a shrill voice. She had said that without those farms, Goldenrod wouldn't have a reliable source of meat. Of course, Landree's favorite meal was lemon and garlic chicken. Landree licked her lips.

"Ugh, I'm so hungry," she exclaimed, throwing her head back.

Jane-Marie turned her neck. A jade pendant lolled

against her silk blouse. "Didn't you just eat lunch?"

Shrugging, Landree said, "I get hungry when I'm nervous."

"Speaking of nerves, I'm still surprised that your parents allowed you to apply for this expedition."

Heat erupted from the back of her neck. Numbness pricked at the edge of her fingertips and traveled up her arms. "About that…".

Jane-Marie released her arm and gasped. "You didn't tell them?"

"I-it's not like I'm going to get chosen anyway!" she retorted, cheeks flushing. "Hundreds of teens applied in this country—thousands if you count transfer students from Irelle and Norlend. The Luce occurs every hundred years. People have been training for this."

"Haven't *you*?" Jane-Marie asked dryly as she cocked a perfectly penciled eyebrow.

"Um, I…" Images of her secret spot immediately popped in the back of her mind. Landree tried, she really did, but it became more challenging over time to fit in training between school and work at the inn. She exaggerated a shrug. "Sort of. It's hard when you're constantly under your parent's thumb. Yours let you attend survival camps in between school breaks."

She shrunk back as Jane-Marie studied her face with pursed lips. It was hard for Landree to believe she also applied. Everything about her best friend was well-manicured, and her mannerisms were more like those in the elite-class— far from the type to trek through unpaved trails without the luxury of bathing. Part of Landree wondered if she simply hated missing out on such a monumental event.

Lifting her hand, Jane-Marie made a snipping motion with two fingers and jabbed at Landree's locks. "I guess that makes sense. It seems like they'd never give you permission in the first place. Like your hair cut, just do it and deal with their wrath later. But in all seriousness, we need to work on your confidence. You're extremely talented, and you and I both deserve a spot."

Both deserve a spot. I highly doubt two kids from the same village or district will be chosen.

Landree shook her head, exorcising the sarcasm from her mind.

Sunlight washed over the duo as they stepped outdoors. Students fanned out as they poured onto a dirt field, often used for sporting events. At the far end stood a stage and podium.

Palm tree fronds waved from each side of the field as a cool breeze danced southbound. Landree stretched her arms into the air and inhaled. Another perfect day. The weather in Camilla was always warm, kissed with humidity in the rainy reason, but the wind always cooled the sweat on its residents.

Situated atop of a massive hill, Goldenrod's southern border boasted views of the ocean. Squinting her eyes, Landree spied a strip of sand in the distance. It certainly wasn't walking distance by any stretch of the imagination, but it was better than nothing.

Landree rarely ventured outside her village, and one major exception was when her family took a week off from work to visit the famous Bleeding Heart beach. Located in the southernmost point of Camilla, it was once a bustling fishing village. After a tidal wave obliterated the homes and drove the residents away, it stood abandoned for many years until Camilla's monarch converted it to a profitable holiday destination.

Caressing the seashells strung across her necklace, Landree recalled wading the shores in search of clams and crabs. As her parents haggled for a reasonable price to stay for the night, she had stumbled upon the most beautiful scalloped shell. Its opalescent inner surface glistened in the light. Who knows how many different types of shells lay on the shores of other islands?

The memory comforted Landree, easing the anxiety that shook her bones. If she got selected for this expedition, she would be able to answer that question in a few short weeks.

In the beginning, the constant fear of inciting her parent's wrath hampered her from indulging in the fantasy. In the last week, Landree's attitude started shifting. She warmed up to the idea of exploring caves and jungles with her best friend in tow. Charting paths on maps and unearthing artifacts tantalized Landree. It drew her in, as if filling a void she never knew she had. While her parents forbade this trip, they surely would have to forgive her after the fact.

Right?

Lights exploded in Landree's eyes as she walked into someone.

"Watch it," a voice growled.

Rubbing her nose and looking up, Landree blinked out a tear. "Sorry, Nick."

Sweeping his ink-black hair to the side, the boy scowled. He wasn't much taller than her, but the boy always held the perfect posture. Never slouching, he proved more intimidating than his peers. "It's Nicholas, not Nick. You don't know me."

Landree blinked rapidly, searching for words that evaporated from her throat. His tone stung like the hornet that found its way into her room last week when she forgot to close the window. Nicholas transferred to Goldenrod from…

Shoot, I can't recall.

Squaring her shoulders, Landree lifted her nose. "You've been in my class for a year."

"So?"

Before she could respond, he turned around and ended the conversation.

Landree's lips parted, completely dumbstruck.

"I think he likes you," Jane-Marie quipped.

"You're kidding, right?" Folding her arms across her chest, Landree fumed. True, she didn't know much about Nicholas other than his one-year tenure at the same school, but it gave him no right to be so rude.

A hush in the crowd expanded as footsteps slowed to a halt. The two girls situated themselves eight-hundred feet from the stage on the left side. Straining her neck, Landree made out Mayor Erebus huddling with her two teachers, Dr. Barnes and Ms. Clio. She found it amusing that Ms. Clio obtained the same level of education as Dr. Barnes, but she didn't request the title change.

Students around her whispered amongst themselves, their features illuminated with excitement. Except Nicholas. He stood even father to the left of the podium, yawning and unfazed by everything.

In her periphery, Landree spotted a gangly boy with straw-colored hair. Grant. She whistled and waggled her finger. Grant was a troublemaker, a rebel, and she was not. Yet despite their polar-opposite personalities, he was another childhood friend, supporting her through the awkward years of adolescence.

He jogged up to her, emerald-eyes shining as he winked. "What's up, pretty lady?"

Jerking her head in the opposite direction, Landree cleared her throat. "See that kid? Have you spoken with him at all?"

He rubbed his cleft chin. "On occasion, but we don't hang out or anything. Nicholas, right? He made it very clear that was his name."

Landree snorted.

"Alls I know is that he sits in the back like I do, but he still pays attention to lectures. Nicholas keeps to himself, which is kinda weird, but I will say he's got a badass piercing."

A black pearl stud protruded from his earlobe. It shimmered with such radiance, as if it generated its own light. Once it caught her eye, Landree couldn't stop staring...until Nicholas turned his head. She sucked in a breath and looked away.

"Hello, students of Goldenrod Village!" a baritone voice boomed.

Landree jumped in place and clutched her chest, cursing herself for getting distracted. Jane-Marie and Grant stood on both sides of her, shaking with laughter as Mayor Erebus situated himself at the podium. A yellow sash draped across his beefy shoulders, stretched to the point of ripping. His protruding belly had expanded since he was elected two summers ago, and yet, his clothes remained the same size. Landree felt embarrassed for the man. Clearly, he demonstrated zero shame.

Dr. Barnes stood to Erebus' left while Ms. Clio stood to his right. Dr. Barnes wore his standard frown, unapologetically observing his students with a look of disapproval from his hawkish nose. Ms. Clio hugged a clipboard, skin paler than usual. She occasionally snuck peeks at Dr. Barnes with restrained envy. When Ms. Clio caught Landree's eye, the village historian gave a quick wave.

Waving back, she couldn't help but wonder how Dr. Barnes had been selected as the expedition's chaperone. Ms. Clio seemed just as qualified and even assisted in updating the official map for the Republic of Camilla. She lived and breathed history and anthropology while Dr. Barnes tinkered with his hydropowered clocks. Plus, she was way more personable.

Erebus dabbed his forehead with a handkerchief and adjusted his collar. "We live in exciting times—our generation has the honor of witnessing the next Luce. Its curtains of light appear on our shores and provides the only way to the island of Amicita. Queen Baneberry has mandated that only the best travel there and take advantage of the month-long opportunity. On top of that, I have incredible news, one that should be announced by someone as prominent as myself, and not scribbled on a piece of paper and posted."

A lively buzz swarmed the crowd. Landree shifted her weight from one foot to another. Her stomach squeezed, threatening to regurgitate her lunch.

Jane-Marie squealed and shimmied. "Someone from Goldenrod *definitely* got picked!"

Why am I terrified? I should be excited!

By now, students formed groups surrounding those that applied. One…two…Too many too count. It should've been no surprise that the number of those striving to make the expedition was significant. Self-doubt gnawed at the tattered fringes of her confidence. As she scanned the crowd, Landree spotted Amelia hugging her book against her chest and circling in place. The backs of her peers faced Amelia except for a statuesque red head.

"Hey isn't that, uh…It's the Norlend transfer. Brenna, I think?" Landree asked, raising her voice.

Jane-Marie's lips thinned. "Yeah. Her parents probably sent her here just so she could qualify," she said bitterly.

"We don't know that." Landree fumbled for words. As soon as The Luce had been predicted five years ago, a record number of students from Norlend and Irelle flooded the country. Because it was a phenomenon specific to Camilla, some viewed this as a political threat, a topic she avoided at all costs.

There was something about seeing the two girls standing alone that bothered Landree. She whistled and waved.

"What are you doing?" Jane-Marie hissed. She tilted her head toward a smattering of seniors who stared at them.

She shrugged. "Forming our own clique, I guess."

"Grant and I aren't good enough friends?" Jane-Marie bemoaned, exaggerating a sigh and flopping a hand over her forehead. Her silver bangles on her wrist clacked for added dramatic flair.

"Of course you're good enough. What the heck does that even mean? You're friends with almost everyone." Landree fought the urge to roll her eyes.

"I'm just kidding."

"Keep me out of this," Grant snorted.

"Shut it, guys," she spat as Amelia and Brenna approached.

The two starkly contrasted one another. Amelia was petite, blonde, and tan, while Brenna was built like a warrior—tall, and muscular with fierce eyes.

Landree wiped her clammy hand before extending it to the Norlend native. "I figured we could lose our nerves together."

Brenna's brow relaxed and the edges of her lips twitched. "You shared some garlic bread when some first-years sent my lunch flying. You also work at Camilla Viewpoint Inn. Landree, correct?"

"Guilty," she answered. Memories flickered in her mind like a dying candlelight. "Oh, yes! Those boys were jerks."

An awkward pause expanded between the group. Landree shifted her left foot backward until she nudged Jane -Marie.

"Yes. That wasn't right," she blurted.

Landree turned to Grant who was already shaking her hand. He bowed his head to kiss it, but Brenna jerked it away, lip curling.

"We don't do that where I'm from," Brenna said curtly.

Landree stared at Grant incredulously. The gesture wasn't unheard of, but it certainly was odd for him. Brenna didn't seem like his type—she stood at around his height and wore no make-up or jewelry. She was no waif.

"Sorry. Just trying to make a good impression," he replied, puffing his chest.

Landree chewed on her nails, laughing nervously. "We can always kick him out of our circle."

"Look! Who's that?" Amelia piped up, drawing everyone's attention back to the stage.

A beast of a man emerged from behind the trio of adults. Towering over Erebus, the man clasped his hands together in front of him with white-knuckled intensity. His peppery beard stretched across his scowl, trimmed without a hair out of place. Embroidered wildflowers decorated his shoulder caps, one representing each district. Thin, copper chains dangled from the decor, indicating some form of military position. A glistening broadsword sat on his hip. Behind his weathered eyes displayed...boredom.

"Not sure." Landree's breath was shallow. Her heart hammered in her chest. All other thoughts vanished—

nothing else mattered. Was the mayor going to utter her name?

Erebus continued to boom, his voice just as loud as the silent man's uniform.

"Goldenrod Village has always slept beneath the shadow of other much larger towns, despite the fact we produce the majority of this countries' meat, leather, and linen. One could say we're responsible for dressing this nation," Erebus rambled, tugging at the lapels of his overcoat.

Audible groans rose from the crowd. Even Ms. Clio was caught mouthing, "Just get on with it, already." Dr. Barnes played with the stray hairs of his comb-over, while the stranger approached the mayor. He tapped on Erebus' shoulder and handed him a scroll.

"Yes, sorry. Everyone, this is Colonel Thamni. He was hand-chosen by Queen Baneberry to lead the expedition, and what a fine fellow he—"

The colonel cleared his throat and gestured to the scroll. Mayor Erebus flushed, muttered an apology, and unfurled the parchment. "Let's see here. The Republic is committed to the research behind The Luce and Amicita for the better-ment of its people. While citizens from Irelle and Norlend aren't excluded from participating in the fifth expedition, all knowledge reaped from the exploration is first and foremost meant to serve the best interest of the Republic. The expedi-tion's missions are to map out the geography, secure a relia-ble route to and from the island, document significant histor-ical findings, and...return with artifacts that require further study which includes, but is not limited to, precious gems.

Phew, that was a mouthful!" He turned to Thamni and chuckled, only to be met with a stony glare.

"C'mon," Landree muttered.

"I see that everyone is eager for the announcement, so let's get on with it. All six volunteers selected for The Luce expedition to Amicita come from Goldenrod!"

Gasps, shouts, and cheers blended into a cacophonous uproar. Many students stomped the ground, *whooping* in celebration, and kicking up plumes of dirt.

"No way. This had to be rigged," one student said.

"Who care if it's rigged if it's our village!" exclaimed another.

The announcement sucked the air from Landree's lungs. She locked eyes with Jane-Marie, both their mouths hanging agape. Grant laughed.

"That's impossible," he blurted.

She exchanged glances with the rest of her group. "So, all students *and* the chaperone are from here?"

Pushing her glasses up the bridge of her nose, Amelia flipped through her book. "Never in Camilla's history has this occurred before. In fact, the last time someone represented Goldenrod was—"

"Never," Nicholas said in a matter-of-fact tone, appearing by Landree's side like a shadow. His black pearl stud earring shimmered in the sun.

Landree nearly jumped out of her skin. Nicholas yawned, ignoring her death stare. "And this doesn't surprise you?" she asked through gritted teeth.

"Shh. He's about to announce the names. You wouldn't

want to miss yours," he drawled.

Heat rushed to her cheeks. "N-no. I don't stand a chance against all the other candidates." When he turned his attention back to the stage, she leaned toward Jane-Marie and whispered, "Who does he think he is?"

Before Jane-Marie could share her theory, Erebus waved his arms in the air.

"Quiet, please. It's time!" Erebus plucked a palm-sized scroll from his breast pocket. He lifted an eyeglass to his left eye, then unfurled the parchment.

Each passing second seemed to drag on longer than the last. Jane-Marie wove her fingers in between Landree's and squeezed. She squeezed back. Everyone waited on bated breath. The only sound that could be heard was the rush of water pressing against the school's waterwheel.

"The first citizen selected is Grant Aster."

Landree's stomach hit the ground. Incredulous shouting pierced through the undulating whispers that ebbed and flowed throughout the field. The conversations surrounding her wormed their way into her ears as undistinguishable white-noise.

How did the laziest kid in the school get selected?

She turned to find Grant just as floored as she was. He slapped his palm against his forehead as his eyes bulged.

Words accumulated in the back of her throat like sludge. "I didn't even know you applied."

"I submitted it last minute…as a joke," he replied, voice cracking. "That wet blanket Nicholas dared me to."

"*Why*? That's so stupid—"

Mayor Erebus cut through the noise. "Next: Amelia Lightheart, followed by Jane-Marie Perch."

Landree winced at the crushing pressure of her best friend's squeeze. Her senses overloaded—both excitement and jealousy collided in her ribcage. Amelia had worked her way to the top of the class, so that made sense, but as much as she loved her best friend, she didn't know what Jane-Marie had over her. For years, Landree chopped wood, hunted, and practiced rappelling off large boulders in the forest—all a means to build her strength and survival skills to compensate for lack of book smarts. Her cold sweat returned as her breathing grew labored.

"...Brenna... Um. Brenna Coil...coilia—"

"Brenna Coilean," the Norlender corrected.

More words tossed around the crowd. The most common one, "foreigner". However, Brenna still stood proudly, facing Erebus, whose blanched face came to no surprise to Landree. She wanted to congratulate Brenna, but her head spun.

There were two more names left. Landree rubbed her eyes and tried to focus. Her tongue clung to the roof of her mouth. Suddenly, she felt thirsty. Hot. Suffocating. Like she should just dive into the river instead of finding out who the last chosen ones were.

"Nicholas Yamanu."

Nicholas tilted his head slightly. He smirked.

What was I thinking? That my stupid little 'training camp' was going to qualify me?

"And finally, Landree Larksbur."

A mixture of excitement and dread forked through Landree. Her surroundings blurred in swirls of color. She couldn't make out what anyone was saying to her. Multiple hands patted her back.

"W-what?" she blurted.

Her thoughts careened out of control as other students pushed her forward. Erebus said something, but all her senses were distorted by shock.

"There she is," Erebus barked. "Now that all the names have been called, I welcome them to approach the stage."

Blinking rapidly, she realized her fellow students ushered her onto the platform, and she now stood wedged between Grant and Nicholas.

Jane-Marie paraded to the end of the line, waving and blowing kisses into the crowd. Brenna continued to stare ahead, completely stoic. Landree groaned and pressed her palm against her forehead.

What are my parents going to say?

Mayor Erebus clapped his hands slowly, lifting his hands to encourage the crowd. A sea of applause rose steadily, to the point where it was deafening.

"Let's hear it for the 5th expedition team! May they bring glory to the Republic!"

CHAPTER

2

The throwing knife lodged itself into the canvas target with a satisfying thud. Swallows scattered from the brambles nearby. Landree sniffed as she jogged toward the center of her secret hide-away. It really was the perfect spot: shielded by thick oak trees, vines, boulders, and a steep hill. Fiddle-head ferns danced with the wildflowers that peppered the dirt patch. She always took care not to step on any.

Landree's lips twisted into a frown as she wrenched the knife free—her aim was all over the place.

I can't focus.

Backing up for another round, Landree tried to ignore her trembling hands. Her thumb grazed the cool leather handle as she raised her arm. It was a handy practice tool. A patron had left it behind many years ago, and she pocketed it when wiping the table down.

Squinting her eyes, she honed in on the target's red dot. The bull's eye seemed to blur and split in two as her attention waned in and out. She shouted in frustration and hurled the throwing knife, sending it flying in a wide arc, over-shooting the target by five feet.

Landree plopped onto the ground and hung her head. It had been an hour since Mayor Erebus announced the six student volunteers for The Luce expedition to Amicita—and they were all from Goldenrod Village. Instead of excitement and a sense of accomplishment, all she experienced was shock and disbelief. So much so that once the mayor finished his speech, Landree raced to the woods without another word. Jane-Marie and Grant yelled after her, but her legs wouldn't stop.

"I should feel happy. Proud," she croaked.

Birds chirped above in reply. A pair of squirrels tumbled to her left, fighting over a nut. This was her peaceful place. Lifting her chin, Landree calculated that she had less than an hour until sunset. Less than an hour to face her parents. She grimaced. They forbade her to apply for the expedition, citing it was a colossal waste of time—and dangerous to boot. Yet, she did so anyway.

It was time to clean up. Landree stood and dusted her slacks. As she tucked the target underneath a network of overgrown roots, she mulled over the fateful day. Fresh from her parent's lecture, Landree had told them she was going to a study group. Instead, she met with Ms. Clio and requested an application. Landree flinched at the memory—she forged her mother's signature and beefed up her resume.

Yes, I had some training. Just…mostly self-taught.

Cleaning her throwing knife with a rag, Landree clicked

her tongue. What had she expected? Of course she always wanted to be chosen. In the last five-hundred years, The Luce allowed people to travel to this mysterious island four times, and they only scratched the surface. Amicita was still full of secrets, ripe for discovery.

As she holstered her throwing knife, Landree gazed endearingly at the ropes tied between the treetops.

Freedom.

It was the idea of freedom and exploration that compelled her the most. Filling out that application seemed to placate her desires, and every night since then, Landree reassured herself that she would likely not be chosen, so no harm done.

The orange and purple glow of dusk filtered through the leaves. Landree snapped from her thoughts and sprinted east. Her heart hammered in her ribcage, sending blood rushing through her ears to the point she could barely hear her own thoughts. It was time to face her parents.

The pungent scent of pickled garlic burst from its flesh as Landree sliced through a clove. She wiped her nose with her sleeve, peeking over her shoulder at Rose. Her mother scuttled in and out of the kitchen with pitchers of wine. She hadn't said much to Landree since she returned home—just to prep for the dinner rush, and her father was seeing to a snake that made its way to a guest's room. Landree had insisted speaking with them privately but was told "later".

Anxiety circled her head like a gnat. Goldenrod was a small village, and while the inn catered mostly to travelers, the last thing she wanted was someone else spilling the news to them.

Ouch!

Blood leaked from her finger in ruby droplets onto the cutting board. Landree sucked on her finger as she raced toward a wash bucket.

"Can't you pay attention instead of daydreaming?" Rose squawked as she appeared by her side with a clean rag.

Landree chewed on her lip silently.

"Really. You've helped your father skin boar and deer many times, and yet you hurt yourself with the simplest tasks. Can you imagine if you were part of The Luce expedition? You'd die on the first day!"

An unbearable heat flushed through her body. Landree couldn't wait any longer. The conversation would be unpleasant no matter what.

After applying pressure, Rose secured some gauze around Landree's wound. She remained on her knees and blinked through her auburn bangs. Creases formed around her eyes. "Maybe that's what you're upset about. A customer just now told me they announced the results, and every student selected was from this village. You must feel extra frustrated because of that."

As Rose stood, Landree grasped onto her mother's grease -stained sleeve. "I need to talk to you and father. Together. Now," she choked out. Her eyes stung as she forced tears back.

They're going to disown me! And forget about actually going.

Rose scoffed and pulled her arm away. "We're still in the dinner rush. It'll have to wait."

"No, mother. It must be now!" she exclaimed, rocketing to her feet.

"Fine, then." Huffing, Rose lifted the hem of her dress as she sped through the double-doors.

Laughter erupted from the dining hall. Jovial voices exchanged tales of adventures over food and drink. This inn was a stop in their journey. Staring at her feet, Landree could only think of how trapped she felt. Her parents undoubtedly would want her to run the place when they grew old—not just cook and clean, but to manage the business as well. It wasn't the worst fate, but Landree wanted to experience more before she was permanently bound to her family duty.

What am I going to say? How am I going to say it?

Rose returned with Spear. Their features were pinched in irritation. Her father's hands and apron were soaked in blood.

"What do you need to say that's so urgent? I have a dead animal outdoors that's decaying as we speak," he snapped. Known around the village as Spear, he always lived up to his nickname. Tough and quick-witted, Spear applied his life principles to parenting.

A lump formed in Landree's throat. Her heart raced, just like when she stood on stage. She clenched her hands and released. "The student volunteers for the expedition were announced," she squeaked.

"That's it?" Spear asked, tapping his boot. Caked mud crumbled onto the floor, earning a look of disapproval from Rose.

Folding her hands behind her back, Landree rocked on her feet. "Do you know who were chosen?"

"They may as well be nameless. Queen Baneberry is out of her mind trying to sell the idea of teens aiding the exploration of an island. That's way too risky for our youth," he spat.

Rose nodded, wringing a napkin in her hands.

She couldn't utter another word. All Landree could do was lift her hand.

Another round of uproarious laughter leaked from the dining room, filling the void of silence between Landree and her parents.

"How could you possibly apply without our consent?" Spear scoffed.

Shame lanced through Landree's body. When she opened her mouth, no words came out.

In a beat, Spear blanched, and his hazel eyes widened. "You...forged our signature, didn't you?" His voice rose steadily, deep and unwavering. "You're only fifteen. You're not capable of making decisions on your own, and now you've volunteered your life up. You're going to die out there!" Spit flew from him mouth as he slammed a fist against a counter, leaving a bloody imprint.

Rose knitted her eyebrows but remained silent.

Landree stepped backward until she hit the wall. Her lips trembled. At most, the expedition was simply a pipe dream—the thrill of filling out the application alone filled her with excitement, much like when she cut her hair short. "I-I wasn't serious about it—"

"Your father's right. You should have gotten our permission," Rose interjected. Venom filled every syllable.

"But you would never say yes."

"Because it's a foolish idea! There's a reason why the government asked for secondary school–aged children. They're strong and dumb." Spear rubbed his hairless scalp as he turned away from his family.

The words slammed into Landree's chest like a battering ram. In one fell swoop, Spear cut her down, reducing her to the Neanderthal he assumed all teenagers were. And yet, instead of allowing herself to be completely swept away in self-doubt, a part of Landree refused to budge.

I have to prove my parents wrong.

Frustration and defiance surged in her veins, but she knew there was only one way to defuse the situation. Averting her eyes, Landree steadied her breath. "I'm sorry,"

Rose lifted her hands and sighed. "I don't know what to do with you."

"Not another word," Spear thundered. "You're not going, and that's final! You're excused for the kitchen. Now go to your room and do your homework."

Landree shuffled past her parents, pausing briefly to courtesy. Met with silence and disapproving faces, she pushed through the double doors and waded through the crowd. Everything blended together in shades of brown as tears welled in her eyes.

"Ungrateful! We raised her so she can leave the family business to dig up rocks in a foreign country?" Spear's baritone voice boomed from the kitchen.

Landree picked up the pace.

"She should be focusing on her studies, and now she'll fall behind!" Rose shrilled.

Their voices faded as she broke into a sprint, not stopping once until she reached her room.

When she locked the door behind her, Landree leapt onto her bed and buried her face into the pillow to smother her sobbing. Every quip from her parents felt like a dagger to her heart. Her parents always painted the picture of her future, as if Landree had no say. Their expectations were sky-high and yet took every shot at her confidence.

Landree never admitted it to her parents, but her heart rejected the idea of managing the inn. She wasn't sure exactly what she wanted to do, but she knew what she didn't want. Perhaps that's what drew Landree to Amicita. It wasn't just because Jane-Marie wanted her to. Amicita was Landree's ticket, even if temporary, out of the inn. It was a chance for Landree to grow and develop on her own. If she was lucky enough, she may even find her purpose on this journey.

After brushing a stray tear from her eye, Landree shifted over her bed and reached under the mattress. A wad of parchment sat wedged between the floor and the bed. After she unfolded the paper, she smoothing it lovingly. Nostalgia filled her veins. Landree stared at a map of Camilla.

It was Ms. Clio's. Once she received an updated copy,

she had offered it up to anyone in her class. Landree chuckled. Amelia hadn't moved to Goldenrod at that time, but if she had, she may've beat her to the punch. Although Landree wasn't the most bookish, maps fascinated her. The intricate lines and shading made it a work of art. Moreover, it represented adventure, a potential story worth unfolding on this singular piece of parchment.

Every village and district was accounted for, but Landree's curiosity expanded beyond Camilla's borders. Cross-hatched lines represented the sea, encompassing the entire island. According to Ms. Clio, the Republic of Camilla stretched 300 miles in all directions. Landree traced her finger from the northern most port— a bustling international trading post that never slept, around the rocky west coast, and stopped at Arrowhead Point. The ink faded over the years thanks to Landree's fascination of The Luce. Her thoughts drifted back to Amicita. Its map has yet to be completed.

Both the Queen's scientific and religious advisor had agreed, for the first time in their lifetime, on the date of the next Luce: right in the middle of the dry season. Landree rolled onto her back and clutched the map to her chest. Two weeks away.

A pebble pelted her window. Landree dropped the map and jolted upright. Another small rock smacked the window. Peeking outside, she spotted Jane-Marie waving from behind a pile of burlap sacks. Landree lifted a finger to her lips then tip-toed across her room. She pressed her ear against the door and heard no signs of her parents. Tickled with excitement and worry, she flew back toward the window and opened it gingerly.

It creaked.

Landree held her breath. If her parents ever found her sneaking out, she'd be done for. Not that Landree snuck out much, and if she did, it was to chat with Jane-Marie and munch on sweets.

She hopped out of the window, paused, and sighed with relief. Hugging herself, Landree approached her friend, who was picking at a hole in one of the burlap sacks.

"Mm, what are these?" Jane-Marie asked.

"Those are dried fruit and nuts for the guests," Landree said, smacking her best friend's hand. "Stop it!"

"Oh, like they'd miss a handful! If anything, they'd think it was a mouse."

Landree cracked a half-smile. "What's up?"

"I heard the shouting." Jane-Marie tilted her heads toward a stone path. "Let's walk."

"Have you been eavesdropping?" Landree hissed, breaking into a light jog to keep up.

Jane-Marie shrugged. "I knew that your parents weren't going to be happy about the news. Someone's gotta look out for you."

"Yeah, well, they'll get over it—"

Jane-Marie patted her on the back. "That's the spirit."

"No." Landree stopped. A cool breeze whistled between the two. "I'm not going."

"What do you mean?" asked Jane-Marie, eyes widening.

Landree dropped her gaze and traced a circle in the dirt

with her foot. Regret welled in her chest. "I'm just not," she finally replied.

Furious with herself, Landree jammed her hands into her pockets. Until now, she always allowed her life to be dictated by her parents or peers. Sure, she was still young, but she felt her parents stifled her ability to thrive. She was always terrified to commit to a decision, unless approved by Rose and Spear.

She wouldn't understand.

Jane-Marie talked back to her parents all the time, but if Landree did that, she'd likely be grounded until she was thirty.

Frogs croaked and crickets chirped. All Landree wanted to do was run home and tear up the map. It was useless to dream.

"You're going." Jane-Marie grasped her hands. "We leave on horseback the day after tomorrow. Stay with your parents, then sneak out the following dawn!"

"I can't do that!" Landree shrieked. "My parents would have a conniption."

Jane-Marie wrapped one arm around her shoulder and dragged her down the winding road. Male voices echoed in the bamboo forest. Landree cast a woeful glance at the schoolhouse in the distance.

"Just think about it. Your parents may prevent you from leaving on the official departure, but once they let their guard down, you're free to leave. Don't think of it as running away. You'll be back, and they'll be forced to forgive you."

Landree grunted.

"The odds of them forgiving you are certainly higher than them granting you permission," Jane-Marie corrected. "Maybe you can bring back some precious gems as a gift to help patch things up."

Chewing on her lip, Landree entertained the idea. Jane-Marie stopped at the edge of the bamboo forest and plucked a lantern from behind a cluster of shoots. She pulled a flint from her pocket and ignited a flame.

"That's your parents only oil lantern," Landree said pointedly.

"Will you just relax?"

As they slipped through the initial line of bamboo, Landree returned to her thoughts. "Even if I met up with you afterward, wouldn't it be a touch suspicious that I showed up to the exploration group unannounced?"

"Just tell them your parents changed their mind. Girl, listen. Unless they invent a mechanism to communicate faster than fowl, you won't be found out until we're well into the passage. There's no turning back from there."

An orange glow snatched Landree's attention. Squeezing her way across another hundred feet, she discovered a path that opened to an alcove. Bamboo surrounded a sizeable boulder that jutted from the soil, forming a circular patch. Grant, Amelia, and Brenna sat in the clearing.

"Oy, look who it is. The wet blanket," Grant blurted, cheeks red as cherries. He sat cross-legged, hugging a pitcher of wine.

Landree turned to Jane-Marie. "Really? You took me

here?"

Her friend shrugged. "We decided to celebrate! Everyone's here. Well, except Nick."

"Nicholas," Landree corrected.

A collective laughter rolled through the group. Landree relaxed her shoulders. Grant held up the pitcher.

Holding up a hand, Landree replied, "I'm fine, thanks."

"Then just sit with us and chat," Brenna said. Her wild, auburn hair resembled fire in the light of the collective lamps. "Honestly, Grant's the only one who's drinking anyway."

"You're that Norlend girl," Jane-Marie chirped as she took a seat among the group.

"I prefer to be called by my name," Brenna replied, eyes narrowing.

"Hey," Landree said, extending her hand.

Brenna gripped it and squeezed. Hard. Landree clenched her jaw as sparks of pain shot up her forearm.

"Come, sit." Grant patted an opening next to him. "You know I was joking."

"I can't stay long." She pinched her nose as the acerbic scent of wine wafted from his breath. Her mind still swam with the events back at the inn—her parents' harsh words... and her growing desire to defy their expectations.

An awkward silence settled on the group like a mist. Grant took a swig of wine and passed it to Brenna. She declined and the pitcher landed in Jane-Marie's lap. Landree hugged her knees into her chest, already calculating when she should return home.

Not that there's much to do there, either.

"Landree says she's not going to Amicita. We need to change her mind," Jane-Marie announced.

She glared at her best friend. "It's not my call."

"But why? It's such an honor," Amelia said. "My older sister is well on her way to becoming a scholar, and this was the only way to top that."

"My parents won't let me go." Shaking her head, Landree steepled her fingers while carefully selecting her words. "I... applied without their permission, so it's my fault."

"Her parents are all work and no play," Grant added, shooting a wink at Brenna.

Ignoring the gesture, Brenna turned to Landree. She absentmindedly rubbed her hands to the fire. "This trip is no vacation, though."

Nodding eagerly, Amelia piped in. "Many would kill for this opportunity. Many people from my country moved to the Republic even before the Luce had been predicted just to have the chance of being there at the right time. You heard Mayor Erebus. It'll be our responsibility to fill in the blanks of the map that the pioneers before us couldn't finish—"

"Document any signs of past civilizations—" added Brenna.

"And confirm its resources," Jane-Marie concluded, pointing at her jade necklace. "We can't forget that. Amicita is rumored to be rich in precious gems, so much so, it could really revitalize the country's economy."

"The world's economy," Brenna said.

Everything they say makes sense, but why can't my parents understand that?

Grant placed the pitcher onto the ground and patted her back. "We're finally entering an age where we're viewed as adults. The last thing I want to see is your life dictated in the same manner as when you were a child."

Nodding, Jane-Marie rested her head on Landree's shoulder. "You were chosen for a reason."

"That's the thing! Why was I chosen? I'm sure there are way better candidates out there."

Brenna cracked her knuckles and gazed at Landree with a solemn smile. "Stop doubting yourself," she said gently.

Those words didn't drag her down like her parents'. Instead, it propped her up, adding a lightness within she hadn't felt in a long time. Gazing from left to right, all Landree could see were warm faces, void of judgment and expectation. Like sipping spring water on a summer's day, she felt reinvigorated. Her self-doubts and fears were far from washed away, but it nourished the voice within.

Maybe I am deserving of this trip. Maybe I should still go.

"I gotta get back," Landree said, jerking her thumb back toward town.

Four pairs of eyes were trained on her.

"And?" Jane-Marie clasped her hands together.

Without another thought, Landree straightened her shoulders and nodded.

The group clapped and whistled. Jane-Marie grabbed her shoulder and shook it wildly. A smile crept onto Landree's lips. A blip of excitement returned and blossomed in her chest.

Making decisions for myself wasn't the end of the world after all.

Landree said her good-byes. Despite the boost in morale, she insisted on walking home alone so she could collect her thoughts. Landree hugged herself, shuddering in the nonexistent breeze. As the sound of her friends faded away, so did her confidence.

Can I really do this?

Landree turned onto the main road. The cobble-stone streets were now vacant, free from oppressive wooden carts and scores of feet pounding away at its surface. The faintest scent of roasted nuts lingered. Flames from the lamp posts cast a warm glow across storefronts, and seashells strung between archways clacked in the breeze.

A swift movement caught Landree's eye. She stopped a block short of her family's inn and leaned back, peeking down the alley she just passed. This archway was adorned with conch shells. A shadow danced against the walls, growing and shrinking in the amber light.

Goldenrod village rarely experienced issues with burglary or violence. If any crime was committed, it was from an outsider—a man or woman that never identified with any town or village. Of course, the benefit of tight-knit communities was that everyone looked out for one another.

And yet, curiosity struck Landree. The village was also known for its sleepy-town status. Moreover, she couldn't identify a body to the shadow. Biting her lip, Landree slipped into the alley.

She continued to chase the shadow, insistent on finding its owner. Landree tripped over a loose stone and clambered against the wall. Her nails scratched the rough, uneven surface. Steadying her breath as a cold sweat broke out, Landree lost chase. Her nostrils flared in frustration.

"Clumsy fool," she muttered.

The air thickened. The temperature plummeted and clung to Landree's skin like a clammy hand. Before she reacted, the feeling dissipated.

"What are you doing here?" A voice snaked into her ear and tickled her ear drum.

Landree nearly jumped out of her own body.

Nicholas appeared by her side.

"I could ask the same about you!" Landree scolded.

Lifting his sculpted chin, Nicholas studied the outline of her face. "Tutoring lesson with Ms. Clio."

Landree narrowed her eyes and crossed her arms. "She offers tutoring?"

"Someone as smart as you wouldn't know about it, so consider that a blessing," Nicholas quipped. He hoisted his backpack and pushed past her. His black pearl earring winked beneath the moonlight.

Nicholas strode confidently through the alley and knocked on a single-level home constructed of clay, stone, and hay. Oak branches tied in neat bunches fanned out to complete the ceiling.

When the door opened, Landree spotted Ms. Clio. Her sallow cheeks looked worse when illuminated by candlelight. She bowed her head and let Nicholas in.

Landree scratched her head. Judging by her stern expression, she'd been expecting him. After chewing on her lip for a moment, she shrugged and turned around. A pompous classmate was the least of her worries.

CHAPTER

3

The Luce: Day Zero

Washing her hands vigorously, Landree scanned the kitchen. The dishes were cleaned, pantry restocked, and the food scraps lay in the bin by the backdoor to feed the neighbor's livestock. After drying her hands, she wiped the sweat from her brow. It was nine o'clock in the evening, and all the inn's patrons had finished their meals and dove into their buckets of ale. Of course, Rose wouldn't allow Landree to handle ale or wine. She chuckled and shook her head. Landree didn't understand what the big deal was.

Rose burst through the double doors. She whipped a cloth tied from her hip and scrubbed the nearest counter. "It's time to start closing the kitchen."

"I'm already done," Landree announced triumphantly.

"Very funny," her mother replied without looking up.

"No, really. I've done everything on the checklist. Can I

go to my room now? I have a reading assignment from Ms. Clio."

Rose knitted her brows and glanced around suspiciously. "Why?"

Heart slamming against her ribcage, Landree studied her mother's face. "It's...my job."

"You never get all your work done without a dozen reminders." Features now contorted in confusion, Rose dropped the cloth onto the floor. "You're not moping around because the expedition left without you?"

Landree tugged at her collar and forced a smile. "Father told them I wasn't allowed to go. They didn't leave me."

"You're dismissed. Study hard then, and go straight to bed after," Rose ordered.

Bowing her head, Landree closed her eyes, relieved. She tried to quell the twinge of guilt within. When she re-opened them, she said, "I will."

I hope you can forgive me.

Avoiding eye contact, she sped past her mother and into the dining area. Men and women laughed in the glow of the candlelit chandelier. She had spent her entire life growing up observing strangers come and go. Where had they come from? What drove them to travel across Camilla? Whenever she had asked her father this, he would tell Landree to go study.

Landree swept past the velvet drapes and ambled down a hallway of rooms. Soon, she was lost in a daydream.

It always started with a valley. Landree would stand at the crest of one hill, overlooking a vast river. Wildflowers bloomed in colors and patterns she'd never witnessed before: some with pink spots on white petals and others producing black berries with yellow stripes. Falcons circled in the sky, searching for mice and rabbits that scampered by her feet.

Each day, her daydream progressed. Slowly making her way down the rolling grass that tickled her knees, Landree felt an urge, a voiceless beckoning, to swim in the river. When she drew near, a fish with rainbow scales leapt from the water and waved its tailfin. A school of minnows swirled downstream like a plume of smoke. Rocks rested on the sandy bed, visible from its crystal-clear surface. Landree extended her hand, longing to connect with the river.

A cold, metal doorknob filled her palm instead.

Landree blinked. She stood in front of her bedroom door, reverie vanishing like steam from tea. It was time to interrupt her flights of fancy and work toward discovering a real-life valley, unmarred by human presence for millennia. Landree glanced over her shoulder. Nerves rattled in her stomach like beans in a tin can. Reassured that neither of her parents followed her, she entered her room and grabbed her satchel.

Taking count of her belongings, doubts crept up her spine. She weighed the consequences of leaving home. It was a lot more serious than cutting her hair. There was no rule or law against that—Rose simply wanted her daughter to have long hair, and Landree paid dearly for simply going against her mother's wishes. She tried to shrug off second-guessing herself, but her worries only screamed louder.

"Flask with water. An extra set of clothing. Throwing

knife. Um. And…and…"

Landree swatted at an invisible fly that circled her head.

"C'mon, girl. Make sure you have everything you need. You won't be back for a while."

Back…

How would her parents react upon her return? If Amicita was as rich in resources as history touted, Landree planned to bring them diamonds, emeralds, and rubies. They'd have to forgive her.

A tattered corner of parchment poked from beneath her mattress. Landree pulled the map out and gingerly placed it into her satchel.

Landree's heart flew up her throat when a firm knock echoed into the room. Before she could reply, Spear flung the door open. Landree's breath hitched. She swore her parents loved to rip her door open as if they hoped to catch her in the act of doing something wrong.

"I was just looking for my book," Landree blurted. "To study."

Spear pulled up a stool with one hand, while the other remained hidden behind his back.

"Of course," he replied.

Heat seared the back of her neck, and her tongue clung to the roof of her mouth. Moving as slowly as possible, Landree slid her satchel out of view. After inhaling deeply, she faced her father. "What do you have behind your back?"

"Nothing special," Spear answered, shifting around in his seat. His softened tone contrasted his square jaw and bushy beard.

A square pastry sat in his palm, still steaming. The sweet tang of mango and red bean mix made Landree's mouth water.

"Is that a Heesu bun?" She clapped her hands together. "I haven't had one in over a year! Wait, isn't that only for special occasions?"

Spear dropped it in her cupped hands. "Right. I, er, you deserve it."

Staring at the bun, Landree's shoulders slumped. Many fond memories were folded into these festive layers of dough and deliciousness. She met her father's gaze, noticing a sheen in his eyes.

"I got it after I met with Erebus about, you know." Spear fumbled with his words.

Landree placed the Heesu bun on the table and wrapped her father in a hug. His shoulders stiffened.

"Thank you," she whispered into her ear. Landree inhaled deeply, memorizing the notes of freshly pressed linen and smoke.

Spear sniffed but replied coolly. "You're welcome."

"And I'm sorry."

He pulled back and looked out the window. "About what?"

Landree bit her lip. "Nothing."

"Well, don't stay up too late studying." Spear strode toward the door. He paused. Without looking back, he added, "I know you'll make us proud."

When the door clicked shut, Landree hung her head and groaned. The still-warm peace offering beckoned her taste buds. She stood, glancing at the Heesu bun, then at her satchel. An uneasy sensation sloshed in her stomach.

It'd feel wrong to eat this and leave.

Guilt wrestled in her veins and rooted her into the ground. Minutes passed as Landree toiled with the decision.

It's not too late to change your mind.

Familiarity and routine tempted her. If she stayed behind, her life would carry on at its typical, boring pace. At the same time, a voice in the depths of her mind cried for freedom and adventure.

I was chosen to go.

After a deep breath, Landree reached past the pastry and grabbed her seashell necklace. After securing it around her neck, she equipped her satchel and crept toward the window.

The cool, evening air kissed her face as Landree slid the window open. She promptly hopped out and took off toward the stable without looking back.

Landree wobbled in place. She strained to keep her eyes open as her mare trotted south. After successfully sneaking her out of the barn, they galloped without pause until the two moons shone directly above. Landree did not protest when her mare began to whinny and slow down.

The two moons, Adin and Deva, overlapped almost perfectly. Over the last year, the moons inched closer each night, amplifying their icy glow. When Queen Scarlett Baneberry's advisors had confirmed the heralding of The Luce, the entire Republic celebrated. In fact, the queen shut down the country for a whole day. Ever since then, when Adin and Deva rose hand in hand like lovers, Landree would gaze up at them in awe. No one understood how the alignment of the two moons had to do with The Luce.

Ms. Clio should've been the chosen chaperone.

Pulling out her map, Landree chewed on her cheek. Reality dragged her down to earth. The thought of reuniting with the excavation team provided the only strength to fight off exhaustion. Even her stomach growled a few times, pulling her thoughts back to her parents.

"We got to be at least be halfway." The challenge was recognizing a narrow path that split from the main trail with only the light from the moons and her lamp. She punished herself mentally for forgetting to bring more oil. Landree had to strike the balance between caution and speed, and she worried if she would make it to Arrowhead in time.

It had been a couple years since Landree traveled beyond her village borders. Other than the one family trip to Bleeding Heart, Landree accompanied her mother to a few business trips to neighboring towns. While she was luckier than most kids in Goldenrod, she couldn't declare herself 'well-traveled'.

Landree clung to her cloak. Without the daytime hustle and bustle of the village market, Landree was left alone with her thoughts, and as the reality of her actions sunk in, her thoughts shouted louder.

"I actually ran away from home. No note, nothing."

Her parents would wake up to find her bed cold and empty. How far would that effect ripple?

"I...made my choice," Landree said, forcing deep breaths. "I'll return with fame and riches, and they'll forgive me."

Not that Landree cared for either, but if that's what could buy their forgiveness, then so be it.

Dirt crunched beneath the rhythmic clopping of hoofs. The ambience of the Camillian forest soon lulled Landree to a state of calm. The mare reared its head and neighed.

"How much slower can we go? I'm sorry, but we can't stop for anything," she cooed and patted its mane.

The mare stopped and pawed the ground, shaking its head.

"What is going on?"

A twig snapped.

Landree's eyes snapped wide open. Her muscles tensed.

Leaves rustled, but there was no wind.

The hairs on the back of her neck stood. Her mare backtracked, whinnied once more.

"Woah, there. Steady."

The mare bucked, sending her crashing onto the ground. The sound of hooves making contact with a body alarmed Landree. The lantern crashed beside her, and the flame snuffed out. However, even without the lamp, two yellow eyes glowed in the darkness. Rolling onto her stomach, Landree spied a silhouette of a creature arching its back.

It lunged at the mare once more, latching onto its hind quarters. The mare bucked and twisted until it managed to slam itself, along with the predator, against a palm tree. The mare bolted into the woods, kicking up clouds of dirt.

Landree's mouth ran dry. The predator pulled itself back onto all fours and growled. Moonlight washed over its muscular frame, revealing a massive wildcat. She felt around for her satchel. Fingers grazing leather, Landree attempted to steady her breath. When her fingers found the hilt of her throwing knife, she inched back onto her feet, never once taking her eyes off the wild cat. It stopped and snarled.

"You must...be...hungry," Landree said, voice barely a whisper.

Standing at full height, she continued to lock gazes with the creature.

The wild cat leapt forward. Landree swallowed her shriek and waved her blade in front of her. "Stay away! Back off!" she yelled as forcefully as possible.

The glint of the blade caught the cat's eye, and it paused once more. Adrenaline flooded Landree's body, illuminating every single panic signal in her brain. Her thighs grew taut, ready to sprint. Despite her body's instinct to run away, her gut grounded her in place. Spear often warned her about wolves and wild cats. If the wild cat shared any traits with their domestic counterparts, chasing its prey would be a welcome challenge.

"Yes. I'm big and scary. Be gone!" Landree waved her arms. "Go!"

A guttural growl escaped the wildcat's throat. It blinked and folded its ears back. Landree held her ground, flicking the blade with her wrist. She knew the humble knife couldn't take down the beast, but she hoped it could at least deter it from attacking. Without breaking its gaze, the wildcat slinked across the trail and into the line of trees. However, its eyes watched her in the shadows.

Landree's mouth fell agape. It had been the closest call in her life, and she hadn't even left the island yet. She scooped her satchel and took one step back. Then another. Landree continued to face the hidden creature until she vanished into the other side of the trail.

Her heart continued to race. Landree had to navigate her way through the woods unscathed. Battling nagging thoughts of regret, she tried to locate the moons through the mess of branches that arched above. Their position provided her with a rough direction south. Straining her ears, Landree pulled out her flask of water. Her hand shook so violently, she could barely wrap her lips around the neck of the bottle. After taking a swig, she swished the water in her mouth and focused on thoughts of Amicita. Landree already took one large leap when she left Camilla Viewpoint Inn. She needed to make it to the expedition at all costs.

Panic will only get you killed.

After securing her flask and adjusting the strap to her satchel, Landree took her first steps southbound. She gripped her dagger tightly. Every rustle or creak sent her nerves on edge.

One hundred feet. Two hundred feet.

As she progressed, her fears eased its hold on her. Although she never spotted those glowing, yellow eyes again, she was determined not to let her guard down. Landree forged ahead with a single mantra.

You're going to make it.

Minutes stretched to hours. Landree's legs ached in protest, but she pressed on—stepping over felled trees and side-
stepping gnarled roots. Every time she was tempted to rest,
Landree dangled the prize of Amicita in front of her: mountains and rivers she could map out and name, ancient ruins
she'd unearth, and decisions she could make on her own.
Someday she could be a patron at some inn, swapping stories with other travelers.

Landree followed the moons with an undying thirst until
she couldn't see them anymore.

Dawn was approaching.

Pale yellow infiltrated the navy-blue sky. Stars blinked
out one by one. Landree picked up the pace. When the first
rays of daylight poked through the ceiling of branches, she
broke into a light jog. Her stomach sank. Even though the
wildcat was long gone, time was now her enemy.

The thought of the expedition ship departing prodded
Landree into a sprint. She ignored the fire burning within
her lungs. Landree couldn't even feel her legs, so she pushed
harder.

Landree's stomach flew into her throat. Her foot caught a
rogue stone, and she flew face forward. She broke her fall
with her forearms, but her environment circled around her
as she tumbled down a slope.

She landed at the base of a sizeable hill, mouth full of
greens and soil. Landree spit them out and cradled her head
in her hands. She fought the stinging in her eyes as tears

pricked the corners and saturated her lashes.

"I'm not going to make it. How c-can I even get back home now?" Landree sat up and pounded the ground. "Idiot! You should've stayed and enjoyed that Heesu bun!"

A sweet scent interrupted her rant. Landree lifted her head and sniffed the air. For a moment, she thought she was hallucinating. Instead of mango and red bean, a luscious combination of plantains and coconut made her salivate.

Landree mustered every last ounce of strength and staggered toward the source. She winced as she squeezed between two thick trees. Scratch marks burned all over her body. Her clothes were damp with sweat. Her satchel caught itself between some branches. Landree tugged and pulled, but it didn't budge. Growing, she yanked harder.

"What the hell?" Landree shouted.

As she wrestled her satchel free, wood snapped and grass rustled behind her. Landree ducked, freeing herself from her satchel and swung her knife in front. "I'm big and scary!" she screamed.

"Landree?"

Brenna blinked incredulously at her.

Landree gaped, speechless.

"What happened to you?" Brenna asked. She pushed the blade away and pulled one of Landree's arms around her shoulders.

"Am I here? Arrowhead Beach?" Landree muttered, eyes darting around wildly.

Brenna jutted her chin in the direction of a cluster of people and crates. Approximately twenty men and women in navy tunics and scimitars tied to their hips with a silk sash scurried to and from the shoreline. They carried crates and sacks filled to the brim over their shoulders. The students of Goldenrod village mimicked their adult counterparts. Everyone chatted amongst themselves except Nicholas, who waved at Brenna.

A tall ship was anchored off shore, but even its polished wood and intricate carvings couldn't outshine The Luce.

Pillars of light connected sea to sky like a sheer veil. Every inch of its existence twinkled gently like dewdrops. When the rays of the sun filtered through The Luce, a kaleidoscope of color washed onto the sand. Dolphins sung and leapt at its base.

Landree's mouth grew slack. The camber of this literal guiding light stretched into the infinite horizon, blazing a trail south. Until today, Landree only saw depictions of the phenomenon in books that Ms. Clio had her class read over and over again. The faded colors of print didn't do it justice.

"Good thing you're big and strong," Landree collapsed into Brenna, words slurring.

Brenna chuckled. "It's quite a sight, isn't it?"

"Is that Landree?" a soft voice asked.

Ms. Clio appeared from the crowd. Her cropped hair clung to her face, already shining with sweat. When she spotted Landree, her clipboard tumbled from her hands.

"What are you doing here?" Landree asked. "Where's Dr. Barnes?"

Sighing, Ms. Clio signaled for the other students. "It's a long story, but a last-minute arrangement has been made, and I'll be the new chaperone."

Grant, Amelia, and Jane-Marie dropped their things and wrapped Landree in a blanket. The salty air tickled Landree's nose. Her lips twitched into a smile.

"I'm really glad you're here," Landree replied.

Ms. Clio's eyes shined behind her glasses. After picking up her clipboard, she scribbled something down.

"Good thing they didn't find a replacement for you," Amelia said. She brushed her golden hair from her eyes and rolled up Landree's shirt sleeves and examined her scratches. After a beat, she turned to Ms. Clio.

"Have they packed up the first aid supplies yet?"

Ms. Clio shook her head. "We're behind schedule. Colonel Thamni is still trying to calm Captain Giles down. I guess half the crew didn't show up. They're nowhere to be found."

As Ms. Clio scurried toward a wooden barrel, Landree spotted two men arguing, their faces inches apart. The man to the left crossed his arms and stood straight. His rolled-up sleeves exposed weathered arms. Scars covered his cheeks, spreading up and across his shaved head. The other man waved his arms frantically as profanities tumbled from his mouth. The navy tunic and scimitar told Landree that he was the ship's captain.

Grant appeared next to Ms. Clio with a crowbar. After a crack and pop, she rummaged for some bandages and a jar of salve.

"Stand aside, kids," Ms. Clio quipped.

Amelia shifted over and asked, "Can I observe?"

Ms. Clio nodded and started washing Landree's scrapes and cuts. "Maybe we should send a hawk to notify her parents that she arrived safely. I don't know why Spear and Rose would change their minds so suddenly and let their daughter travel alone. Unless they didn't change their minds." She shot Landree a knowing look.

Laughing nervously, Landree fumbled for a response. Jane-Marie's shadow washed over them, spewing excuses on her friend's behalf. Landree closed her eyes gratefully, too tired to enjoy her best friend's elaborate story.

"Fine then. Help gather her things and re-seal the medical supplies barrel. Leave us be. Run now," Ms. Clio barked. Shifting her focus back to Landree, she continued in a whisper. "You shouldn't have snuck out."

Landree tensed. Ms. Clio could easily send her home. The thought made her sick. After all this effort, Landree refused to turn back now.

Ms. Clio winced. She dropped the gauze pad and gripped her stomach. Amelia rushed to her side with new gauze.

"Are you alright?" Landree and Amelia asked simultaneously.

She nodded, gritting her teeth.

Footsteps crunched on the sand. Landree glanced up and spotted Nicholas. He too knelt by Ms. Clio's side, his long lips stretching into a frown.

"You mustn't overexert yourself. Let Amelia finish the task. Landree's injuries aren't that serious." He paused, avoiding Landree's gaze. "And I don't think we should worry about anything else other than getting everything and everyone on the ship. Time is precious."

"You're right," Ms. Clio replied, struggling to finish her sentence.

Even though Landree should've felt relieved that he convinced Ms. Clio not to notify her parents right away, she found his level of influence odd.

He's just a student like Jane-Marie and I.

While Nicholas guided Ms. Clio from her seat, his black pearl earring caught her eye. Its glow pulsed like a heartbeat. Landree held a hand to her forehead and groaned.

I'm seeing things. I think I need some sleep.

"Almost done," Amelia said warmly as she rolled up the extra gauze. "Looks like you're joining us after all."

CHAPTER

4

Eighteen days left of The Luce

Staring into the bucket, Landree wondered what exactly she had eaten for breakfast. The contents swimming in her vomit didn't at all appear like rice soup. Her stomach squeezed in protest as she retched. The foul smell didn't help. Lifting her head, Landree focused on a peg on the wall.

The wooden panels creaked and groaned. As the ship swayed gently, Landree shut her eyes for a beat. The constant rocking ever since she stepped foot onto the expedition vessel never bothered her until now.

"How are you feeling?"

Jane-Marie popped out from her sheets, rubbing her eyes. Her mop of ebony hair resembled that of a bird's nest.

"Revisiting my breakfast," Landree murmured. She cringed at the acidic taste building at the back of her tongue.

Yawning, Jane-Marie swung her legs around and dangled them off the edge of her cot. "At least you didn't get seasick like Ms. Clio and Nicholas."

"He's a little puke himself," Landree replied, dipping her head into the bucket and emptied the contents in her stomach. *What's left of it, anyway.*

"Maybe he likes you. Boys show their affection in mysterious ways." Jane-Marie's melodic laughter filled the cabin.

"Please quit it with that." Landree wiped her mouth and leaned against the wall. She shifted uncomfortably. Most of her injuries from her journey to Arrowhead healed, but she still carried sizeable bruises.

"How are *you* feeling? You had a few nasty panic attacks the first few days."

"Small spaces are not my friend, but I'm finding ways to cope—meditation and plenty of time alone and on deck."

Jane-Marie was the only one left in the cabin. Three lanterns that strung across the ceiling had been extinguished, and the curtain covering the lone porthole had been tied back. The room reeked of garlic and mixed with the salty, moist air in the most unpleasant way. Slightly smaller than Landree's bedroom, the female student quarters managed to fit all four girls and their belongings. Blankets were folded and smoothed out on Amelia's cot. Jane-Marie's were bundled into a ball at the edge, while Brenna's cascaded onto the floor.

"Ugh. That's how insects get into your bed," Jane-Marie said, pinching her nose.

Landree flushed. There had been quite a few mornings

where she didn't pick up after herself. Without her parents breathing down her shoulders, she realized how difficult it was to be responsible without prompting.

"How did you get to sleep in?" Landree asked, hoping to divert her friend's attention.

"I just felt like it."

Raising her brows, Landree said, "Wow." The storm in her stomach settled long enough for her to stand. "I'm going to empty this and get to work."

"Sure thing."

When Landree stretched her arms and yawned, she caught a whiff of her body odor. Cringing, she missed the luxury of a warm bath, scented with lavender oil, that she could take at her leisure. There were a lot of things she'd taken for granted ever since she stepped foot on this ship.

Lifting her bucket, Landree squeezed by Jane-Marie. The scent of frankincense tickled her nose.

"Did you pack scented oils?"

"Yeah, I packed a few. Can't stand to be stinky," Jane-Marie said.

Landree flushed with embarrassment. "Sorry," she murmured. "I...uh...never thought to pack that."

"You smell fine," Jane-Marie quipped as she rummaged through her pack of clothes.

Once Landree made it to the exit, she noticed a pendant hanging from the doorknob. It was Amelia's. A lion's paw woven from yarn. On the first night aboard the vessel, she had explained it was an Irellian symbol of good luck. Landree could only think of her encounter with the wildcat.

One hallway and staircase later, Landree dumped the contents from her bucket and scrubbed it clean. The crisp sea air lifted the fleeting bits of drowsiness. The ship glided against the waves, never straying from The Luce's path. Its golden glow continued to shine, never dulling once for the last ten days. Every night before bed, Landree found a secluded spot on deck and stared at the fabric of light. They were never close enough to touch. She learned the hard way the first night. Landree had climbing onto the railing, with Jane-Marie holding onto her ankles. She had slipped, banged her forehead against the wood paneling, and dealt with another lecture from Ms. Clio.

Landree sighed. She imagined it feeling like satin.

"Oy!"

Scrambling to her feet, Landree searched for the familiar voice.

"Are you feeling better?" Ms. Clio asked. The edges of her cracked lips pushed up her cheeks. A red bandana adorned her head, and her faithful clipboard was tucked beneath one arm. She'd started wearing bandanas since embarking on this trip.

Landree couldn't tell if it was a trick of the eye, but Ms. Clio's brown hair seemed thinner. Ms. Clio had been pulling at her strands whenever her hands weren't preoccupied with her quill.

A wave crashed into the tall ship head-on. Landree's stomach summersaulted under the undulation. "Yes."

Studying her with hooded eyes, Ms. Clio clicked her tongue. "Alright. Please drink some water before you attend to your duties. I want you to join Brenna in adjusting the sails with Captain Giles."

"Then, the usual?"

"Of course," Ms. Clio replied warmly.

Landree studied her eyes. Their edges were tinged with yellow. "Are you alright?"

"I'm fine. Once I get a proper meal on me, I'll look good as new."

No sooner had she turned around, Ms. Clio tapped her shoulder.

Holding a fist to her mouth, Ms. Clio coughed. She lifted her index finger and smiled apologetically. "I've held off asking you, but it's important for me to know the truth. We're in the middle of the ocean. Secrets and lies are no good here. Why did you sneak out to join us when your father notified Thamni that you weren't going?"

An uncomfortable heat washed over Landree as she chewed on her nails. From the second she rose from her cot in the morning to the moment she lay her head against her lumpy pillow at night, dread dogged her steps about whether Ms. Clio would revisit the topic since they set sail. And yet, after all this time, she didn't understand why Ms. Clio waited this long.

"I-I know this looks bad. It wasn't my intention to disobey my parents." Words bottlenecked at the tip of her tongue. She bit into her cuticles until they bled. She didn't understand why it was so hard to speak her mind. "This is a once in a lifetime opportunity for me. I love my parents, but I needed to make this decision on my own."

Ms. Clio sighed. Landree stared at the crow's nest and braced for a lecture.

"You're still young, and I don't approve of what you did." The historian released her grip. "However, I appreciate your honesty. Although the manner in which you joined us was foolhardy, I'm still glad you made it. I have a feeling we're going to need someone like you."

The muscles in Landree's neck relaxed. While a brisk wind chilled her skin, her chest filled with warmth. "Thank you," she replied. "How's the sea chart moving along?"

Pushing her glasses up with her index finger, Ms. Clio tilted her head back and forth. "It's coming along, but I'm not confident in its accuracy. As expected, our compasses haven't been responding since we entered The Luce, and the constellations seem to appear in a different location each night. Not by much, but enough where it doesn't make much logical sense. My theory is that The Luce distorts the lighting and creates the illusion of the constellations shifting. So, I've been mapping things off based on the position of the eclipse." A fire lit in her gray eyes. "I've been studying my theory for about fifteen years. If I crack this mystery, I'll be the first person to map a route to Amicita without guidance from The Luce!"

"That's brilliant," Landree replied breathily. "I hope it works!"

Ms. Clio bowed her head slightly, failing to hide her pink cheeks. "Carry on, now. Thanks for speaking with me."

"See you around!"

Landree's steps felt lighter as she skipped across the deck.

Soon, she'll reach Amicita and prove her worth. She fantasized her name permanently scribed in history books as one of the few who rediscovered the once forgotten island. The things she'd discover could change the world, from much needed resources to relics of historical significance. That's the Landree that would be remembered, not some manager at a sleepy inn, and this level of impact drove her to work hard every day since she arrived on the ship.

The sun beamed proudly, free of any oppressive clouds. The morning was cool, yet comfortable. Any remaining sickly feeling had finally swept away. She waved to the captain, dressed in the same garb since day one, who had been chatting with Brenna.

"Morning, young lady," Giles said, wiping his brow with a dirty handkerchief. "Glad to have you assisting me. I need you and Brenna to adjust the foremost sail as needed while I help my son mend the torn one from yesterday's storm. Do you need a refresher on how this works?"

Squaring her shoulders, Landree shook her head. Out of all the students, only Nicholas and Grant had sailing experience, although Amelia made it known several times that she read about it. The thought drew a smile from within Landree. Captain Giles had no choice but to train everyone else. He never found out why his boatswain and half his crew never showed up. He had gotten into a thundering shouting match with Thamni, demanding to wait an additional twenty-four hours for them. Thamni eventually won—threatening charges with treason if Giles held up the Queen's time-sensitive mission.

"Perfect. I'll leave you capable women to work, then." With a tip of his cap, Giles hobbled toward the stern, whistling his favorite tune. Giles' weathered boots squeaked comically as he puffed his chest out and saluted his men.

"Nice guy, smells like he crawled from a pit of rotten food." Brenna tied her hair into a bun and smirked. Her biceps bulged beneath her tunic.

"I really admire how strong you are," she bemoaned. Brenna already was built like a boulder, but she seemed to grow stronger while Landree lost weight.

Brenna rolled her eyes. "Let's go. Giles' other men are working the second and third mast."

With minimal staff, the six students were assigned daily duties on the ship—manning the sails, cleaning the dishes, repairing things that broke, just to name a few. It kept Landree and the rest busy because Ms. Clio and Thamni filled their evening with orientation sessions to prep them for Amicita. Ms. Clio educated the students on the discoveries from past expeditions, and whenever she grew winded—which happened often—Thamni stepped in a ran through protocol.

The morning cruised by with little effort. After the storm, the wind shifted in their favor, allowing ample time for Landree and Brenna to move at their leisure. The raw sensation of rope in Landree's hands and the squeaking pulleys lifted her spirits. She barely noticed that, by this point, her palms were heavily calloused.

"So, when did you move to Camilla?" Landree asked.

After securing a knot with a grunt, Brenna leaned against

the ship's railing and drummed her fingers against the polished oak. "When I was five or six? I spent more of my childhood in Harebell. You know, the trading post in the north."

Landree nodded vigorously as she joined her side. "I've never been. What's it like?"

Brenna scratched her pointed nose. "There was this main road that stretched for miles, hugged by clusters of homes with clay-tiled roofs, sheltering side-roads from view. Lots of folks bustling about, too busy to mind their manners. There were lots of us there…" she trailed off.

"Lots of…little kids?"

"No. Lots of immigrants," Brenna said, looking down. Even when she stooped over, Brenna still seemed to tower over Landree.

A pregnant pause spread between them, the only connection was their elbows, grazing one another. They both stared into the horizon, a line of dark blue cut in half by The Luce. The usual background noise of barking orders and shouting commands had silenced, allowing the scrubbing noise of deckhands to come through.

"Maybe I'll develop a nice tan," Brenna said, voice brittle. "…So people can stop remarking on my ghostly complexion."

Landree bit her lip. "I think you look beautiful as you are. What I mean is, the tan will fade eventually, but it's how you behave that people will ultimately remember you by."

"You poor, naïve child."

WINDS OF AMICITA • 73

"You're the same age as me!" Landree blurted.

Brenna rested on one elbow and faced her. Strands of red hair escaped her bun and tickled her heart-shaped face. "You know what I find amazing? That no one can navigate to Amicita without The Luce. Compasses just go haywire."

The topic change threw Landree off, but she managed a nod.

A bell rang above.

"Sounds like lunch," Brenna added. She fumbled for words. "Would you like to sit next to me?"

"Sure!"

Brenna's features brightened. Together, they made final adjustments to the sails for Giles who replaced them for the afternoon.

Landree made her way to a rectangular room below deck. After her morning bout of nausea, she was ravenous, and as long as it wasn't rice soup, she was excited to eat anything. Almost as excited as getting to know Brenna more. The statuesque Norlend native had kept to herself since their departure from the Republic. The only person who bothered to try and get to know her was Grant, and his primary goal was to... bother her. Landree wasn't sure if he liked her or not, but she knew Brenna couldn't care less.

As they waited in line for their meal, a light in Landree's mind illuminated. Grant's heritage was Norlender as well. Running a hand through her hair, she scoured her memory, trying to remember if he was born in Camilla or not.

"Bread and dried venison," the chef croaked.

"Thank you," she replied. Brenna stood a few feet ahead,

waiting. After the cook dumped a meager portion onto Landree's plate, she sat next to Brenna at a round table for eight. A group of deckhands nearby picked at any remaining crumbs of their plates—some resorting to licking them— or tossing dice around while pounding their tankards on the table. These men and women worked hard, so in turn, they played hard.

"I heard you are a great cook," Brenna began. "Tell me some of your favorite recipes."

"Only one." Landree gestured to her plate. "Flavorless jerky." The two girls snickered.

"But really, I enjoy making this citrus strew. It sounds bizarre, but hear me out. You marinate the meat in orange juices and peels, then brown it in a pot. Then, I make the stock from what's left there. It involves a bundle of spices, a touch of lemon juice, oh, I could go on and on."

"This sounds way better than what we've been eating on the ship!"

"Agreed. How I miss the food at the inn..." Landree trailed off. Her fingers gravitated toward her shell necklace. Landree wondered what her parents were doing, and if they missed her. Or the more likely—if they were still furious that she left. The thought made her heart ache. Despite her decision, Landree still missed home terribly. She often reminisced over clean sheets, delicious food, familiar hallways, and, although rare, her parent's hugs. She shook her head. "Anyway, do you have any favorite dishes?"

Brenna rubbed her belly. "My mother used to cook a traditional Norlend meal. It's steamed trout that had been—"

"There you are." Grant popped out from the mass of navy. His blonde hair was slicked back, and forehead covered in grime. A crooked grin stretched across his face as he fixated his gaze on Brenna. She clamped her mouth shut.

I haven't seen you around in a while!" He drew a seat across from them. "I was afraid I'd forgotten what you'd look like."

"It's a small ship, Grant," Landree interrupted.

Brenna cleared her throat and tore off a large wad of venison. Grant nodded to Landree.

"How's it going? I've been fixing a broken step in the men's quarters with the carpenter. Dirty job but someone's gotta do it." He winked at Brenna who took particular interest in a speck of dust on the table.

"Not too bad. I think I ate something funny, but I'm better now."

"So, Brenna. What do you think it's going to be like on Amicita?" he purred.

Landree rolled her eyes and bit into the slice of bread. A resounding crunch told her it was days old. She fantasized noshing on a fresh harvest in Amicita. In her daydreams, vegetables and juicy berries grew in an abundance. Even fields of wild grains.

Amicita.

The island that sat at the end of The Luce went years without a name, and it was the fourth expedition that imparted it with the name Amicita. Along with fresh food, Landree hoped to discover its original, and likely much better, name.

"Can I sit here?" Amelia asked.

Landree broke free from her daydream and raised her glass of water before taking a sip. Jane-Marie wasn't too far behind. Even Ms. Clio moseyed her way to the table. Brenna remained silent.

"I hope you don't mind," Ms. Clio said. "I'm sick and tired of sitting with the adults. If you call sailors adults."

"No worries. You're much cooler than Dr. Barnes," Jane -Marie chirped. Her eyes shined and her cheeks had a healthy, peachy glow.

Picking up the stick of venison, Ms. Clio frowned. She put it down. "So, are you guys ready? We're almost there."

Everyone nodded vigorously.

"It certainly is the most historical visit in history. We have students that represent the three major countries: Republic of Camilla, Norlend, and Irelle. I do say that, despite the ruckus it caused to get us here, it's a huge step in a more global focus on the world."

As if on cue, Amelia pulled out a book and thumbed through its pages.

"Where did you hide that?" Jane-Marie exclaimed.

"Is it true, Ms. Clio, that the first event occurred just over five-hundred years ago?"

Ms. Clio nodded. Everyone around the table scooched closer, much like children clustering around a campfire, eagerly awaiting a bedtime story.

"The first documentation came from a fisherman out of Arrowhead. In an oral attestation, the fisherman witnessed the sea vibrate as 'heaven's light' cast from the sky and carved its path through the waves."

"Sounds like a made-up tale." Brenna wiped her greasy hands on a napkin. "But the fact that this occurred every hundred years on the dot can't be a coincidence."

"Hence Camillians' obsession with clocks and calendars," Jane-Marie added proudly.

"I wonder what possessed them to follow this path, let alone figure the timeline out?" Grant asked.

Ms. Clio pursed her lips. "You haven't been paying attention in class, haven't you?"

Grant shrugged unapologetically.

"Really. You were chosen over hundreds of students. If you applied in hopes of joining the expedition, you should've taken upon yourself to memorize the history and its significance that has led up to this moment." Ms. Clio's rounded glasses almost slid off her mousy nose.

Folding his arms behind his neck, Grant said, "I'm in it for some blood-pumping adventure and making a fortune so that I will never have to work a day in my life."

Amelia's nostrils flared. "You realize you're admitting this to the chaperone of this expedition."

"Everyone has their own agenda." His emerald eyes flashed. "The queen of this all-too-perfect Republic claims this is in the name of research, but we all know that there are other agendas. Norlend wanted representatives to mine precious stones for wealth in order to catapult them into a world superpower. Irelle, the superstitious state that it is, seeks this mythical power that is supposedly resting within those gems. You should know."

Amelia slammed her glass against the table. "You're insufferable."

"And you're naïve," he replied coolly.

The table fell silent, absorbing the collective chatter from the rest of the room. Landree's stomach soured, losing her appetite.

"Well." Ms. Clio swallowed her last piece of bread. "We are due to arrive on Amicita in a few more days. I need to prepare for our evening meeting, and perhaps I can correct some assumptions that've been made."

"I'm gunna relax before the meeting," Landree replied in succession. "See you all there."

After a lukewarm bath, Landree arrived at the main cabin a half-hour early, eager to soak in some peace and quiet. Her footsteps echoed as she entered the bare room. Stain-glass shards hung from the ceiling, reflecting multiple swatches of color across the scuffed floor. Eight worn stools sat in two rows of four, facing an oak desk and leather-bound loveseat. Tea-stained charts were strewn across this desk. Ms. Clio had poured over previous accounts, trying to document their journey thus far.

Most of the items on the desk belonged to her, as opposed to Thamni, who seemed to have packed very little. He also said very little outside his evening prep sessions. All Landree learned thus far was that he was the right-hand man to the queen. While Ms. Clio was the primary chaperone to the student volunteers, Thamni existed to make sure things "get done".

Whatever that means.

Between that and Grant's words at lunch, Landree experienced an itch of curiosity that she couldn't satisfy by speculation alone. She shrugged. Maybe she was overthinking it, and Thamni was just another political lackey. It was unfortunate since Thamni was the hard edge to the otherwise flexible dynamic of the expedition team.

Landree crept up to the desk. She traced her fingers over the various papers, quills, and tools, and found the map Ms. Clio had been working on. At the top right-hand corner, she had written *The Republic of Camilla* and drew crosshatches around the letters. Various numbers and symbols were scribbled down both ends of the scroll, things that stumped Landree. Thin lines connected one end to another, and when they intersected, Ms. Clio had etched a question mark. The pattern of question marks curved its way to the midpoint of the scroll, leaving the bottom left blank. Landree scratched the back of her neck, catching a tangled knot with a nail.

Ms. Clio is so smart. I hope she cracks the route to Amicita.

"I never took you for an early bird."

A gravelly voice shattered the silence, sending goosebumps erupting all over Landree. She swung around wildly, shooting both hands in the air.

In the corner, Nicholas sat back, perched against a bay window like a cat. His all-black attire further highlighted his pale complexion. His ice-blue eyes stared past his bangs, laser-focused on her.

"How long have you been sitting there?" she seethed.

"Why do you look like you're about to punch someone out?" he shot back.

"Because…" Landree took a deep breath and forced her shoulders to relax. "Never mind."

Collapsing onto a stool, Landree hung her head. She should've remained in the sleeping quarters until the meeting started.

Landree blew a few strands of her hair from her eyes. "What's your deal, anyway?"

"No deal. Just meditating. We're almost there."

The last three words send butterflies aflutter in her stomach. It felt surreal. "Why'd you apply for this expedition?"

"I don't have much going for me in the Republic."

Landree found herself nodding. She cleared her throat and sat up straight. Nicholas continued to stare.

"Plus, my uncle always told me that I have ancestral ties to this island. It calls me," he said in a dead voice.

A chill spread beneath her skin. "Humans haven't been documented to have lived there for hundreds of years. How would you know?"

Nicholas tapped his stud earring. "This."

The black pearl.

It oozed mystique, catching not only her attention, but the attention of everyone else in the school. Piercings were fairly common, but no one has ever seen a black pearl before. Part of her wanted to ask for more details, but the other part didn't want to encourage him. "What do you know about Amicita?"

Running a hand through his hair, Nicholas scoffed. "What a stupid name."

Landree shrugged. "Okay…Until we discover its true name, it's Amicita. Like you could come up with any better."

Nicholas leaned forward and stretched. "There's a reason why humans, or any other intelligent species that used to roam the world, don't exist there anymore. And yet, because the land is rich in precious stones, it's become the focus of the three most powerful countries in the world. Makes one wonder if 'Amicita' should be explored."

"Sounds like you're actually against this." Landree chewed her fingernails. She knew it was a bad habit, but she couldn't help it.

"I'm not against it, but only an imbecile would believe the Republic, Norlend, and Irelle didn't have their own agendas, whether it is for financial gain or an interest the mysterious powers some gems may hold."

Landree bit down hard. Metallic fluid saturated her chapped lips. She shook her hand, trying to distract herself from the throbbing pain. "You too? You and Amelia are the most bookish of the group, and you both are willing to entertain the existence of magic? Seriously?"

A crooked smile spread across his face. When Nicholas' lips parted, voices and footsteps tumbled from the hallway. Within moments, Landree's classmates and Ms. Clio entered the cabin.

Ms. Clio's eyes brightened when she spotted Landree.

She waved with one arm, while the other cradled her stomach. Amelia sat front and center, still reading the same book. Grant followed closely behind Brenna. Jane-Marie trailed the group, glowing from her bath. A maroon dress lined with fur hugged her curves. Landree felt confident that Jane-Marie was the only person who packed leisure outfits.

"Hey, you look nice," Landree said to Jane-Marie who sat to her right.

Jane-Marie flicked her braided hair over her shoulder. With a wink, she replied, "Thank you. It's nice to feel human again."

"Agreed." Landree chortled.

Amid the chatter, Thamni finally entered the cabin, closing the doors behind him. He donned a dark-green jumpsuit and leather boots. Lifting his square jaw high, Thamni marched with heavy steps toward the front. His tall stature and tan skin contrasted greatly to the mousy, pale teacher. Landree smiled—despite the physical differences, Ms. Clio held her own.

A cool rush of air brushed past Landree to her left. Nicholas took the vacant seat on her other side. Landree pretended she didn't notice.

"How's everyone doing tonight?" Ms. Clio addressed the students.

Everyone answered at once, making it difficult to tease out a specific word. However, the tone was shared among everyone: untethered excitement.

"Great." Ms. Clio fumbled for her glasses.

Landree squinted her eyes. She noticed Ms. Clio's hands

were trembling.

"We're a few days behind schedule due to some inclement weather and unfavorable winds, but I believe we are close to our destination, so I'm going to review the rules for disembarkment. Oh. Amelia, did you extinguish the lamp in your room?"

Heads turned. Amelia snapped her book shut. Shrinking into her seat, she nodded.

"Good. Now, after speaking with Thamni and Captain Giles, we should arrive at Amicita as early as tomorrow. In preparation, we'll load our supplies onto deck at first light."

As Ms. Clio continued speaking, Amelia turned and cast Landree a dirty look.

"I didn't say anything," Landree replied, shaking her head wildly. Amelia had consistently forgotten to extinguish her lamp after reading, and Jane-Marie reported it multiple times. It caused palpable tension throughout the trip, and Landree chose to avoid the drama at all costs by keeping to herself.

When Amelia turned back around, Landree fanned herself. Too many little things were distracting her from focusing. She already struggled not to analyze Nicholas' cryptic replies.

"The second expedition documented that The Luce takes us to a rocky beach in the north. There, we'll establish a base and focus on breaking into smaller groups."

Thamni stood beside Ms. Clio. His gaze traveled from one student to another. He did this each meeting, as if sizing up which one was worthy of belonging to his party. Landree prayed she ended up with Ms. Clio. Thamni produced a scroll and passed it to Ms. Clio, immediately wiping the excited expression off her face.

"Again?" she murmured.

Thamni nodded, stone-faced.

Unfurling the scroll, Ms. Clio sighed. "As a reminder, by the decree of Queen Baneberry, first of her name, the Republic of Camilla has and will continue to own all expeditions to the aforementioned country named Amicita," she said in one monotone breath. She threw Thamni a pained expression, but he nodded rigidly. "The Republic is committed to the research behind The Luce and Amicita for the betterment of its people. While citizens from Irelle and Norlend aren't excluded from participating in the fifth expedition, all knowledge reaped from exploration is first and foremost meant to serve the best interest of the Republic. The expedition's missions are to map out the geography, secure a reliable route to and from the island, document significant historical findings, and...return with artifacts that require further study which includes, but is not limited to, precious gems."

The last few words met with resistance as they escaped Ms. Clio's lips. She placed the scroll on the desk as the group broke into murmurs. It was the same statement Mayor Erebus had read, and Landree felt Ms. Clio would've rolled her eyes if she weren't under Thamni's scrutiny. The document was nothing but a cold, empty statement that somehow drove Landree to more suspicion about the Queen's intentions. If anyone pursued this expedition purely for the sake of knowledge, it was Ms. Clio, and judging from her curled lip, she likely thought that 'mission statement' was a load of crap.

Grant snickered and whispered, "Yeah, right."

Landree's found herself nodding. Maybe he was onto something.

"Anyone have any questions?" Thamni asked.

Amelia's hand was raised before he finished his sentence. Landree chuckled inwardly while Jane-Marie sighed loudly.

"Why is Queen Baneberry only sending one ship? Why not an entire armada?"

"Smart question." Thamni folded his arms behind his back and strolled to the front of the desk. Leaning back, he grabbed a wooden model of the ship. "If you can recall, The Luce shines for 28 days and provides the only path to Amicita. The ships must sail completely within the veil of light or else they are doomed to be lost at sea. It would be inefficient for a hundred ships to sail single file in the limited time provided. Part of our goal is to succeed where the last four had failed—uncover a solution to this challenge. That's what happened to the third group. They took many ships and stayed too long. I intend on leading a focused approach. There *is* an answer to that navigational puzzle somewhere on that island, and I intend on finding it."

A grin spread across Ms. Clio's cracked lips. "If you recall in our history lessons, the civilization that once inhabited Amicita believed that gems such as diamonds and rubies held deep ties with the earth and its elements," she croaked. Although she sounded parched, it could not mask her childlike enthusiasm.

Thamni waved her off. "That's mythology, Ms. Clio. I thought we were all about the facts here."

"Oh yes, of course. Just wanted to provide some background." Her bony fingers fidgeted. "One can extrapolate the potential effects of its rich minerals could throw off our compasses."

Resting her chin on her hand, Landree fantasized about possessing supernatural powers. She immediately thought of her secret hide-away and the rush of hair as she glided between trees.

Yes. I wish I could fly.

"If there are no more questions, let's review our strengths and divvy up tasks." Ms. Clio's face brightened as if a switch flipped. She pulled out her clipboard and scribbled down suggestions while taking votes. Who was proficient in reading maps? Who wanted to be the note-taker? Did anyone learn self-defense?"

Of course, Amelia raised her hand for everything. Landree forced herself to look straight ahead to prevent herself from comparing her abilities to others.

"I'm familiar with Amicita's various lore," Nicholas said.

"I've studied multiple languages and have drawn maps before," Jane-Marie added.

Everyone's voices swarmed around Landree's ears. The adventure was about to begin. Everyone must rely on one another for a successful mission—and for survival. So many questions arose in her mind, and the one that rose to the top:

Did I really deserve to be chosen for this trip?

CHAPTER

5

Seventeen days left of The Luce

The valley... It's so close. But why is the earth shaking?

Landree jolted awake, launching herself upright. She collided headfirst against someone's else's skull. She yelped as lights exploded in her eyes.

"What the hell?" Nicholas shouted. He covered his left eye and backed up a few steps.

The blurred edges of his body shifted into focus. Deckhands flew about behind him, paying the pair no mind.

"What happened?" Landree yawned, her back ached from napping against a wood crate. Although her lumpy mattress was no better.

"While you were snoozing, everyone else has been preparing to disembark." Nicholas beckoned her to stand.

Someone snorted. Landree caught Thamni shaking his head in her direction as he dragged a rope across the deck.

He wore the same jumpsuit as the evening prior. His closely shaved head shined from beneath the sun.

"We're here?" Landree stood, knees cracking, and teetered toward the edge of the ship. She leaned against the railing.

The sun melted into the horizon, spilling pink, periwinkle, and violet onto the sky's canvass. A seagull cried and hovered around the tall ship then took off toward a russet-colored blob in the distance.

She rubbed her eyes, waking up bit by bit. "That's Amicita?"

Nicholas stood beside her, resting his elbows against the railing. His black pearl ear piercing glistened. The edges of his eyes softened. "Yes."

Her stomach squeezed at the realization. "My dream is finally coming true," Landree trailed off.

Nicholas grunted. "If it's so important, then have some sense of urgency. Get downstairs and pack up."

He stiffened his back, giving him the appearance of a wooden pole, and marched off. Landree folded her arms and watched him vanish below deck. Even during the voyage, Nicholas kept to himself as if he enjoyed his role as an enigma.

Captain Giles bellowed an order, snapping Landree from her thoughts. She scrambled toward the cabin, grinning from ear to ear.

When Landree opened the door to the women's quarters, a sea of arms flinging clothing greeted her. Brenna's head poked up from behind a bedpost.

"Where've you been? It's time to carry our belongings upstairs."

"Can't we just get the boys to do it?" Jane-Marie asked with an exaggerated pout.

No one paid her mind except Landree who replied, "We don't want them to get big heads and think they can do more than us!"

Amelia side-stepped them, armful of tunics and hair wraps. Her hair bounced in thick curls over her face. She blew some strands so she could see. "That's the Irellian way! Women are seen as a pillar of strength. It's refreshing to see it in other cultures."

"Where are my glasses? Glasses!" Ms. Clio exclaimed from the hallway. Moments later, a sharp crunch silenced her.

Landree found her corner and stared at her empty cot. She had packed only what she could carry in a satchel which sat by her feet.

"Looks like I'm already packed." Landree tossed her pack across her shoulder.

"Watch it!" Brenna exclaimed.

Landree froze. Her bag barely missed a trio of candles on a nightstand. Her muscles burned as she inched away.

"Who left these candles lit?" she asked. "It's very dangerous!"

Jane-Marie padded into the room. "I think it's Amelia. She was reading, again, when Ms. Clio announced it was time to pack up."

"She couldn't have blown them out?" Brenna growled.

After tying her hair back, she bent at the knees and hoisted two boxes.

"I was hoping to get another chapter read if I finished early." Amelia appeared a few feet behind Jane-Marie.

"Just don't forget to extinguish it when you're done!" Brenna barked.

Amelia provided some long-winded excuse, but Landree shifted her back to Brenna, whose legs visibly shook.

"Do you need help?"

"I'm fine." Brenna grunted. "…but thanks."

Over the next hour, Landree helped her friends carry their packs on deck. With each trip, the blob in the distance transformed into a larger-than-life island. Jagged mountaintops with steep cliffs made her heart flutter. She imagined her dream valley on the other side waiting patiently.

Ms. Clio broke the team of six students into two in order to transport the larger items to the deck. Sweat dripped from her hairline, and she repeatedly rubbed her eyes. Landree shot her a reassuring smile, knowing that the pressure Ms. Clio was in hadn't been exactly fair.

Landree also felt badly for Captain Giles. No one figured out what happened to half his crew. She didn't mind lifting heavy objects and completing whatever task was required to advance; however, for a once in a century trip, it wasn't the best use of her time. And judging by Thamni's face, he wasn't thrilled either.

Thamni stopped to speak to Ms. Clio, his under bite reminding Landree of a bulldog. He folded his hands behind his back and puffed out his chest. Ms. Clio opened her mouth to reply, but her knees buckled. Thamni hooked one arm around hers and guided her to a seat. When Thamni caught Landree's eye, he scowled.

"No stalling. Get to work!" he commanded.

Brenna, Grant, and Landree were tasked with carrying crates filled with wagons parts that they'd assemble on shore. While her arms burned and legs shook, Brenna and Grant made the hard work seem effortless.

When they transported the last crate, Landree collapsed onto her knees. Panting, she fanned her face with her hands to no effect.

Grant leaned over toward Brenna. "I like a strong woman."

Landree cringed, and Brenna smacked him across the cheek. Rubbing his jaw, he peeked back at Landree and winked.

"You're an idiot," Landree mouthed.

A whistle cut through the thick air. Landree stood, still catching her breath, and congregated with the other students. Sweat stains blossomed through everyone's tunics and slacks. Landree loosened the strings to her collar. The air increasingly grew humid.

Jane-Marie crinkled the bridge of her nose. Leaning over toward Landree, she whispered, "Do you smell something?"

"Maybe the chef is cooking again," she replied.

"Right before we disembark?"

Landree shrugged. The heavy air made her yawn.

Ms. Clio stood next to the foremost mast, clutching her clipboard like it was her newborn child. She rubbed her eyes as she took count of the team.

"Can you see alright?" Jane-Marie asked.

"Yes. Things are a touch blurry without my glasses, but I packed a spare. It's… in one of these many crates." She gestured to the maze of boxes then resumed rubbing her eyes. "I wanted to go over first-contact with you again."

Ms. Clio cleared her throat and studied the document in her hands. Her nose grazed the parchment before making a satisfactory hum. "Amicita has been around for thousands of years, visited by outsiders only four times in the last half-century. One troop failed to return safely. In order not to repeat this error and maintain the safety of our citizens…and citizens from other countries, I must relay the following rules."

Landree's chest swelled in excitement. She felt like she was floating in a dream. As much as she tried to focus on Ms. Clio, Landree often found herself staring past her and at the mountains. Some corners formed a perfect edge. Landree knitted her brows. Natural landmarks didn't have perfect edges. She turned to catch the attention of her friends.

Jane-Marie bounced on the balls of her feet while Amelia clasped her hands together and pressed them against her lips as if in prayer. Grant was preoccupied with antagonizing Brenna, leaving Nicholas to himself. He crossed his arms as he shifted his weight back and forth, drumming his fingers repetitively. Despite the surrounding distractions, Nicholas' eyes were fixated on the floor. His eyes and nose twitched sporadically, and his lips moved as if he was talking to himself. Even his pearl earring seemed like flicker, matching his anxiety-inducing behavior.

"Creep," she muttered.

"Landree, could you please pay attention?" Ms. Clio strained her voice to combat Giles shouting commands at his crew.

"Yes, ma'am," she replied bowing her head. A peppery heat stung her nostrils. She rubbed her eyes.

"As I was saying, The Luce vanishes after one full cycle of Adin and Deva's eclipse. One month. Once again, I must emphasize that no person has ever successfully traveled to or from Amicita without The Luce. Even though I'm excited to report that I'm close to breaking through the route's mystery, I don't want to risk anything. Captain Giles and his crew will remain on the ship to prepare for our exit or notify us if something's amiss. Giles?"

Murmurs broke through the group.

"You smell it, too?" Grant asked.

Brenna coughed in response.

Boots pounded against the deck. Nicholas met Giles halfway, painting a picture of stark contrasts: a youth strolling nonchalantly and an old man hobbling so quickly, he seemed in danger of tripping over his own boots. When Captain Giles came to a halt, he doubled over and hacked.

"F-fire, lad." He grasped Nicholas' tunic and craned his neck in the direction of the crow's nest. "Fire!"

Thamni pounded his fist against the railing. "What the Deva is going on? What fire?"

Ice cold dread doused Landree. Turning to Jane-Marie,

she said, "That smell."

"Smoke." Her eyes widened.

The tinkling of glass shattering followed a gust of wind. Landree instinctively ducked while Grant and Brenna screamed. Smoke billowed from the sides of the tall ship in ominous tendrils of gray. All at once, a bell chimed and deckhands scattered across the deck with buckets dangling from the crooks of their elbows.

Thamni cupped his hands around his mouth and shouted. "Save the horses!"

Landree took after Giles, but Thamni held her back. His meaty hands encompassed her entire arm, and yet his grip was gentle. "Let them handle this. Stay close to Ms. Clio and the other students," he said firmly.

Frustration boiled beneath her skin, but Landree obliged.

The wind continued to pick up. Landree huddled between Jane-Marie and Ms. Clio as a groan resonated below them. The floorboards vibrated. Giles doubled back to fill another bucket of water, but his leg broke through the floor. He squeezed his eyes and cried out. By now, smoke poured from the main cabin's double doors, hungry to be set free. A handful of deckhands fell through the deck in a sea of shrieks of anguish.

Thamni sprinted toward the captain and pulled him out, revealing a hellish hole where sweltering heat poured forth.

"How did this happen?" Thamni asked, shaking Giles' shoulders. Sweat flew everywhere.

"Alls I know is that it wasn't the kitchen, sir. I was there when I smelled smoke. Regardless of how, we need to abandon ship. It's eating up the entire mid-section, which'll mean it'll snap in half before it sinks!"

A wave crashed into the tall-ship. Landree flew off her feet, landing on Jane-Marie. A dark mass spread across the deck like a storm's shadow. When Landree looked up, confusion gripped her. The sky was clear. In the background, Amelia argued with a deckhand, waving a book in her hand. Brenna and Grant supported Ms. Clio from both sides. Their gazes darted back and forth, eyes wide. Nicholas stood farthest from the group, leaning against a crate. His arms were still crossed as he tapped his foot. Landree's lips tightened.

Jane-Marie whimpered. Cupping her cheek, Landree said, "We're going to get through this."

With another snap, the cabin doors collapsed. Fire roared from the fissure. Everything around Landree tilted back. The nose of the ship kissed the water as it made its slow descent. Men and women slid past Landree. Each time a wave hit the boat, it sent those deckhands into the sea.

Heart racing, Landree reached for those closest to her. In one hand, she grabbed Jane-Marie, and in the other, Brenna. In the line of vision, Grant hugged the mast as Ms. Clio and Amelia grabbed onto each of his legs. Landree caught Grant's eye. It was the first time she'd ever see him cry. Nicholas scratched at the wood, inching past Landree.

"We have to let go or else the ship will drag us into the bottom of the ocean!" he exclaimed. Nicholas' hair glued to his cheeks. Dirt and grime masked his features, but he stared at Landree knowingly. "It won't be easy, but we need to jump and swim. Now!"

A scream split the air.

In another cascade of cracks and snaps, the middle mast fell, fire gnawing at its base. The solid mass barreled toward Landree and her friends, its multiple white sails fluttering like an eagle diving for its prey. Landree rolled to her side, narrowly missing the mast. It slammed into Nicholas, pummeling him, back-first, into the wall. Landree shrieked in horror and lost her footing. She began to slip but refused to let go of her friends. One of the masts' rope caught on Brenna's foot.

"We need to jump," she shouted.

Jane-Marie nodded, sobbing loudly.

Swallowing the lump in her throat, Landree tensed her thighs and kicked.

Landree's stomach somersaulted, every ounce of air squeezed from her lungs. When she crashed into the ocean, her skin stung. Landree opened her mouth to scream but only bubbles rose from her mouth.

Her friends' grip broke away from her. The salt water burned her eyes. Landree squeezed them shut and fought toward the surface. However, no matter how hard she stroked her arms, Landree sunk further into the ocean depths.

Panic chilled her soul. She fought the stinging sensation and searched for the source. While her right leg kicked in tandem with her arms, her left leg remained straight. The knee was locked, and Landree was unable to move it no matter how hard she commanded it. She could've sworn someone, or something, pulled her leg like an anchor, but all she could see was darkness.

Her mind became fuzzy, but tendrils caught her eye. Seaweed? Yet, Landree could not spot the ocean floor. Black as a starless night, they swayed with the tide. One by one, they twisted and fastened themselves to her leg. The harder she fought, the tighter they clung. Landree's thoughts grew disoriented, and she had feared she would never step foot onto Amicita.

Hands grasped her armpits. The force pulled while the dark reed resisted. Landree opened her mouth, her last breath escaping her lips.

CHAPTER

6

Sixteen days left of The Luce

Warped sounds magnified. A shrill, high-pitched tone battled against the deeper, slower paced one. Landree felt as if her body shifted along with the sound waves. An incredible pressure rammed into her chest. Again. More shouting. Human voices.

Salt water erupted from Landree's throat as she curled onto her side. Everything burned. She continued to retch as her body awoke in tremors. Grains of sand glued to her lips. Strands of her chestnut hair fell in stiff clumps over her face. As she gasped for air, the voices became more defined.

"She's breathing!"

That baritone voice. Must be Grant.

More shrieking and squealing. "Mother of Deva! Landree!"

Jane-Marie's voice, thick with emotion, pierced her ears.

Landree's stomach twisted, shooting the last of seawater rushing out of her throat...and onto Jane-Marie's lap. Her friend gagged but hugged Landree nonetheless.

As Landree gained consciousness, her limbs trembled. Her tunic and slacks felt stiff as it dried. "I-I'm alive."

Jane-Marie brushed her hair aside. "Yes, you are."

Grant knelt by her side, canteen in hand. "I'm sure you're sick of water, but I discovered a stream feeding into the ocean nearby. Take tiny sips."

Grasping the canteen, Landree nodded weakly. Although the sun hadn't risen yet, the temperature was mercifully mild. "What happened?"

Grant hung his head and sighed. "Our ship caught fire. It spread like nothing I've ever seen."

"It consumed the cabins, disintegrating it from its core," Jane-Marie added.

Finally sitting up, Landree took a swig of water and scanned her surroundings. They were on a beach, comprised of smooth pebbles instead of sand. Wreckage from their ship dotted the area.

Pieces of wood. Clumps of sails. Broken boxes, contents within likely waterlogged. A silhouette wandered from pile to pile, checking for salvageable items. The person's stooped shoulders didn't instill confidence in Landree.

To her left, a few figures huddled over twigs. A spark glowed and fizzled. Thamni's voice rose and fell with disapproval. Ms. Clio muttered as she continuously struck a flint. A couple more sparks jumped and landed into a nest of twigs and grasses.

Other bodies flew to the infant light. Ms. Clio chided them, hovering over the flame as if it would snuff out with the slightest movement. Landree's shivers became more violent, so Jane-Marie and Grant helped her toward the fire.

"Oh, thank goodness you're safe!" Ms. Clio exclaimed. The orange light accentuated her sallow cheeks and puffy eyes. "I'm sorry we don't have any blankets. Everything is... well. You know."

"Is it true? Everyone made it to shore alive?" Landree asked.

"Everyone but a few of my good men." Captain Giles appeared like an apparition. He had been the one drifting from one wreckage pile to another. He scratched his unruly sideburns and chewed on his lip. Although he remained stoic, his red eyes spoke of sorrow. "No horses made it ashore."

Ms. Clio scanned the group. "Where's Amelia?"

"Here." Amelia's usual pep to answer a question diminished to a hollow whisper. She wobbled and sat down next to a vacant spot next to Ms. Clio. Amelia's blonde hair cascaded down her back in wild curls, covering much of her torn outfit. She stared into the flames, eyes vacant.

The group fell silent. Expressions of anger and blame were deafening. Landree shifted in her seat, somehow growing even more uncomfortable.

"What's next?" Landree raised her voice as she hugged her knees to her chest.

Clearing his throat, Thamni stood. "Safety is our priority, and it's clear we're stranded. We need to start rebuilding at first light."

Giles barked in laughter. He held his belly, highlighted by his wet clothing that clung to its generous curve. "Rebuild a *ship*?" We will be lucky to get a vessel to fit us all in a few months! Not to think of creating one that could withstand a deep-sea voyage."

Thamni glared at Giles. "*The kids*," he muttered.

"They ain't kids or else they wouldn't have been chosen for your stupid trip. Mules to do the country's bidding—"

Thamni stormed up to Giles and snatched his collar. He yanked the captain to his eye level and snarled. "What other choice do we have? There are certainly less people now than there was supposed to be in the beginning."

Shoving a finger in Thamni's face, Captain Giles growled. "That's my crew you're talking about."

Landree hugged her knees tighter, trying to quell the anxiety threatening to burst from the seams as she observed the standoff. The tension had become so palpable, she figured even a machete would have a tough time slicing through. It at least removed the spotlight from Amelia, who repeatedly blamed herself for the situation they were in. While the evidence was damning, Landree wasn't fully convinced.

The fire now danced wildly. Ms. Clio, Brenna, Nicholas, Jane-Marie, Grant, and Landree all watched the two men with bated breath. Amelia didn't move a hair as she continued to stare at the fire—expression hauntingly blank.

"Boys," Ms. Clio drawled with a hint of warning.

When Thamni released his grip, Captain Giles lowered his finger and broke eye contact. He kicked up some pebbles with his soggy boot. "Fine. There may be a *slim* chance we can survive if we can make it to any of the Pekering Isles. That'd serve a halfway point to Camilla, and if we're lucky, we'll run into a tribe that'd be willing to help us. Ain't no way we'd make it to the Republic in one shot." Giles snapped his fingers. Five of his deckhands lined up beside him.

"Then, let's not waste any time." Thamni slapped his hand against Giles' back.

Shoving his hands in his pockets, Captain Giles muttered, "This is a sign we shouldn't be meddlin' with this cursed island."

Landree sighed. A simple fire took down an entire ship, transforming this expedition into a fight for survival. It was a terrible situation, and she wouldn't have been a part of it if she hadn't snuck away from home. She lifted her trembling fingers to graze the ribbed surface of her shell necklace.

My parents. I wonder how they're feeling.

"If we're going to find a way home, we'll need supplies. Lots of it," Giles said. "We'll continue to salvage what we can from the ship, but it won't be enough."

"You won't find anything useful here."

Landree's mouth parted in shock to hear Nicholas chime in.

Giles folded his arms against his chest. "Excuse me?"

Nicholas sat farthest away in the circle, just enough to keep his features shrouded by night. It sent chills up Landree's spine. She shivered.

Is he not cold?

"We're marooned on a stone beach. I explored at least a mile in both directions. There's barely anything close by." He nodded toward the fire. "We were lucky to gather enough to build that!"

Resting a hand against her cheek, Amelia whimpered. "And the guiding light, The Luce. It'll vanish in less than a month's time. If we even manage to re-build a vessel, it'll surely be well beyond that time frame."

The bioluminescent glow of The Luce extended from the depths of the ocean a few miles from shore. The aura seeped into the night sky like a turquoise fog. The light shimmered indifferently.

"I'd remain silent if I were you!" Grant's voice hammered against Landree's skull. He leaned forward, swaying menacingly. "The girls were talking about how you left a candle lit while we were preparing to disembark. How else would our ship combust into flames?"

The muscles in Brenna's jaw tightened. Amelia glanced between her and Grant.

"It could've come from the kitchen—" Amelia's voice wavered.

Ms. Clio gripped Amelia's hand tighter. "That's enough. We don't have proof of how the fire started."

"Are you seriously taking her side, Ms. Clio?" Grant asked. He turned to Giles. "What are your thoughts? You've sailed all your life, haven't you?"

One of the sailors that stood behind Giles raised his hand. "I'm the cook. The kitchen was shut down after lunchtime. Moreover, I didn't cook any hot meals all day." He peered at Amelia apologetically.

Landree's mouth ran dry as Amelia broke into sobs. While Ms. Clio rubbed her back and cooed soothing words, Grant's features twisted in fury. It seemed like every person in this encampment was unraveling. Landree's gaze fell on Nicholas last. He sat back, poised and indifferent like a feline.

"That's enough!" Thamni thundered. "I can't handle any more of this nonsense. It doesn't matter how the fire started at this point. We are here, and we must work toward a solution."

"He's right." Landree peeped. "Our original plan was to venture into the four main regions of Amicita. Maybe...we can adjust our plans. Split into groups and search for the materials and food that we need."

"Well put, child," Thamni said. "Giles and his crew will remain here to collect and tinker with what they have while we break into groups to search for material. I defer to Ms. Clio and Amelia on where we'd most likely find what we need."

Amelia straightened. "Me?"

"Ms. Clio will need assistance, and I've read your record, Miss Amelia Lightheart. You excelled in all subject matters in school, and you take a particular interest in Amicita's history. We can't run around a landmass blindly." Thamni stumbled over his last words. Rubbing his thick caterpillar eyebrows, Thamni groaned. "We'll strive to make it before The Luce vanishes. If it does, we can give Ms. Clio's map a try."

"It's gone." She swallowed audibly. "My map. It went down with the ship, b-but, I'm sure I can recall most of it."

"But no one has safely navigated back without The Luce," Jane-Marie bemoaned.

"We'll utilize what knowledge we have and do our best. That's all we got. Let's reconvene in the morning. I need to take a walk."

The expedition leader brushed past Giles, shoving a little harder with his broad shoulders. Giles fired curses beneath his breath and commanded his deckhands to follow him in the opposite direction.

Landree's chest tightened. Ms. Clio was left with her students, and her incessant fidgeting betrayed her buttoned-up exterior.

"It's alright," Landree offered. "We're all capable of handling ourselves."

Jane-Marie nodded. "We can pretend like we're on the same mission we left Camilla with…"

"Except more is at stake." Grant's head fell into his hands.

The fire started to dim, its source of fuel disintegrating into ash.

Landree released a bitter laugh. "Maybe if we're lucky, we can discover some mystical powers that could aid us."

Nicholas, who was playing with some object in his hand, looked up. His ice-blue eyes seemed to shine with newfound interest. "Unless those same powers lead to our demise first," he added in a gravelly voice.

"Ms. Clio, can you please tell him to stop that? Magical powers are nothing but a fantasy. There's nothing based on fact. Historians couldn't fully explain Amicita's history, so it became a prime target for story tellers!" Amelia exclaimed.

Landree narrowed her eyes. Amelia was the one who had been swept off feet with the fantasy of magic powers. It almost seemed like she was at constant battle with herself between her love for logic and fantasy.

"Let's all act like adults like Giles believes we are." Ms. Clio paused, frowning. "I would say try to get some rest, but I understand we're nowhere near the comfort of our beds. But...please do try."

Landree turned to Jane-Marie. Her friend already curled into a ball on her side. She accepted her extended hand and snuggled up close. Every rock pressed against her body in protest, but Landree shifted her body until the pebbles conformed to her curves. Jane-Marie squeezed her hand.

"I'm scared," Jane-Marie whispered.

Pins and needles rolled across Landree's skin. The asymmetrical landscape unsettled Landree, instead of exciting her. Instead of wondering what artifacts and treasures lay hidden on the other side of the mountain, she now feared the threats that hungered to consume her and her friends. If her parents were here, they would've showered her with, "I told you so." Landree was no longer just as risk of failing, she faced the risk of dying in an alien world.

"Me too," she replied, forcing her fears into the back of her mind. "But we'll be okay."

Starting past Jane-Marie, Landree watched the fire fade. On the other side, Nicholas sat up straight, facing the ocean. Even though all was quiet, his lips moved as if he was talking to himself.

"I hope," Landree added as she yawned and shut her eyes.

CHAPTER

7

Fifteen days left of The Luce

"Would you hurry up?" Nicholas grunted. He struggled with a massive pack twice his size.

Fiddling with her shell necklace, Landree struggled not to lash out at him. All she wanted was to be left alone. She missed her sleepy village and the Camilla Viewpoint Inn. She even missed her parents, despite their controlling and nagging nature. Landree inhaled deeply. The salty air filled her lungs, but she couldn't shake her exhaustion. Thamni, Grant, Amelia, and Brenna stood opposite her. The sun hovered over the horizon, bringing much needed warmth after a night being soaked to the bone.

Thamni and Ms. Clio ultimately decided to split into groups of two. Their best chances of finding enough resources lay directly to the east and west end of the beach. Giles hadn't said a word since sunrise, digging tirelessly into piles of wreckage. It was as he had expected. Barely anything was salvageable. Gulls cawed and circled over the sailors while the waves lapped indifferently.

"We all understand our mission?" Thamni's thick voice steamrolled across the group.

Everyone nodded.

The lines in the corner of his eyes softened. "Don't get the white signaling powder wet. Be swift but safe. Exploration and excavation is no longer a priority."

Brenna stood to his left dressed in a charcoal jumpsuit. Her fire-red locks were braided tightly without a hair out of place. She tossed a wood pole back and forth between her hands. She had whittled into a make-shift spear at some point overnight.

On the other hand, Amelia hadn't spoken or looked anyone directly in the eye since sunrise. She fixated her ashen expression toward her sandals that she salvaged. Its golden straps wound across her ankles and up her calves, which were covered in scrapes. A bow and quiver was strapped to her back.

Finally, Landree's gaze landed on her childhood friend, Grant. For once, he wasn't antagonizing Brenna. He folded his arms against his chest and nodded at Landree. The hilt of a dagger peeked from beneath his baggy and soiled tunic. Landree's thumb grazed her hip, where her dagger sat. It was heavier than her throwing knife, but she had lost it in the fire. The dagger felt awkward to handle at first, but Landree figured she'd get used to it over time.

Hopefully she wouldn't need to use it for self-defense.

A pang of guilt resonated in the pit of her stomach. Her father was the one who initially taught her how to handle a knife. Although training had been meant for hunting, Spear included a few moves for self-defense. Landree felt far from confident, but it was one skill she had over Jane-Marie. She only hoped Amelia, Grant, and Brenna knew how to handle their weaponry.

Why is it so hard to say good-bye? I'll see them again soon enough… Right?

A hand gently pulled her back by the shoulder. "It's time to go," Ms. Clio said.

An uneasy sensation writhed beneath Landree's skin. Although many pointed their fingers at Amelia for the fire, the manner of which it spread seemed supernatural. Landree pulled at her pant legs. It hadn't fully dried, but other clothing options didn't fit her petite frame.

When she had undressed to dry up a little, Landree discovered warped bruises that circled her calves right where those reed-like shadows had gripped her. She hadn't shown anyone. How could she possibly explain what happened beneath the waves?

"Could you be any slower?"

Landree glared at Nicholas. "Fine," she hissed, waving good-bye to the other group.

Ms. Clio led Landree, Jane-Marie, and Nicholas across the rocky beach. They shuffled west in silence for a few miles. The burden of their journey weighed heavily on everyone's shoulders, not to mention the sense of failure. Landree couldn't help but wonder how Thamni felt—how he was going to report back to the Queen that they blew their expedition. One that could only happen once every hundred years. It made her task of facing her parents less impossible.

Still frightening though.

When the shoreline ended, Ms. Clio paused to pull out a scroll. She squinted and sighed. After a beat, she handed it to Jane-Marie.

"Could you look at this for me?" she asked. "I, uh, never found my spare pair of glasses."

Jane-Marie nodded and studied the parchment. Landree snuck a peek over her friend's shoulder. No longer smelling of frankincense, Jane-Marie stank like the rest of them. She shed a dress for tunic and slacks that belonged to one of the deckhands. The markings on the map appeared as incoherent scribbles. Lines didn't connect. Hatch-marks covered most of the entire island.

Ms. Clio flushed. Her hands gripped her backpack.

"From what I could see, yes, we should be able to bypass these cliffs. The downside is, I can't pinpoint where," Jane-Marie said.

The cliffs towered ominously to their left. Jagged charcoal-colored peaks riddled the mountainsides like the spiny backside of a porcupine. Landree broke into a cold sweat.

"You mean the others need to traverse through that death trap?" she asked.

"So it seems. But, like you, I've never been here before." Ms. Clio rubbed her face. "I'm sorry. Just... struggling. We haven't been traveling for more than an hour or two, and we've already reached an impasse."

"Over here!" Nicholas shouted. His lean figure scaled a boulder. At the top, he disappeared beneath a felled tree. He poked his head back out. "I see a path."

Jane-Marie scratched her head. "How did he get there so quickly?"

Shrugging, Ms. Clio padded toward the boy.

"I would've taken anyone over him," Landree growled.

She struggled to grip the faint indents in the boulder. Landree's left foot slipped, and she bit her tongue as her bruise throbbed up her leg. The pack she carried pulled at her in protest. Her breath grew shallow, and her muscles burned. Panic fired from her nerves as her fingers began to slip.

Jane-Marie grabbed her. The duo struggled, but Landree finally reached the top.

"Thank you," she said, pressing a hand against her forehead.

"No problem." Jane-Marie breathed heavily. "Imagine when we find material for a ship?"

Landree shuddered. "I don't even want to know."

After squeezing through the fallen tree, Landree whistled at the endless stretch of boulders. Thankfully, all the winding paths led downward instead of up. Land stretched as far as the eye could see.

"We're located at the very edge of these mountains." Ms. Clio shaded her eyes with a hand. "If we can safely get to the bottom, we should follow those plains."

Nicholas started walking without another word.

"What exactly are we looking for?" Landree asked.

"Anything, for starters. Sources of food, sturdy trees…a means to cut down trees…" Ms. Clio's voice trailed off. After clearing her throat, she followed Nicholas.

Landree and Jane-Marie eyed one another.

"This sounds impossible," Jane-Marie said, crestfallen. The map crinkled in between her fingers.

As much as she wanted to agree, Landree steeled her nerves. "Let's just try and get there first. I'm sure Giles and his men will find tools in the wreck. They have time to search really, really well."

Plastering a fake smile on her face, Landree did her best to portray courage. Jane-Marie pocketed the map and nodded.

"Okay," she said.

Somehow, Landree tricked herself to settle into her own false sense of security. She and Jane-Marie hiked west, trailing behind Nicholas and Clio.

Fourteen Days left of The Luce

Landree met the base of the mountain with gratitude. Dirt crunched beneath her feet, scattering plumes of dirt between her companions. The grass that greeted them grazed their knees. Their silvery tips quivered in the breeze. Leaning her head back, she welcomed the dry heat.

Hill after hill, Landree forged along. Even Jane-Marie, who typically chatted her ear off, hadn't said much.

By the time the sun peaked in the center of the sky,

Landree's stomach rumbled incessantly. She didn't spot anything in the wild that was edible.

"Can I eat some of my rations?" Landree asked.

Stopping, Ms. Clio turned to face her. Landree blanched. Her teacher's veins were visible on her neck and face, and her skin appeared so dry, it could flake off with any sudden movement. Ms. Clio even tried to hide her persistent tremors by pocketing her hands, but it had become more prominent since they set sail. Landree opened her mouth to say something, but Ms. Clio cut her off.

"You've become adults in my eyes as soon as we arrived on this island. You're welcome to any amount of your rations, but just remember, they are *your* rations. No one else's. And you must make them last."

Releasing a nervous laugh, Landree shook her head. "I'll wait."

"Maybe you should eat something," Nicholas commented.

Landree secretly thanked him.

When Ms. Clio took a step forward, she flung her arms out and wobbled in place. Everyone rushed to her side, catching her before falling face-down.

"Woah. Maybe I should," she uttered weakly. "It's like blood rushed from my brain all at once."

Racking her brain for ideas to help, Landree supported Ms. Clio until she could sit. Nicholas pressed his two fingers against the underside of Ms. Clio's wrist.

"I hope she's okay," Jane-Marie said, clasping her hands together.

"Get her a flask of water," Nicholas demanded.

After shoving the container into his hands, Jane-Marie added, "*You're welcome.*"

Nicholas ignored her as he gingerly balanced the opening to Ms. Clio's lips. Landree raked loose strands of her teacher's hair away and supported the back of her head.

"How about some venison, please?" Landree asked.

"Right away," Jane-Marie replied.

After a few heart racing minutes, Ms. Clio was able to sit up by herself. Relief spread through Landree's limbs, but she still felt restless. Even though her teacher grew progressively worse since the trip started, she had noticed signs of illness earlier than that, and if that were the case, why did Ms. Clio accept the chaperone position?

"Have you seen a doctor before this trip?" Landree asked.

Ms. Clio's eyes narrowed. "No. Why?"

A lump formed in Landree's throat. "You've seemed un-well lately."

She tossed a panic look at Jane-Marie who shrugged.

"I just forget to keep hydrating," Ms. Clio answered. Her elbows cracked as she lay on the ground, head against one of the backpacks. "Nicholas. Take Landree to search for food and water. Jane-Marie, could you set up camp? I'm afraid this is as far as we're getting today."

"Now hang on a second. I don't agree with this—"

Nicholas hooked Landree's arm and tugged her away from Ms. Clio. She wrestled her arm free and glared at him.

"Why'd you do that?" she hissed.

"Let her rest," he answered nonchalantly.

The two waded through the tall grass. Nicholas took long strides, forcing Landree to jog in order to keep up.

There was so much wide-open space, and it missed the hustle and bustle that usually filled her ears. At home, Landree would always hear bells jingling from cattle and hagglers squabbling over merchandise. The hum of the village transformed into this ever-present background noise that Amicita lacked. However, Landree's concerns continued to shout loudly between her ears.

"Don't you see what I see? She's visibly sick. Ms. Clio should've stayed behind with Captain Giles. Not only is she slowing our progress, but more importantly, she's putting herself at risk."

"We need her knowledge."

Tugging at her hair, Landree ground her teeth. "But she's no good to anyone if she's dead."

Whirling around, Nicholas jabbed a finger in her direction. "We're all as good as dead if we can't find a way out of here."

Landree slouched, shoulders deflating. She didn't have any energy to argue further. The mission ahead was too daunting. The picture-perfect adventure story transformed into a survival nightmare...complete with an irritating and socially inept companion.

Nicholas beckoned her to continue exploring.

"How are you staying so cool about this?" Landree asked, tone saturated with defeat. She stared at the back of his head, wishing she had the key to unlock his thoughts.

"There's no point in panicking," he replied while pausing to inspect a broken twig. "We're involved in something bigger than all of us, something you have yet to understand."

Landree tilted her head. His words struck a chord within her.

I wonder if he knows more than he's letting on.

"Follow me. I think I see a structure there in the distance," he whispered.

As she followed close behind, Landree recalled the evening he claimed to have been tutoring with Ms. Clio.

But she's tutored Grant before.

Then, there was the time he persuaded Ms. Clio against notifying her parents about her arrival at Arrowhead Beach. While grateful, it seemed unusual that her teacher agreed with his suggestion without another thought.

But maybe she was considering that already.

Landree also caught him muttering to himself a few times.

Some people talk to themselves and are totally normal. Right?

They reached a shack, or what remained of a shack. The oak panels rotted away and collapsed from the back. A sign lay half-buried beneath the greenery. Nicholas bent down and ripped it free. He used his sleeve to wipe the dirt away.

"It ends with Post. My guess is trading post?" he asked.

"What do you mean by something bigger than all of us?" Landree asked.

Dropping the sign, he kicked the termite-infested wood aside until he located a crawlspace. He snuck a peek at Landree with a glint in his eye. "This island is a dangerous place."

"I think after the fire we all understand the gravity of being stranded here," she grunted as she wormed her way through the hole, doing her best to avoid getting hit in the head with his boots. Light, fluffy soil padded her elbows and knees, filling her nostrils with a magnificent earthy smell.

Crops would grow like crazy on untainted land like this.

When she emerged on the other side, Nicholas greeted her with a hand. She ignored it and stood on her own.

Circling in place, Landree drank in the shelves, warped from moisture and time. Shards of porcelain plates and rusted iron trinkets scattered about. The entire shack was about the size of her bedroom, and the ceiling sagged a few inches—grazing the crown of Nicholas' head.

"I don't think we'll find anything edible in here. Or materials to construct a boat for that matter."

Nicholas played with his pearl stud. Locking gazes with her, the edges of his lips twitched as if about to say something, but his creased brow expressed concern.

"What?" Landree asked.

He ran a hand over his face and through his tangled, dark hair. The walls of the already claustrophobic room seemed to squeeze them closer together.

"Amicita needs to remain isolated to the world," he said in a matter-of-fact tone.

Landree choked on her own spit. "That's a joke, right? Part of the queen's mission statement is to solve the puzzle on how to navigate here.

Bringing a fist to his mouth, Nicholas bit his knuckles

and sighed.

"Hey! Don't get frustrated with me, mister. I'm not a mind-reader or a master of riddles," Landree shot back, poking his sternum with her finger.

"The Luce appeared for the first time five hundred years ago. Documents from Amicita's previous inhabitants never mention it, even though eclipses have occurred since the creation of time. It had to appear for a reason, and I believe it's a warning." Nicholas turned and rifled through a crate and pile of moth-eaten curtains piled on the ground. He seemed to be looking for something smaller, more specific, instead of food and water. That, or he was losing it. Landree rubbed her chin, both amused and confused.

Brushing past her, Nicholas shook his head and cursed beneath his breath. "Nothing," he answered. "Let's keep moving, and I'll keep talking."

"A warning for what?" Landree followed him back outside. As much as she felt he was speaking nonsense, she couldn't help but find out more.

"I'm not exactly sure, but it's related to the mythical stones of power."

"I can't believe it," Landree shouted, throwing her hands into the air. Bushes rustled as startled field mice and rabbits darted from their hiding places. "That's *magic*, not reality. And I thought you were a serious kid—"

"That's enough!" Nicholas snarled.

A silver flash blinded Landree for a brief second as a whirring sound blasted over her like a tornado. The hairs on the back of her neck stood. Fear like she never experienced before clogged her veins like sludge. Her throat clamped up, so she clawed at her neck. Realizing nothing was there, Landree cleared her throat and steadied her breathing, but her adrenaline continued to surge throughout her body. She blinked the stars out of her eyes and studied her surroundings—no signs of disturbance, not a blade of grass out of place.

"What the hell was that?" she asked, fighting the urge to hyperventilate.

Nicholas jerked back, so Landree could only see his profile. Lifting a hand, he cupped his hidden ear and remained silent.

"Tell me what just happened!" Landree insisted through gritted teeth.

"You're the one that doesn't believe in the supernatural, so clearly, you're imagining things," he replied slowly.

Nostrils flaring, Landree turned to the left, then the right. Crows nestled on the branches of a dying birch. Dragonflies hovered over the occasional flower. The silver grass continued to sway in its sleepy rhythm, lulling Landree's spiraling anxiety with its gentle rustling.

Was I really imagining it?

She stared at her hands and flexed her fingers. "But it felt so real. Like a shadow suffocating me."

"We don't have much time before sunset. I've spotted an overgrown trail. Let's follow this for about a mile, and if we find nothing, we'll turn back," Nicholas said, finally relaxing his posture. Dirt and dust clung to every crease in his slacks and tunic.

Landree looked down and frowned at her soiled outfit.

"Fine, but I'm not letting this conversation go."

Nicholas grunted.

They continued down their linear path. All the while Nicholas dashed left and right, inspecting any barrels or boxes he discovered. Each time, he returned empty-handed, clenching his angular jaw like a disappointed child. Landree poured her focus into the landscape, searching for signs of anything edible. She passed over spotted lavender mushrooms, a species she'd never seen before. None of the trees she encountered bore fruit.

"You know, if Ms. Clio needs to consume more rations to keep her health up, I'm sure the rest of us can skimp out short term. I'm more worried about water supply," Landree concluded as her gaze lifted toward the sun melting into the horizon.

"Good thinking. Let's check out the line of oaks over there. There's got to be a water source nearby that had supported those that once lived or worked here."

His words almost bowled Landree over. "Did you get hit in the head? That's the nicest thing you've ever said to me," she said.

"Don't get used to it," he said with a sniff.

When they changed directions, sunlight reflected from Nicholas' earring. It always seemed to have a life of its own, but now it looked rather dull. A thought struck Landree.

"Where did you get that black pearl?" she asked.

"My uncle."

"Why?"

He jutted out his lower lip, clearly annoyed. "It's a family heirloom."

Landree ticked off the facts in her mind as they wove through the tree line. "And you say you're a descendant from someone who apparently grew up here."

"And?"

She picked up the sound of trickling water not too far ahead. Her heart leapt with excitement when she discovered a bubbling brook beyond a cluster of boulders. The two dropped to their knees and fished for their empty canteens. Landree giggled as she savored the first gulp. She licked her dry lips and sighed. While she went for another refill to bring back to Ms. Clio, Landree sat back on her knees and watched Nicholas.

"Let's say I believe you. What do you think this warning is?"

Nicholas splashed water over his face. "My ancestors meant to banish all powers that could've inhabited gemstones on Amicita. Something tells me they failed."

CHAPTER

8

Thirteen Days left of The Luce

A restless sleep haunted Landree. After returning with Nicholas, all three students tended to Ms. Clio who proceeded to insist that everyone get an early night's rest. When Landree tried to pull Jane-Marie aside to talk, her best friend pleaded for her to wait until tomorrow. The disheveled hair and dark circles that plagued the underside of Jane-Marie's eyes said it all. That left her with Nicholas who rolled over on his sleeping mat with his back facing her.

The journey thus far had been the most physically demanding challenge Landree ever experienced, but she struggled to fall asleep after her time alone with that mysterious boy.

Magic doesn't exist, and even if it did, why didn't he say anything to Thamni? The world would flip over on its head if they discovered precious stones that granted powers of the elements.

Owls hooted and crickets chirped, serenading Landree as she got lost in her thoughts.

The morning fog rolled through the plains as the group packed up their belongings in a symphony of yawns. Landree eyed Jane-Marie who stumbled about camp like a lost specter. Once breakfast was handed out—a handful of dried fruit—they proceeded west. Struggling to stay awake, Landree fell last in the pack. She still wanted Jane-Marie's take on her conversation with Nicholas, but she conceded to the fact that it'll have to wait till later.

Besides, Jane-Marie would tell me he's full of it. What's the point?

The landscape morphed as they ventured further into the wilderness. Moisture collected in droplets on the grass. Frogs croaked, and parrots clicked their tongues. A damp, musty smell hit Landree square in the nose, jolting her awake in the most unpleasant way. She retched.

"Anyone else smell that?"

"Yes," Jane-Marie replied, pinching her nose.

The ground softened with each step. Thicker weeds replaced that of the silver-headed grass. Insects with long wings and buzzed to and fro. Landree swatted at one and shuddered when she made contact with its hairy body.

At this point, it didn't matter what silly ulterior motive Nicholas had. Landree only cared about returning home safely.

That's the real threat—being stranded on Amicita forever.

"Look! Trees!" he exclaimed.

Landree's breath hitched. She needed to find supplies for Giles as soon as possible. She bolted past her group, ignoring Nicholas' cries of protest. Excitement looped in her mind. Trees meant wood. Possibly food!

One of her boots sank into the ground. It suctioned her in place, sending her flying face-forward and splattering into mud. A sour taste saturated her tongue. Landree pushed onto her elbows and wiped her eyes.

Birds with thin beaks and stick-like legs took flight in a sea of white wings, cawing in annoyance.

"Imbecile!" Nicholas shouted.

An arrow whizzed into the air, striking one bird in the chest. Feathers rained onto the earth as the injured fowl struggled to fly. However, its wings gave in, and it landed a few feet away from Landree.

"You're the imbecile," she retorted. "You could've hit me with that arrow."

Nicholas strolled toward his kill. "Doubt it. Last I checked, you were face down in the mud."

Landree growled, pushing Jane-Marie away, who had been trying to pull her up.

"For once, can you stop acting like an insufferable ass?"

"For once, can you take this seriously?" Nicholas clutched the bird by its neck.

Jumping onto her feet, Landree ignored the pain in her calves. She stalked up the him, only to be met by Ms. Clio's arm.

"That's enough," she warned.

Landree's stomach growled. The putrid stench of the mud that covered her sickened every fiber of her body. Every little thing bothered Landree, and Nicholas stood on the opposite end of her rage. She balled her hands into fists as they shook.

"You're immature and incompetent. I can't believe someone like you was chosen to travel to Amicita!" Nicholas exclaimed.

"You don't even know me," Landree snapped. "I was just as worthy of this trip as you are!"

Nicholas' lip curled. "You're going to be the downfall to everyone you love and care about."

"Stop it! We're all we have. Like it or not!" Ms. Clio's eyes flashed in warning.

Jane-Marie hugged Landree, but she gently pushed her away.

"Fine." Landree swung her pack around and rummaged for a linen cloth. Burying her face, she closed her eyes as tears wet her lashes. Emotions ran through her veins like a wild animal. Landree knew what was at stake. Her life. The lives of those stranded in Amicita with her. The pain and sorrow that would befall her parents. It was too much to handle, and this jerk dug his insults right where it hurt the most.

After a few rattled breaths, Landree finished wiping her face. She had questioned her worth since Erebus called her name, but she refused to let Nicholas knock her down a peg. He wasn't the judge of her worth. Finally, Landree tucked the soiled towel into her pack and nodded at Ms. Clio.

"Let's keep going," Ms. Clio said. "These trees are dead."

As the hours dragged on, the pools of mud expanded into lakes of goop. Rotted-out trees stuck out in odd angles. Landree glared at the back of Nicholas' head as their surroundings warped into a swamp. She wished she could grab him by the collar and shake him as hard as she could. Or maybe if she told everyone that he believed in magic rocks, they'd lock him up and call him insane.

"Huh. Look at that," Jane-Marie remarked.

Flowers with five white petals bloomed around a decayed tree trunk. Six stones stacked on top of one another in perfect balance. An engraving decorated the top stone: a swirl that unfolded into a wing.

"Ms. Clio. Do you think this was the work of a society that once lived here?" Landree asked.

The historian's blood-shot eyes widened. Excitement flashed across her face like a lightning bolt. Bringing a fist to her lips, she cleared her throat. "Maybe. But this isn't our priority anymore."

Landree slumped her shoulders.

Jamming his hands against his hips, Nicholas circled in place. "The sun will set within the hour. We need to set up camp here."

Ignoring him, Landree addressed her once more. "What can I do to help?"

"Not sure if it's possible, but all of you try and gather enough supplies for a fire. I'll start plucking that crane."

Nicholas bowed his head in response. Landree tugged Jane-Marie's sleeve, guiding her away.

When out of earshot, Landree fumed. "Nicholas is insufferable. I wouldn't be surprised if no one but his parents love him."

Jane-Marie shifted her pack uncomfortably. Strands of her hair danced in the tepid breeze. "I think his parents are dead."

"What?" Landree exclaimed. She side-stepped and reached for a lone branch. Almost everything in this swamp was dead or dying. Gathering dry, healthy wood or tinder for a fire was going to pose more of a challenge than she thought.

Jane-Marie shrugged. "That's what I heard from other students. It's all gossip, so I never thought more of it."

"Oh. That reminds me. I had the strangest conversation with him yesterday. Listen to this. He believes The Luce is a warning and his mission is to stop—"

Something splashed in the swamp. Then a gurgle. Landree scanned the area, but the water remained still as glass.

"This place gives me the creeps," Jane-Marie said.

Twilight continued to stretch across the sky, painting the muddy landscape violet. The breeze died down, and the humidity weighed on them like a guilty conscience. The air felt as stale as the swamp water. A chill crawled beneath Landree's skin, and she lost track of her thoughts.

A shadow slithered in the corner of her eye.

"Hey. Did you notice something?" she asked slowly.

Jane-Marie froze in place, hand lingering by the hilt of her dagger. "The crickets stopped singing. No croaking frogs or those irritating bugs."

As if sucked into a vacuum, all traces of sound vanished. Even the sound of her breath grew faint. Landree's hand flew to her throat.

Am I imagining things?

"We gotta head back," she said. Urgency laced her voice.

Jane-Marie nodded.

They headed in the direction toward camp. Darkness nipped at Landree's heels. When she glanced down to discredit her irrational fears, she gasped. Their footsteps had vanished.

Digging her heels into the moist earth, Landree panicked. "Isn't this where we came from?"

The strip of land they stood on appeared undisturbed my human or animal.

"Th-that's impossible. Let's just keep going." Jane-Marie took off.

"Wait! I don't think we should be running blindly."

When Landree didn't hear a response, she broke into a sprint down the twisted path. In another couple hundred feet, an unfamiliar fork split the trail.

"Jane-Marie, stop! I think we're lost."

However, her friend continued to run, taking a sharp right. Landree's hands fell to her knees as she caught her breath. Her lungs burned in protest, but she chased Jane-Marie. Adrenaline coursed through her veins. They had to stop and assess the situation. Pumping her legs harder,

Landree inched closer. When within arms' reach, she hooked her arm around Jane-Marie's and yanked her back.

"What in the Deva are you doing?" she yelled, shoving her face into Jane-Marie's.

Her friend's blue eyes were wide and round. Color drained from her face as her chin quivered.

"We need to get back to camp. We need to get back to camp!" she repeated over and over.

Landree grabbed Jane-Marie's shoulders to stop her friend from rocking in place.

"You got to keep it together. I know it's scary, but…"

The silence that shrouded them was deafening. Searching for clues, Landree studied their immediate area. All the life-less trees, vines, and rocks all looked the same—except for a lone tree stump with a perfectly straight stack of stones. The white flowers that bloomed around it fed her traces of hope.

"See? I recognize that. We're close," Landree said, shaking her finger at the tiny rock tower. "Don't give up."

Although Jane-Marie continued to rock, she nodded. Guiding her with a hand against the small of her back, Landree led Jane-Marie along the path that extended beyond the stump. Wiping her brow with her free arm, Landree prayed Ms. Clio or even Nicholas was nearby.

"Hello?" Landree's voice echoed. "Ms. Clio?"

"Anybody?" Jane-Marie joined in.

Darkness filled the gaps between the plants and trees. She couldn't make out a silhouette. Even as the eclipsed moons rose, the swamp seemed impervious to its light.

"Landree…" Jane-Marie whispered. Her voice slowed as

if the two syllables were dragged through molasses.

She didn't reply. Landree just walked faster, assuring her-self that her group was on the other end of this trail. She struggled with speaking as well.

"Nicholas?" As much as he irritated the hell out of her, Landree swore she'd hug the boy if she could spot him.

Everything looked the same. Vague edges and curves re-peated themselves in a nerve-wracking pattern. Minutes passed, but Landree was no closer to finding camp.

Jane-Marie stopped. "Look."

To their right was a stump…with six rocks lined on top of one another with the same white flowers.

"We're traveling in circles." Landree's voice oozed with terror.

Birds scattered into the sky. Ripples danced across the water; however, there still was no sound. The ripples intensi-fied as if something massive approached them.

In a whirring gale, a cacophony of sound erupted and knocked Landree off her feet. She covered her ears and clenched her jaw. Shrieks and groans echoed loudly in her ears—she could barely make out her own thoughts.

Jane-Marie screamed. She waved her dagger in the air. What she was swinging at, Landree didn't know.

As sound normalized, Landree hopped onto her feet. She drew her own dagger and tried to find what Jane-Marie was staring at.

"What's going on?" Landree shouted.

A black mass zipped between the two girls. It hopped onto a ledge before diving into the water. Bubbles rose to the surface one by one, increasing in intensity as if the swamp had begun to boil. In an updraft, a wall of water and weeds shot upward, and a creature with massive claws revealed itself.

It screeched as it landed near Landree. It shook its thick mane, dousing her in water.

She brandished her blade, but fear rooted her feet to the ground. Landree grimaced, unable to determine its species. Its feline features were distorted with a razor-sharp beak and bat-like wings. It stretched out its front limbs.

Before Landree could register another thought, it pounced at Jane-Marie. Her friend fell back with a scream while furiously swiping her dagger. Releasing a deep cry, Landree swallowed her nerves and launched herself onto the creature's back. Her grip slipped as she tried to grab onto its slimy feathers.

Landree struck the beast with her blade and twisted. It released a deafening screech and flew back on its haunches. She slammed into the ground, wind knocked from her lungs. Landree gasped for air and fought to stand.

She charged again, but this time ducking a hefty swipe of its claw and shoving Jane-Marie out of the way.

"Are you okay?" she asked.

Jane-Marie panted and nodded. Her gazed drifted past Landree as a shadow washed over them.

"Look out!" Jane-Marie pushed Landree.

The creature swooped over her and wrapped its claws around Jane-Marie's shoulders. She struggled, hair incompletely unbound and whipping around her head. Jane-Marie tried to stab its leg, but it locked her arms in place.

Feathers rained over Landree. She raced toward Jane-Marie, extending an arm, but the creature flapped its wings and shot into the sky. Landree stumbled over her feet and landed on her knees.

"Stop!" she screamed as they vanished into nothing but a speck in the sky.

Jane-Marie's cries amplified. Landree looked up, spotting the winged monster diving downward. She reached for her hip and cursed, realizing her dagger was still lodged in its flesh. Landree watched helplessly as the creature drew near with no signs of slowing down.

The creature veered right and dove into the swamp. Landree drew a sharp breath and ran toward the rippling water. Wading into the swamp, she pushed against the weeds and mud.

Knee-deep.

Thigh-deep.

The ripples flattened, but it didn't resurface. Landree's heart rammed against her rib cage. She was only a hundred feet away, but anxiety gripped her throat. The swamp remained at hip level with no signs of growing deeper. Landree strained her eyes, it was now so dark that the line between land and sky became inseparable.

"Jane-Marie!" she shouted but was only greeted by her own echo. Landree covered her mouth as she reached the spot where the creature dove. The surface reached her waist.

A headache forked through her skull. "This is impossible. Where could they have gone?"

Landree didn't know how long she stood there. Shock and horror threaded her body from head to toe. Her world shattered piece by piece. Landree's head continued to throb. She admonished herself—she should've listened to her parents and stayed home.

A soft glow appeared in her periphery. An orb of light bobbed up and down, a beacon in the shroud of night. One by one, sound returned to the swamp. A lone caw mixed in with the symphony of crickets.

"Landree?"

Her stomach squeezed. A male voice carried from the light. Landree waded back to shore, lashes wet with tears.

"Hello?" she responded.

A lanky figure held a torch. The flames highlighted a shimmering object in the person's ear. A black pearl.

"Nicholas!" Landree jogged toward him. "I didn't think I'd ever be happy to see your face."

Looking past her, Nicholas knitted his brows. "Where's Jane-Marie?"

Landree hung her head. Nothing but shame occupied her mind.

"Where is she?" he asked again, dragging each word out.

"It's not safe here," Landree blurted, not meeting his eyes. She focused on his piercing. An opalescent hue reflected off the black pearl.

Was it supernatural? If I tell him, I'm sure he'll try and connect it to his nonsense theory. There's got to be a rational explanation for this.

Nicholas grunted. After a beat of silence, he wrapped one

arm around her shoulders. Landree flinched.

"Let's get back to Ms. Clio. Maybe then you'd feel more comfortable talking about it," he said, voice softening.

Although she still struggled to speak, Landree walked alongside Nicholas, grateful he didn't push. Moreover, grateful he had an ounce of empathy to show for once.

Landree could still hear Jane-Marie's screams. They bounced in between her ears. In one swift movement, the creature spirited her away. It didn't make sense. And yet, Landree held out hope that if the creature was able to vanish without a trace, Jane-Marie could still be alive somewhere.

In a clearing ahead, Ms. Clio prodded a small fire with a twig. She immediately looked up and sighed. Her lips stretched wide and tears filled her eyes.

"You're safe!" She exclaimed, opening her arms.

Nicholas let go of Landree, exposing her neck and shoulders to the evening air. She hated to admit it, but his touch leant a warmth that calmed her nerves. He strode past Ms. Clio and added his torch to the camp fire.

"Jane-Marie is gone," Landree blurted.

Stopping in her tracks, Ms. Clio's face blanched. Her hands fell to her sides. "Excuse me?"

Nicholas ripped into a skewer of meat. "Why don't you both take a seat. Landree, eat something. Then tell us in detail what happened."

CHAPTER

9

Thirteen Days left of The Luce
Amelia

Amelia clung to her map, scribbling down notes. She trailed behind Grant, Brenna, and Thamni, who were walking too fast. It wasn't conducive to capturing every detail. They had been traveling for two days, and they barely reached the summit of the mountain. The trail was steep, filled with thorny brush and uneven terrain. Amelia tried to sample the soil, but Thamni scolded her multiple times to keep up.

It's like a sturdier charcoal. I needed to save some!

"This is rough," Grant said. He paused to sip from his canteen. Wiping his golden hair from his eyes, he turned to Amelia. "Didn't you say the West Team had a path to go around these things?"

Amelia nodded. Even though he was fair-haired, Grant

could never pass for Irellian. Petulant and whiny with wide-set eyes and a weak chin, Grant embodied the stereotype of Norlenders. She glanced past him and at Brenna. Amelia quickly learned that thankfully not all Norlenders were like him.

"What about *us*?"

Amelia bit her cheek. She wanted reach in and yank out his vocal cords.

"Aw, is someone getting tired? I know it's hard, being as delicate as you," Brenna quipped. She leaned against her staff. Her clothes clung to her body, soaked in sweat, but she showed no signs of fatigue.

"How are you smiling?" Grant asked. "You're crazy."

Thamni cleared his throat. Clutching the straps to his pack, he squared his shoulders. "Grant, Amelia is our source of knowledge while Ms. Clio is the West Team's. Both had agreed to the paths taken. Remind me how well you did in your historical studies?"

Grant shook his head. "I'm good."

"I know we encountered a few blocked routes, but we should reach the halfway point today. Then it's all downhill from there. That's if Amelia picks up the pace." Thamni jerked his thumb in the direction of the path. "Everyone needs to hustle as fast they can. I'd prefer to reach an altitude where we don't freeze to death when the sun sets."

A chill zipped down Amelia's spine. "Yes, sir."

Amelia grappled with her frustration. Her parents raised her to always follow orders from elders or superiors, but whatever happened to her thoughts and opinions? Gaining knowledge of the surrounding environment was just as important as plowing right through it.

She had kept to herself most of this trip. The memory of the ship fire dogged her steps. Although no one brought it up, Amelia could feel the responsibility mount her shoulders. It didn't help that Grant would shoot her a dirty look once in a while. Her stomach squeezed. Amelia was certain she had snuffed out those candles. She wanted to prove her case, but she didn't have the time or the evidence. Even so…

Who would want to set the ship on fire?

The group trudged around the bend. Amelia tucked her map into the side-pocket of her pack. If the books were accurate, they'd encounter two deserted cities on their journey. Only one if their first stop contained what they needed.

A gust of wind brushed Amelia's cheek. Her gaze followed it south. Her lips parted at the view revealed between two mountainous peaks. Rust-colored earth fanned as far as the eye could see. In a central cluster, buildings stood like ants. Amelia clapped her hands.

"I think I see our first stop!" she exclaimed.

"If it's more than a day's walk, I don't care," Grant replied without looking back.

Amelia huffed and charged past him. She was sick of staring at the back of his head. When she reached Thamni, she pointed at the land exposed between the mountains.

He nodded, sunlight reflecting off his shaved head. "Keep your eyes on our goal."

"What exactly are we looking for, anyway? I just think it'll be difficult to transport the amount of materials needed to build a vessel large enough for safe transportation overseas," Amelia remarked.

The soot-colored dirt crunched beneath their feet. After a beat, Thamni regarded her with his large, gray eyes.

"We need lots of strong wood. Oak is preferable if they grow here. Scraps of metal too, if possible."

"How many trees?" she pressed.

His jaw tightened. After a deep breath, he replied. "I don't have the exact number. As much as we need."

When Amelia opened her mouth, he lifted his hand.

"Just focus on the directive. You're incredibly brave to take part of this journey. If you think too much, you'll worry yourself to death before you come to a solution."

Amelia bit her tongue. It didn't make logical sense. Thamni's reply was much like one of a devil-may-care adventurer ...or a parent soothing his terrified children when he himself was unsure. She slowed her pace, allowing Thamni to push ahead.

"Hey," Brenna said, appearing on her other side. Up close, she wasn't as "giant" as others described her. She lowered her voice. "I think what he's trying to avoid telling you is that...we don't really have any other choice."

Amelia's face fell.

"Don't tell me you hadn't figured that out with that genius brain of yours," Brenna continued as she shook her head. "Logic is well and good, but when that fails to provide answers—you do have one more option."

"And what's that?"

"Faith."

The wheels in Amelia's head turned, digesting her words. Faith was so abstract. She couldn't measure it, weigh it, or calculate statistics from it.

Faith in what?

Brenna shared a crooked smile. "You'll learn. Perhaps this is the spiritual journey you need."

Amelia chucked. "You sound more Irellian than Norlender."

Brushing dirt from her braid, Brenna snorted. "I wish."

Questions continued to bubble in Amelia's brain, but she swallowed her words and instead soaked up the warm silence.

They continued around narrow twists and spindly thickets. After another hour, Amelia's legs begged for a break. Grant's stomach growled. However, Thamni led the group without looking back.

The incline they traversed leveled off. Amelia wiped her forehead. She had donned a bandana to keep her curls in place. While she was not one to worry about looks, she knew her hair was a complete disaster.

"Can we stop and eat?" Grant asked.

The troop slowed to a halt. Amelia wiped her glasses with the hem of her tunic and pulled the map out. Thamni and Grant exchanged heated words, but she tuned them out. She had made a copy of Ms. Clio's, and it didn't say much. From her studies, Amelia filled in the rest with her assumptions. Tracing her fingers along the path, she calculated their approximate location.

"If my guess is accurate, we're very close to some sort of

gorge or canyon. Given the view from here, we've reached the highest point we need to be."

Grant snapped his fingers. "Perfect. See? Excellent time for a break."

Throwing his pack on the ground, Thamni grumbled. "You children are undisciplined. We have limited rations and are trekking over a barren wasteland. Your body doesn't need food like it does water."

Brenna tilted her head, eyes rolling up and to the right in thought. She knelt, resting her staff against a boulder. "Let's agree to a thirty-minute respite. We all could use it, but we won't idle."

"Sounds ideal," Amelia chimed in. She plucked a quill and bottle of ink from her pack and scribbled more notes.

Thamni grunted. He leaned against a boulder and scratched his head. Once closely shaven, patches of platinum-blonde became more prominent across his skull. Amelia continued to study him closely as he rolled up his sleeves, revealing a lion's paw tattoo under his forearm.

"You're an Irellian?" Amelia blurted.

Thamni's head snapped up. The glimmer of fear faded into anger. "It's a tattoo. Keep to yourself."

Before she could reply, Grant tossed an oval object to Amelia. She flinched, only for Brenna to catch it before it smacked her in the face.

"You need to learn to give people a head's up," Brenna scolded. She sniffed it. "Ew. What's this?"

"Boiled egg. What kind of egg? You can ask Giles when we return." He pulled two more out and extended one to

Amelia.

Brenna peeled the shell, nose crinkling. "That was nice of Giles to share some with you."

Grant's gaze fell. "Share. Right."

Amelia examined the egg. Ignoring Brenna's gagging, she peeled the shell and dug her thumb through the center. She felt a soft lump. Separating the two halves, Amelia discovered a misshaped lump of membranes and feathers. A dark orb, the size of a pea, stared back at her.

"Oh, yuck. There's a...dead...I mean, baby...*thing* inside!" Brenna exclaimed.

Grant shrugged. "It's a delicacy in certain Camillian street markets. I'm surprised you haven't run into them before."

"I'll have one," Thamni volunteered.

Brenna tossed the egg at Thamni then hung her head between her knees. She shuddered and burped. Amelia sniffed hers. Metallic. Earthy. She pursed her lips.

"No?" Grant asked. Specks of egg flew from his full mouth.

Amelia curled her lips and leaned away. "I'll try it if you keep your mouth shut until you're done eating."

Breathing in through her nose and out her mouth, Amelia told herself, *it's just food.* She grew up eating various kinds of cuisine because her family traveled so much. She steeled her nerves, closed her eyes, and opened her mouth.

A piercing howl echoed through the pass.

Amelia leapt to her feet. Wolves with yellow, slit eyes appeared from behind rocks and an alcove above her head.

When it landed, the wolf bared its fangs, but what caught her eye was its two tails.

Had I smudged my glasses when trying to clean it?

Amelia hurled the egg, but it didn't budge. Its eyes remained trained on her.

"Really?" Grant quipped.

"Sorry, knee-jerk reaction."

"Don't turn your back," Thamni muttered. "Maintain eye contact. Most importantly, remain calm."

Amelia retreated until her back grazed the others.

The wolves slinked closer. Saliva dripped from their jaws. Amelia's breath grew labored; her chest tightened to the point where she thought it'd burst. They continued around the group and lined up next to one another, blocking the path down the mountain.

Amelia's features twisted in confusion. "Predators usually circle their prey."

When Thamni stepped toward them, one wolf crouched, ready to pounce. He raised his arms and shouted. "Be gone!"

Amelia and the other kids copied him, puffing their chest out and shouting. The wolves took pause and observed them.

"They're not leaving," Amelia said, barely moving her lips. "It's like they won't let us pass."

"We have no choice. Draw your bow. Brenna, prep your staff," Thamni ordered.

Fighting the tremor that seized her limbs, Amelia reached over her shoulder. Every time the wolf in front of her snarled, she'd freeze.

In what seemed like an eternity, Amelia grasped her bow and nocked an arrow. She was greeted with uncertainty. She didn't want to harm a creature unless she absolutely had to. She inhaled deeply and held her breath. Between the Grant and Thamni's yelling and the wolves' tails twitching, Amelia fought every urge not to release the arrow until the right moment.

"We are going to pass," Thamni exclaimed.

The central wolf howled and pounced. Grant ducked, and Amelia let her arrow fly. It connected in between its eyes, and the wolf collapsed. Amelia coughed a laugh.

"I-I did it."

"Watch out!" Grant shouted.

A body slammed against hers. Drool rained over Amelia as Brenna locked her staff in its jaws. Amelia clawed the earth, attempting to pull herself from the pile. Another wolf dove at her. Brenna wrestled her assailant and rolled off Amelia.

She shrieked, swinging her free arm. Her fist connected with the wolf's snout. Pain exploded in Amelia's knuckles, but the blow bought her enough time to draw and arrow and fire it into the wolf's chest.

It yelped and writhed on its side. A pang resonated in Amelia's chest. Her archery experience extended as far as hay or tin can targets, not a living creature. Thamni stepped in and struck the final blow.

He nodded at Amelia. Scratch marks marred his face. "You okay?"

"Yes," she answered, gaze fixated on the maroon stream leaking from his wound. "Are *you* okay?"

"Just a scratch," he replied gruffly.

"These are interesting looking creatures," Brenna said. She nudged the dual tails from one of the wolves.

Grant scratched his chin. A decent amount of scuff was growing in for his age. "Speaking of food…"

"No time," Thamni cut him off. "We don't know if there's more. We'll prioritize food when we get off this damned mountain."

Grant pocketed his hands and kicked a pebble. Amelia lifted a brow and shrugged. After everyone packed up and Amelia recovered both her two arrows, they set off on the descending trail. Crows zoomed over them, cawing in delight at the meal they left behind. Acid churned in Amelia's stomach as she imagined their beaks ripping apart the wolves' flesh. Her parents had always told her she had an active imagination.

As Amelia trudged along, she picked up an odd scent. She couldn't place a finger on it.

Meaty, yet burnt? No. Like something rotting… much like spoiled eggs.

She poked Grant's shoulder. "Do you have more of those eggs?"

Tightening his grip on his shoulder straps, Grant responded with, "Why?"

Amelia rolled her eyes. "Just tell me yes or no."

Grant paused. "No."

"I'm serious. I smell rotten eggs."

"Oh." Grant relaxed. "No, I really don't."

Brenna whacked him on the side of his head. "Why the hell were you acting like you had 'em, then?"

Cracking a smile, Amelia basked in gratitude for Brenna. While the two Norlenders squabbled, she redirected her attention to Thamni who was audibly sniffing the air. Amelia should've known—judging by his fair hair and the fact she never saw his skin burn from the sun—that he was Irellian. Perhaps what surprised her the most was that Queen Baneberry hired a foreigner. Amelia hugged herself. Maybe her future was brighter than she hoped!

"You smell something off as well?" she asked cautiously.

"Sulfur."

Heat rose to Amelia's cheeks. "I should've known that." She pulled out the map. "Likely near hot springs. This indicates possible volcanic activity," Amelia murmured as she jotted those words down.

"Volcanoes?" Grant wailed.

Everyone ignored Grant as they continued their descent. Amelia pinched her nose as the sulfur scent intensified. Rushing water echoed nearby as well. It ate away at the silence, transforming into an insatiable roar.

"Check this out, kids." Thamni pointed at a clearing.

Steel buildings wobbled in the wind like sleeping giants. Most were stripped down to their frames, the last bits of their integrity held together by rusty bolts. The beams matched the color of the soil. Orange-brown particles danced around the abandoned streets. Amelia's mouth grew slack. A metallic taste crept its way onto the tip of her tongue. Haunting yet awe-inspiring.

What kind of a tribe inhabited here? What happened to them?

"Wow," she finally said.

"Wow, indeed, but I don't think rusted-out metal is going to help us," Brenna said, tone tinged with disappointment.

"Let's scope out the area," Thamni said.

Amelia and the others followed an open path that led them to an arched gateway. Not far from the entrance stood the source of the echoing roars.

A waterfall cascaded from the adjacent mountain and emptied into a basin. Amelia observed its perfectly rounded structure—certainly not nature-made. A circular plaza created an audience-like space to view this waterfall. Two torches stood on an elevated step at the edge of the basin.

"This is…incredible!" Amelia exclaimed.

"Spread out. Search for materials and food."

"Yes, sir!"

CHAPTER

10

Thirteen Days left of The Luce

With the rush of the waterfall at her back, Amelia veered toward a narrow alley with Thamni. Grant insisted on accompanying Brenna, much to her dismay. Many of the buildings Amelia passed were too unstable to risk entering. She scoured abandoned food carts and wheelbarrows, discovering a copious number of rusty axes and swords, but nothing was worth taking.

The setting sun painted the sky with a myriad of colors. Amelia wrapped her arms around herself. Goosebumps pricked her skin. The temperature dipped a few degrees since they arrived at the abandoned city. She sighed.

"We, uh…" Thamni clicked his tongue. "Let's search until the end of this street, then we can turn back and set up camp."

"Okay," she replied half-heartedly.

Even Thamni's strides grew less urgent. His usual stiff posture sunk into itself. When Amelia caught his eye, he straightened.

"So, you're Irellian too?" he asked.

"First generation," Amelia answered cautiously.

Funny. This is the same man who didn't give a damn about small talk.

"My daughter will be a first generation Irellian, too." Thamni's face lit up. "I miss you, little one," he murmured to himself.

"I didn't know you had kids."

He squared his shoulders and tugged at his collar. "I'm sure you can tell, but I tend not to share personal details."

"Well, I think it's neat that an Irellian-born was hired by Queen Baneberry. Many Camillians think Irellians and Norlenders only came to their country for a chance at the riches and glory of this expedition."

Thamni cracked his neck then his knuckles. "…Your family hasn't pressured you to apply simply to further Irelle's power and influence, have they?" he asked.

Amelia glared and huffed. "Seriously?"

He lifted both hands. "I'm sorry. I didn't mean anything by it."

Guilt forked through Amelia as she fidgeted. He wasn't incorrect. It was the only way to outshine her sister. But the opportunity to explore this country came with harsh expectations to bring glory to the homeland. She always found that word funny.

Homeland. But Camilla is my home.

Amelia caught Thamni staring. "Oh, sorry. Um, no I'm not offended."

He chuckled as he knelt to examine a chain that looped through a shop entrance. Its porous, burnt orange surface chipped at his touch. He shook his head. "I realized it's going to be a longer journey than I thought. I figured it would be nice to get to know you guys. Teenagers are crazy, you know that? Who in their right mind for volunteer for such a suicide mission? And I don't mean this mess we got ourselves in—"

More guilt. Amelia had successfully pushed the fire incident into the back of her mind since their first night in Amicita. She recalled the rage in people's eyes.

"I swore I blew that flame out," Amelia blurted.

His lips twisted into a frown.

"I know everyone blames me for the mess we're in, but it makes no sense. A massive tall-ship, even though it's primarily made of wood, couldn't just combust with the flames from a few small candles!" Amelia slammed a fist against a steel beam. Rust rained on her like tainted snowflakes. Frustration simmered in her veins.

Thamni clasped her shoulders. Giving her a gentle squeeze, he shared a knowing look. "I have the same suspicions. I've been around for a long time, and I've never seen a ship, a home—anything, go up that quickly. It's been on my mind since it happened. Please don't beat yourself up over it."

This giant of a man built of only harsh edges spoke softly. His words rested easy in Amelia's mind as the edges of her lips crept up.

"Okay."

He pointed at a wide building near the dead end. "Everything so far has rusted beyond use. Let's finish up."

When Amelia wrenched the sliding door open, she covered her nose with the crook of her elbow. The air within coated her skin like a cloak of moisture. She hesitated.

"What do you think?" Thamni asked.

Normally, Amelia would turn and run as fast as her legs would carry her. Yet this journey forged a new foundation of courage.

After facing a pack of two-tailed wolves, I can handle this.

"May as well do a quick check."

Amelia crept over a raised step. The room was built around its stone structure. She ran her fingers over the uneven walls and skirted around the broken-down ceiling. Flies buzzed in uncoordinated circles.

Something cracked beneath Amelia's boot. She stepped on one of the many shattered pieces to a gemstone. Picking up a shard, Amelia examined its blood-orange center. Warmth pricked her fingers. Yellow flickered within its core.

Or was it the light?

"I've never seen a stone like this before." She followed the trail of shattered stone which led to…

Amelia gasped. She shoved the gemstone into her pocket.

A human skull with patches of long hair, unattached to its body, lay on the floor. Her vision grew blurry as terror seized her limbs.

"A-a real corpse…i-in the flesh!" she exclaimed as her mouth ran dry.

"Well, it *had* flesh," Thamni corrected.

Amelia ripped her glasses from her face and glared at Thamni. Her entire body trembled. "That's not funny!"

He rolled of his eyes and muttered, "Kids."

Wiping fog from her lenses feverishly, Amelia steeled her nerves. After putting her glasses back on, she knelt down. The mere thought of touching bone sent bile up her throat, and yet, her analytical side needed to investigate. She tucked the squeamish feeling away in a mental box and buried it deep in her consciousness, then pulled an arrow from her quiver. Using its pointed end, Amelia turned the skull over. Its dry, paper-thin texture indicated it had long since decomposed.

Crunch!

Thamni cursed. Amelia's head snapped up, finding him in the opposite end of the room. The man stood near a throne, shaking one of his legs.

"Is that a headless skeleton you stepped on?" Amelia asked nonchalantly.

"Why you ask?"

Amelia lifted the skull by its hair. "This is the rest of him. Or her. It's certainly humanoid in form."

"Great," he replied sardonically.

Amelia strode toward Thamni, sizing up the skeletal body beside him. She nodded. "Yup. Very much humanoid given its stature and appendages."

Thamni continued to scour the room without a reply.

After placing the skull next to the rest of its body, Amelia studied the throne. Crafted entirely from iron, its decrepit remains were held together only by its velvet padding. She ran her fingertips over the armrest, robbed of its jewel-encrusted décor, and arrived at a wolf's head.

"This place had nothing to offer. What a waste of time. Let's go," Thamni boomed.

Amelia held up her finger and ignored his audible huffing. "I'm trying to figure out who once sat here."

"You're not satisfied with the only corpse in this room?"

"One can never assume," Amelia said as she rounded to the backside of the throne. Strips of iron twisted and melded into a six-foot figure. Mouth agape, she reached for her parchment. She sketched the image feverishly. "It has the head of a wolf but the body of a human."

"Does it have two tails?"

Amelia shook her head. "It's nothing like the animals that attacked us. Also, there is prominent detail on their mane." She tapped her quill against the braided design. Her mind whirled through the library of books she's read on Amicita. Nothing.

"And yet..."

Thamni cleared his throat. "I know this stuff interests you, and in a perfect world, this is what we would've been doing, but studying a throne is no longer a priority."

Reality snuffed out Amelia's enthusiasm. She slowly rolled her parchment and equipped her backpack. She should've known better and listen to her superiors, but she just couldn't help it. The flame of curiosity flickered within herself, unwilling to change. She silently followed him out of the room, fighting every instinct search the walls for clues.

Thamni held the front door open. "And yet what?"

"Hm?"

"You were mumbling 'and yet' just before we left." His wild brows bent upward, genuine and inquisitive.

"Oh, nothing. I just recall an extinct species, the Foti; however, their fossils were discovered on the Bridge."

"The land between Irelle and Norlend?" Thamni asked.

"Yes. I've read nothing about them here. They could've immigrated to Amicita, but to have a throne and established city... That would be just thrilling!" she exclaimed, eyes widening in awe. After a beat, she caught herself and lowered her head. "Not that it's important."

Thamni dropped his gaze and folded his hands behind his back. His sandy complexion flushed a deeper hue. "No need to apologize. We didn't waste *too* much time."

Smiling inwardly, Amelia grazed her thumb over the blood-orange gem in her pocket that she salvaged. It was enough.

The two trotted down the alleyway, their footsteps echoing in the haunting wasteland. Each time they kicked up dirt, Amelia would taste the metallic residue. She wrinkled her nose as she suppressed a sneeze. Despite Thamni's kind words, the tensing of his jaw muscles told her that he struggled with the lack of results. Each time he examined a building, his posture grew more slouched.

"Why are expedition volunteers teenagers?" Amelia

asked.

Thamni rubbed his hand over his face, then spat into the dirt. Amelia side-stepped even though she was well beyond its trajectory.

"Camilla sees this as an opportunity of a lifetime for secondary students in their final year before transitioning to adulthood," Thamni said in one breath with a thick coat of sarcasm. He glared at the sky.

"You're just reciting from the campaign scrolls."

"Huh. Can't pull the wool over your eyes, can I?"

Amelia trained her eyes on Thamni, refusing to look away. After a few beats, he groaned.

"Alright. You wanna know what I think? They're young and stupid. You follow orders, and you're free labor."

Amelia felt a strange twinge in her chest. His theory was glaringly offensive, and yet it made sense. "But I'm not stupid."

"Perhaps they made a mistake with you," he replied with a snort. "But I meant more like, kids tend not to ask questions. They're meant to do as their told."

"Question what?"

Thamni walked faster and sniffed. "How the hell would I know? Stop asking so many questions."

The sun made its final descent just as Amelia and Thamni met up with Brenna and Grant. The two sulked by the edge of the basin as if they spent the entire day enduring one of Dr. Barnes' lectures about hydro-powered clocks. Grant scooted closer to Brenna, but she mirrored his movement to keep the same amount of distance. Amelia couldn't help but smirk.

"Anything?" Thamni asked.

"Nope," Grant replied. Brenna rested her chin on her knees, eyes sunken behind dark circles. "You?"

"I found this gemstone. I think it's a bloodstone—"

Thami cut her off. "We found nothing."

"What kind of civilization would build a city of iron near two sources of water? This place is sandwiched between the sea and this damn waterfall!" Brenna leapt to her feet and kicked a rock into the basin.

The cogs in Amelia's brain spun in circles. "Well, I found a throne decorated with a Fotian figure—"

"That's enough, Amelia," Thamni snapped.

"What? Why?" she asked, pressing a hand against her chest. "I don't understand—"

Throwing his backpack on the ground, Thamni arched his shoulders and balled his hands into fists. "What did I just go through telling you? None of that nonsense matters. We. Need. Material," he said, ending his last sentence breathing heavily between words.

Amelia shrunk back. Brenna hopped off the basin's ledge and gently placed a hand on her back. "Come, let's get food for dinner while the boys work on a fire."

The continuous roar from the waterfall provided much needed background noise while Amelia and Brenna fished through their packs for tins of nuts and dried apricots. It filled in the empty voids in Amelia's mind that would have otherwise led everyone down a rabbit-hole of anxiety. She didn't mean to irritate Thamni.

"I can't believe we didn't find anything." Brenna pulled out a bag of jerky.

Amelia bit her lip, hesitant to share her discovery. "Well, I did find something, although it won't get us back to Camilla."

Dropping the jerky, Brenna searched another bag, expressionless. "Oh?"

"Yeah. The bloodstone I mentioned earlier."

Amelia produced the fractured gem and displayed it in her palm. It emitted a serene warmth under the twilight. Or was it actual heat?

"That's a rock," Brenna said flatly.

"Not just a rock. This is a piece of the shattered remains of what appears to be a precious gem!"

"…Which is a fancy rock."

Amelia closed her hand into a fist and pressed it against her chest. "Amicita is famously rumored for its precious gems! Gems that may have once harbored magical powers. As someone who signed up for this expedition, I'm surprised you don't show more interest."

"Here we go again." Brenna leaned forward. "I don't get you. You're the bookish type that only believes what can be deduced from logic, and yet, you're also the one that is the most fascinated with the lore."

"It's…a bit hypocritical sounding. Maybe I secretly want the supernatural to be real. Spice things up a bit."

"Listen, it's all greed. Those that are paying for these expeditions aren't interested in its history or tales of whimsical nature. Personally, I signed up so I can get away from my house." She tied the pack with an impatient yank. Eyes trained on the ground, Brenna sighed. "I even considered just staying behind."

Shock rippled through Amelia. "But why—"

"Hey ladies," Grant swaggered in between them. He plopped some canteens on Amelia's lap then placed his arm around Brenna. "Amelia. Why don't you fill us up?"

"What did you say?" Brenna asked. She pointed at the waterfall then tapped her ear.

Grant leaned closer. "I said—"

She elbowed him in the solar plexus, grabbed the canteens, and said to Amelia, "We'll get the water and light those torches. Come on."

Ignoring Grant who rolled on the ground, half laughing and half groaning in pain, Amelia trotted behind Brenna.

"In Camilla, that's called assault," she said.

After flicking her auburn hair, Brenna's upper lip curled. "In Norlend, that's nothing. It's tough love, baby."

Amelia fumbled for words.

"He's an idiot. And a glutton for punishment."

Brenna knelt by the basin, filling one canteen after another. Taking off her bandana, Amelia fantasized jumping into the water so all the grime, sweat, and blood would wash away. She dipped a finger into the water and shuddered. Ice cold, but it didn't dampen her desire for a bath. Perhaps she could sneak one in after everyone was asleep.

After capping the first canteen, Brenna rested her elbows on her knees. "It stinks we found nothing here."

Amelia unfolded her map and traced her nails against the

rough parchment until she reached a part of the coastline that formed a hook in the east. Hatch marks encompassed the area. She tapped at the question mark. "It does, but we still have one more chance. Descriptions elude to a jungle."

"That should do it, then. Right?" Brenna asked, features perking like a watered daisy.

"It's our best bet. A forest in the east and plains to the west. We're bound to find the supplies we need in time."

The two girls glanced at the two moons. Each night, they inched apart, and served as a looming reminder of their deadline. Brenna's smile faded, and she returned to filling more canteens.

Chewing on her lip, Amelia stared at the back of her neck. Brenna didn't seem convinced. Amelia wasn't sure she was convinced herself.

"Do you really think we won't be able to find our way home without The Luce?" Brenna's eyes remained hidden behind her hair. Her voice was fragile—a word Amelia would never associate with Brenna.

Amelia racked her brain. "The expedition that failed to return had a lodestone. And some documents say that other expeditions tried to test their home-made compasses beyond the curtain of light, and it sent them into a perpetual spin. However, if Ms. Clio can remember her findings, we may have a chance."

"Mmm." Brenna capped the canteen.

Uncertainty terrified Amelia. All she had were books upon books detailing four previous voyages, each with varying experiences and results. While it provided her with all the knowledge to get top marks in class, she couldn't answer Brenna with confidence.

Leaning forward, Amelia carefully selected her words. "It doesn't mean it's impossible. We have the tools for navigation, and we have Ms. Clio. We are fine. Totally fine!"

"Hey. Would you mind giving me a hand?" Thamni hollered, straining his voice.

He gestured toward a metal rod with a soaked rag tied at the top that lay near the itty-bitty fire. The flame licked at meager twigs, threatening to extinguish at the slightest breeze. Thamni had been tinkering around the two torches, setting them upright and stuffing them with flammable material.

Amelia kissed the torch to the flame. In a *whoosh*, the torch ignited the cloth that wrapped around its head.

"I packed a flask," Thamni said as if reading her mind.

"Whatever works," she replied and took to the first torch. "It feels warmer already." She smiled and lifted her arm to set the second torch on fire.

"Thanks. Now, it's time for a well-deserved meal."

Grinding metal overpowered the waterfall. Amelia swiveled on the spot, searching for the source of noise. The ground shook, sending ripples across the basin. She pressed her hands against her ears as the screeching intensified.

"Another earthquake?" Amelia shouted. No one answered.

The buildings around them broke into chunks. Beams slammed onto the earth around them. Thamni yelled something, and Amelia took off along the circular plaza, narrowly missing another falling piece of architecture.

Even when the grinding sound stopped, the vibrations intensified. The water in the basin swirled like a whirlpool, as if an imaginary plug had been pulled from the bottom. The waterfall continued to fall into the ever-growing abyss, causing a mix of curiosity and fear buzzing around her.

Brenna's cry snapped Amelia from her thoughts. The silhouette of a creature clamped its jaws against her ankle and dragged her toward the basin. Its glowing red eyes shifted its gaze right at Amelia, taunting her with its unblinking orbs.

"Where'd they come from?" Amelia exclaimed, whipping her head in both directions.

Thamni and Grant stood on either side of Brenna, slashing their daggers in their air. The aggressors had two tails…

"More of them?" Amelia asked, blinking her eyes rapidly. She wasn't sure if she needed to clean her glasses again. Other than their tails and eyes, the rest of their bodies appeared as blurry, dark blobs under the two moons.

Amelia darted toward her pack and plucked her bow from its resting place. She rolled on her shoulder, avoiding a shadow zipping by. When she returned to an upright position, Amelia equipped her quiver and fired an arrow at the wolf attacking Brenna.

The arrowhead shattered at the base of one of the torches. "Damn," Amelia cursed. Steadying her breath, she took aim once more.

"Watch out!" Grant shouted. Bodies collided onto the ground, filling the night with grunts and scuffling in the dirt.

Nails pawed against the ground, growing louder each

second. Amelia breathed deeply, trying to steady her hands. The back of her mind screamed at her to duck, that one of those creatures was about to reach her.

Every moment counts.

Amelia released the arrow. A body slammed into her seconds later, knocking her off her feet. Her glasses flew from her head, and lights exploded in her eyes when her skull connected to the ground. Amelia arched her back in pain. The creature sniffed then released a low growl.

Everything appeared out of focus. Amelia squinted, but other than the same red eyes, she couldn't make out the wolf's features. She shot an arm out and wrapped her fingers around its throat. Instead of fur, the texture was much like a snake's, smooth and cool.

Ignoring the questions that pelted her curious mind, Amelia pushed against the creature. Each time it lunged, its jaw missed her neck by mere inches.

Amelia's hand slipped. Her stomach plummeted as the wolf snapped at her again.

Its teeth scraped her collarbone but snagged her tunic. Amelia's hand flew instinctually to her neck. Once it got ahold of her, the wolf dragged her toward the basin.

Although stunned by fear, she thought of her ancestors. The foundation of Irellian history had been built behind powerful women with a simple motto: "Strength and Courage". Even in her family full of physicians and scholars, they all showed unwavering confidence in their line of work. They never cowered in the face of any obstacle. Swallowing the harrowing odds of death, she blindly felt around until her fingertips grazed the rims of her glasses. She had to see. She had to weigh the risks and benefits then find a solution.

"What are these things?" Brenna shouted.

Amelia fumbled to put her glasses on. As the glow from the torches expanded, Amelia gazed upon the horror before her. While it took on the form of the wolves she encountered earlier, the creature looked like its literal shadow. There were no defined features—just a force of darkness and red eyes.

"Demons?" she yelped.

This was the stuff of nightmares, only belonging in a bad dream or in a story book.

Amelia punched its head repeatedly, reinforcing them with a battle cry. And yet, not matter how much force she used, it seemed to absorb her blows.

The rush of water grew louder. Panic forked through Amelia. She flailed her limbs wildly, kicking up clouds of dirt. No matter how hard she resisted, the monstrous wolf-like form dragged her along like she was its plaything.

In the corner of her eye, Amelia spotted Grant wrestling an identical being that had attacked Brenna. He struck it repeatedly with his dagger, but it only bucked him off its back. Brenna found a split second and just enough room to roll over and crawl toward her staff. It whistled as Brenna twirled it above her head. The creature dove, and the staff missed and crashed into a torch. It teetered, showering Brenna with ashes.

Thamni's voice thundered above as he connected with the shadowy beast that was dragging Amelia. With a twist, he sent it down with a body slam, relieving the mounting pressure against her chest. The crisp air grazed her face as she gasped for breath.

Amelia immediately stood, dizzy from the blood rushing from her head. The shadow beast fought Thamni's grasp, gnashing in her direction. It expressed no interest in Thamni. The creature howled, chilling Amelia's soul with its hollowed-out sound.

The shadow beast that clashed with Brenna caught her staff in its jaws, wrenching it from her grip. It tossed the weapon aside and bolted toward Amelia instead.

Amelia's breath hitched. She reached for another arrow, but the creature sank its teeth into her wrist. Or at least it felt like real teeth. Sharp, white-hot pain seared up her wrist, and like de ja vu, it lugged Amelia toward the basin.

The more she struggled, the tighter it clenched its jaw.

Shouting erupted from all directions. Everything swirled in a mess of dark colors. Amelia refused the give up. She kicked and writhed as she inched closer to the basin. As the dual torches entered her line of vision, an idea popped into her head. Amelia had no idea what these things wanted, but they had attacked when the basin had drained. She connected a boot with a torch. It fell to the ground, and the fire snuffed out.

The grinding returned. Amelia strained her ears—the hollow abyss seemed to fill back up with water.

Amelia opened her mouth to shout in victory, but the shadowy beast tossed her into the air, sending her somersaulting into the basin. As soon as it released its grip, its beady red eyes disappeared into the night. She flailed her arms, desperate to cling on to something.

An arm jutted out and clasped hers.

"I gotcha," Thamni shouted. His head appeared over the rim. Fresh blood seeped from his old wounds on his face. His eyes flashed in alarm as she started slipping.

Amelia swung her other arm and grasped onto him with both hands. However, between her sweat and his blood, Amelia continued to slip.

Muscles twitched in his jaw as he pulled. "Hang on!"

The ledge was within inches of Amelia's grasp. The water's turbulent flow rumbled hundreds of feet below.

"Come on," she said, gritting her teeth.

Thamni's eyes bulged. With a thud, the dark beast with blood-red eyes landed on his back. Before Amelia could re-act, it struck his neck with lightning speed. Spit and blood spurted from Thamni's mouth, raining on Amelia's horror-stricken face. His lips moved with his gaze still fixed on her.

"Nayana," he whispered in a hoarse voice.

As soon as the beast vanished once more, Thamni's grip weakened. Stomach flying into her throat, Amelia plummet-ed into the abyss.

INTERLUDE

I

Are you sure this is going to work? asked the woman.

The boy who was sitting next to her hung his head. *I have no choice. Plan A failed, and somehow the stones of power have awakened.*

Is it all connected? asked the woman.

Everything's connected, the boy said.

The woman hugged herself and shivered. *I don't feel well.*

The boy placed a hand on her shoulder. *One thing I'm sure of is that you'll be okay.*

CHAPTER

11

Twelve Days left of The Luce
Jane-Marie

A headache throbbed in between Jane-Marie's ears like it never had before. She groaned as she rolled over to her side, trying to dispel the pain. A cool surface pressed against her face. She wondered when her mother was going to burst through the door and wake her up for school. Maybe she could fake being sick.

Another boring day.

Her eyelids fluttered open. Instead of facing her favorite windowsill, she was surrounded by a porous, cobalt wall. Jane-Marie lifted her head, sniffing the dank air. Claw marks ravaged her arms. The world swam around her head as she tried connecting the dots.

"Where am I? What—"

She had been laying on a coral platform in the center of a

cavern. The air was laden with salt. Stalactites peered down at Jane-Marie, its peach or tan arms ranged from a few inches to multiple feet. Sitting on her knees, she stared into the water that surrounded her. Its teal hue contrasted greatly to the plain stalactites. Although deep, she could see right through to the bottom. Crabs scuttled against the rocky floor. Strings of seaweed danced in the rhythm of the tide.

This looked nothing like Camilla. No matter how hard she tried, Jane-Marie couldn't recall what had happened. The last things she remembered was resting her head against her pillow, anxious to join the expedition to Amicita.

She shivered as a thought struck her.

"Wait. Am...I here?"

A snuff echoed in the cavern.

Jane-Marie rotated slowly on the spot. Hanging upside-down from the ceiling was a mass at least three times her size, wrapped in bat-like wings. A squeak escaped her lips before she covered her mouth with a hand.

The creature snuffed again and unfurled its wings. Jane-Marie's skin crawled. It exposed its feline body and opened its beak to yawn. The oddest thing of all though, was that it was completely coated by a black substance. It almost seemed like she was staring at the creature's shadow and that the real thing was underwater, ready to leap up and attack. Jane-Marie's gaze fixated on its talons, then stared at her arms.

Jane-Marie's heart raced. She wasn't sure what frightened her more: this super-natural being or the fact she had lost all sense of control. Something terrible had happened, and she couldn't even remember how and why. Her thoughts wandered to Landree.

What happened to my best friend? Nicholas, Grant, Amelia... even that Norlender girl.

A fire lit in her torso, dispelling her initial fears. If this thing wanted her dead, she would've been already. Squaring her shoulders, Jane-Marie steeled her nerves and stood as tall as she could.

"Where am I? What have you done to my friends?" Jane-Marie exclaimed.

The monster blinked awake and stared back intently.

She pointed at her forearm. "You brought me here! Why? Tell me now!"

Its features remained unchanged. "Find a way," it answered in a staccato voice.

After it yawned again, the creature released its grip on the stalactites. When it plunged into the water, it dissolved into thousands of obsidian particles. The cloud of darkness vanished, leaving Jane-Marie alone with the crabs and minnows darting around in confusion.

"You've got to be kidding me!" she shouted, voice ricocheting around the cavern.

Wasting no time, she studied the cavern walls. Unable to determine any openings, Jane-Marie trained her eyes beneath the ocean surface. A pair of manta rays weaved back and forth with grace, circling around Jane-Marie before vanishing in a network of tunnels. She broke into a cold-sweat, and her breathing grew shallow.

You have no choice, girlie.

She rolled up her sleeves and forced deep breaths. Jane-Marie wasn't the best swimmer, and navigating through a dark, narrow space chomped on her confidence.

Refusing to allow any additional doubts to enter her mind, she leapt from the platform. As she swam with broad stokes, Jane-Marie was pleasantly surprised at the mild temperature. When she drew near the tunnels, she decided to follow the path the manta rays chose. Taking the deepest breath she'd ever taken in her life, Jane-Marie dove under water. She kicked her legs forcefully, contorting her body to fit into the underwater corridor.

At first, her elbows and knees constantly scraped the narrow walls. Each time, her claustrophobia flared. A flurry of bubbles escaped her lips as she fought to cry out. Her instincts begged her return to the previous room.

A bioluminescent glow captured her attention. Specks of light blue and aquamarine twinkled on the walls, lighting her way. Jane-Marie's eye's widened at the foreign beauty. The gentle glow of the lights softened the edges of her fear. Ribbons of seaweed tickled her stomach as she pushed through the path that bent upward. More bubbles escaped her mouth as she inadvertently sighed. She admonished her carelessness and continued swimming. It was too late to turn back now.

Jane-Marie's lungs burned as the seconds ticked by. Her mind grew fuzzy. Water pressure thudded against her ear drums to the point where she couldn't even hear her thoughts. Jane-Marie's movements grew more desperate, and she cut her hand against a jagged rock. Fighting the urge to cry out, she made one last push. Light glistened above; however, everything blurred to the point where she wasn't sure if she was imagining things.

Jane-Marie broke the surface and gulped the air hungrily. She paddled toward the ledge, groaning as she pulled herself onto another porous surface. Collapsing onto her stomach, Jane-Marie squeezed her eyes shut, desperately trying again to piece her broken memories back together.

Once she caught her breath, Jane-Marie sat up. She slammed a fist against the ground, still unable to recall anything.

A shimmer of light painted the ground. Jane-Marie's eyes widened as she lifted her gaze. Blue flames danced on top of candles in their holders against the wall. In the center of the room stood an altar with a shield at its center. Oval in shape, the shield appeared untouched. No scrapes or dents. Pearls and a single sapphire decorated the surface. Jane-Marie was hypnotized by the blue gem, radiating more brightly than the pearls.

Indeterminate voices whispered in Jane-Marie's ears. She concluded she was still dizzy from lack of oxygen. Shaking her head, Jane-Marie told herself to focus.

However, there wasn't much else to focus on. Although she survived the underwater experience, Jane-Marie wound up in a room with no doors. Looking over her shoulder, her stomach twisted at the thought of diving back in. Panic forked through her body and her heart beat rapidly.

Did I miss a turn?

She growled and kicked the altar. The granite pillars that

held the slate horizontally toppled, sending the shield crashing onto the ground. Jane-Marie's hands flew to her cheeks.

"Oh, shoot. Sorry, sorry." She mumbled to herself, trying to stand the stone back up, but it was near impossible to keep one standing while she worked on moving the other.

The room shuddered, throwing Jane-Marie onto her seat. Stone ground against stone in a high-pitched screech. The ceiling split open from the middle, and a rush of water filled the room. Adrenaline shot through her veins, filling her with panic.

Jane-Marie fled toward the tunnel she had emerged from. "Where is it?"

She searched frantically for that opening in the ground. Pulling at her hair, she broke into tears.

"What the hell is happ—"

The ocean deluged the room, sweeping Jane-Marie off her feet. She gagged, fighting against the rush of water in vain. No matter how hard she fought, the turbulent water swirled her about. She slammed onto the wall, candleholder digging into her back. Jane-Marie's body screamed.

She clung to the wall until the entire room filled and the current stilled. Her muscles relaxed one by one as she absorbed her surroundings. The ceiling had completely opened, exposing a much larger, darker underwater room. Jane-Marie blinked incredulously at the candles—flames still danced on their wicks with their turquoise hue.

When she let go of the lantern to make her way up, the whispers returned. Jane-Marie glanced down, finding the shield lying on the floor. The sapphire sparkled brighter than before. It made no sense. Nothing made sense.

Without pause, Jane-Marie swam deeper and turned the shield over. She slid her left forearm through the leather straps. As soon as she fully equipped the shield, white-hot heat shot up her left arm and burrowed itself deep in her chest.

Jane-Marie opened her mouth to gasp. Fully expecting salt water to burn its way down her throat, she knitted her brows. Instead, a sensation of cool air funneled into her lungs. Seconds ticked by. Jane-Marie couldn't comprehend what was going on. The sapphire on the shield illuminated the room, filling it with as much light as the sun on a cloudless sky.

Everything appeared fantastical. Then it hit Jane-Marie.

This has to be a dream!

She tested her theory and dared a breath. Inhaling through her nose, the burning sensation of water shot through her nasal cavity, but her body was rewarded with oxygen. Resigning to her theory, Jane-Marie swam up and out of the room.

I've just got to kill time until I wake up.

Fear and anxiety shifted into curiosity. Using the sapphire, she shined the light forward, exposing a ballroom-sized arena. Murals covered the walls, detailed with black pearls, diamonds, and other precious gems. Most images depicted ocean creatures, like the dolphin or octopus. Jane-Marie fixated on one that she didn't recognize.

The creature was rabbit-like and had a fin for a tail. Lapis Lazuli outlined the image and strokes of blue paint portrayed fur.

Jane-Marie continued to explore the room. Various colored coral presented maze-like paths on the floor. Opposite that was a gold chandelier. It swayed ever-so-slightly in the water. Her eyes widened as she took in the sights.

A wave of silver zipped past her. Jane-Marie jerked her head toward the source of disturbance. The tail end of a school of fish scattered, revealing a massive sea creature. Rib -like fins stretched across its seven-foot-long body. It opened its jaws, revealing scores of sharp teeth. Staring unblinkingly at Jane-Marie, the fish flicked its tail, inching closer. It paused, then flicked its tail once more.

Jane-Marie swallowed her fear. If this were a dream, she couldn't truly be harmed.

Right?

The giant fish darted at her, opening its jaws wider. Jane-Marie swung the shield in front, struggling with the clumsy underwater physics. Its teeth scraped against metal, grazing her elbow.

Sharp pain streaked up her arm as she screamed. Bubbles rose furiously to the ceiling as blood oozed from her wound. Shaking the fish off, Jane-Marie bit her lip and watched blood dissolve into the water.

The predator swam seamlessly and looped back for another attack. Jane-Marie swung her free arm and connected her fist with its nose. It hissed and swam off, vanishing into a corridor near the bottom of the room.

Jane-Marie heaved, paralyzed in place. She *felt* pain like no other. She was profusely bleeding from a wound. Dread seeped into the back of her mind.

This was no dream.

Searching for an exit, the only other way out of the room was through the corridor the massive fish swam through.

Alternating her arms and legs, Jane-Marie fought her way toward that corridor. She prayed she would not run into the beast again. However, the fear of being trapped in the sea outweighed his fear of a carnivorous fish.

She continued down the corridor, no longer taking pleasure in the quaint depictions of these rabbit-like aquatic creatures. Jane-Marie's breath grew shallow, unable to shake the unexplainable ability to breathe now.

What if it stops working all of a sudden? At what cost?

Jane-Marie's tears dissolved into the sea. She swam and swam, desperate to find the end of this horror sequence. An opening appeared above. She kicked furiously until she reached a smaller room. Her eyes widened at massive glass windows. Beyond the windows stood the vast sea.

A coral reef extended as far as the sapphire's light reached. Yellow, red, and orange coral decorated the underwater world. Jellyfish bounced up and down as angel fish played peek-a-boo with the eels. Beyond that, pure darkness.

A squeak broke Jane-Marie's train of thought. Rocks shifted on the debris-laden floor. When she swam closer, she spotted an aquamarine fuzz ball twisting and turning. Its lengthy ears twitched in agitation as it tried to free its tail from beneath a boulder.

"The creature from the paintings?"

It froze, black eyes locking its gaze on Jane-Marie's. Its whiskers dropped.

"A human?"

CHAPTER

12

Twelve Days left of The Luce

Jane-Marie rubbed her eyes. She rubbed them a second time for good cause.

"Please don't hurt me!" it peeped, curling into a ball. Held in place from its tail by the boulder, the creature swayed like a buoy.

Jane-Marie swam closer, engrossed with curiosity. It looked like something straight out of a five-year-old's imagination. Dozens of questions filtered through her mind, but she needed to calm it down first. "It's alright," she said gently. "Let me help you."

The creature revealed itself once more, swallowing audibly. "The rock…"

Nodding, Jane-Marie placed both hands on the boulder and kicked as hard as she could. Her muscles strained, pushing more blood from her gash. Lights flashed before her eyes as Jane-Marie grew lightheaded.

"It's no use."

"Use Kai's Sapphire."

"The what?"

It twitched its nose. "The blue gem on that shield," it replied in a matter-of-fact tone.

"What's that going to do?" Jane-Marie narrowed her eyes.

"How else were you able to breathe under water?"

"Good point." Rose Marie swung the shield in front of her. She flushed, feeling ridiculous as the rabbit-like creature watched. After a few seconds of inaction, Jane-Marie lowered the shield. "I don't exactly know what I'm doing."

The creature's ears folded back as he fell into a morose silence. Each strand of his fur swayed in tow with the direction of the current.

"So, the humans *have* forgotten," he finally said. "Focus all your mental energy onto the sapphire. Generate the image of what you desire in your mind, and if you possess enough inner strength, the gem should be able to manifest your desires in its power."

Feeling like an utter fool, Jane-Marie lifted the shield once more. A fuzzy memory tickled the back of her mind.

Wasn't there some myth about magical gemstones in Amicita?

She imagined freeing this creature. How? By moving the rock.

Move the rock.

Jane-Marie tuned out the environment around her. Her arms trembled, but she trained her thoughts to the one mantra.

Move the rock.

Her core tensed as an invisible force tugged her closer to the shield. Warmth radiated from the sapphire, its blue light now flickering in tandem with her pulse.

Move the rock!

A funnel expelled from the shield, forcing Jane-Marie backward. The current rammed into the rock. Her heart raced, feeling as if she had been running at full speed for miles. The rock teetered but remained standing.

With a grunt, she threw her whole self against the shield. An explosion of air bubbles erupted and blasted the rock into smithereens. The sapphire flickered, light dimming to a faint glow.

The creature swirled in circles, but Jane-Marie couldn't move her muscles. She had no energy left. Jane-Marie tried to speak, but her lips barely moved. Suddenly, she was overcome with exhaustion.

"Hold on, I'll bring you ashore!" Its voice echoed as Jane -Marie floated to the ocean floor.

The world swam around Jane-Marie in shades of blue and gray. Her thoughts came and went in incoherent threads. All she understood in that moment in time was that some rabbit-dolphin hybrid was jerking her around the ocean.

Absurd!

When the creature reached the shore, it kicked the shield from Jane-Marie and hopped onto her stomach. The impact forced water from her throat and nose, jolting Jane-Marie from her trance. She hacked and gagged, forcing out more water.

Everything stung. Jane-Marie grimaced.

"Are you okay?" the squeaky voice asked.

"Yup," she replied. Jane-Marie belched, and emptied the last of the ocean water from her insides. "How the hell did I survive?"

"You're welcome," it quipped, shaking its body to rid its fur of water.

Jane-Marie sat on her knees and waved a hand in resignation. "Sorry."

Its ears twitched, showing off its shell earrings. "You clearly know nothing. Do you even know what I am?"

Water dripped from every strand of hair, falling into her eyes and on her lips. Wet sand found its way in between her fingers and up her back. Everything was incredibly uncomfortable, and she wasn't in a mood for guessing games. "Water bunny?"

"My name is Lepus, and I am a Kai."

Jane-Marie stared. "A what?"

The Kai's chest deflated. "So much for the glory of a mythical creature," he muttered.

"I'm sorry, I've never heard of a Kai in any fable or tale." Jane-Marie wrung her hair. "Either way, thank you for saving me."

"Well, you saved me first." Lepus brushed his fur against

her shivering body.

A smile crept onto her lips. Jane-Marie reached out and petted his back. Lepus froze, gaze darting back and forth. She retracted her hand.

"Sorry."

"That's...fine. Let me get something for you. I'll be back shortly."

He hopped across the unadulterated, white sand. A few stone cottages dotted the beach. The walls were painted various colors, resembling much of the reef beneath the ocean surface. Jane-Marie also made out a shimmering gate. If she saw correctly, it was a gate made from gold.

The landscape was breathtaking, an idyllic destination for a vacation if it weren't for its eerie silence and suspicious string of storm clouds pushing its way inland.

Jane-Marie dropped her head between her knees. Although her senses returned to normal, she still couldn't remember how she woke up beneath the ocean. Everything happened all at once, and now she was left to deal with these questions alone. She shivered uncontrollably.

What happened to me? Why can't I remember the trip?

Kai's Sapphire caught her eye. It sat on the shield, dull and lifeless as a gemstone should be. Mystery shrouded the sapphire, but Jane-Marie had a feeling it could aid her in her journey to find her way back to her friends...even home. She needed all the help she could get—there was no way she was going to be stranded on an empty island alone.

When Lepus returned, he covered Jane-Marie with a blanket.

"Sheep's wool," he mentioned, as he fussed over her elbow.

"I didn't mean to offend you," Jane-Marie said softly.

"It's quite alright. We haven't co-existed with humans for hundreds of years. I guess it's vain to believe that we could fade into history while humans write songs about us. Some Kai even allowed glimpses to sailors, just to send them into a tizzy."

Wrapping the blanket around her tightly, she smiled. "Very nice to meet you. My name is Jane-Marie."

"What brings you to Deran, Jane-Marie?"

"To where?"

"Deran…" Lepus narrowed his eyes. "This island."

Her hand flew to her mouth. "Oh goodness! We've been calling it by a completely different name for years!"

Lepus shook his head and chuckled. "That doesn't surprise me. Previous visitors have gone right for the precious gems, never bothering to read the historical scrolls tucked away in the palace."

"A palace?" Jane-Marie scooched closer. Normally history lessons bored her to tears but hearing it from an adorable rabbit-like sea creature was much more appealing.

Lepus crossed his front arms and bounced on his tail. "It's no longer a palace, that's for sure. I wasn't alive around that time, but my grandfather told me it was made from gold—a gift from two tribes that once lived in Deran." Lepus stopped bouncing. "My ancestors belonged to one of those tribes."

"What happened to them? So, none of the Kai live here

anymore?" Jane-Marie tilted her head to the side.

"The Kai have a complicated past; however, I will say that over the years, there weren't many reasons to stay."

"Then why are you here?"

His fur bristled as his gaze lifted toward the sky. He shook it off then crept on all fours, circling the shield. "I was actually in search of this. I know I can't physically wield a shield in a sense that humans can, but it's not the shield that I need." Lepus brushed his cheek against the sapphire, and the light within flickered then faded.

Jane-Marie chewed on her cheek. "And why's that?"

"This Kai's Sapphire once belonged to the matriarchs of Deran, along with three other stones that were gifted to them. After multiple wars...and other horrific incidents, a Queen Isabel determined the magical components should no longer exist. After she passed, the tribes held onto them in case her successors ever changed their mind." He sighed. "Of course, this kingdom no longer exists, but the Kai check in on the stone from time to time."

"But if Queen Isabel banished the stones' powers..."

"I'm getting to that. My family and I have detected unusual activity the last five-hundred years—"

The Luce!

"—like the powers were somehow returning, and I believe the recent seismic activity was a sign of a looming threat. With no one left in Amicita, I figured that if Kai's Sapphire powers truly returned, I could borrow it and—."

"Threat?" she interjected, gripping her knees with white-knuckled intensity.

Lepus huffed. His tail thrashed back and forth. "You're like a child. What am I saying? You *are* a child!"

"Excuse me, I'm not a mind reader!" she exclaimed.

A gale caught Jane-Marie before she could keep speaking. Stiff strands of her hair whipped off her face, and sand rained against her cheeks. A wall of gray clouds rolled in from the south, casting darkness on the land.

"A storm builds," Lepus shouted. Nudging the shield toward Jane-Marie, he continued, "Let's seek shelter in the nearest hut!"

She jumped to her feet, snagged the shield, and trudged toward shelter. The sand slowed her pace, but she pressed forward. A fine mist transformed into a downpour. Palm trees bent to the will of the wind. Every time a raindrop splashed on her neck, Jane-Marie shivered. The rain was as cold as ice.

Another gust of wind nearly tore the blanket from Jane-Marie's body. Hugging both the blanket and shield against her chest, Jane-Marie pumped her legs to reach the final few feet. She rammed into the door with her shoulder and fell in.

"Reckless human! You nearly broke the door and undid the patchwork I did for your elbow!" Lepus hissed as he struggled with the lock.

"Are you seriously going to criticize me now?" Jane-Marie growled. "Or maybe you just aren't fond of humans!"

Lepus rolled his eyes. "Please. I may not have interacted with a human in over a hundred and fifty years, but it's a well-known fact that they don't even like people within their own species."

Jane-Marie strode toward the window, refusing to engage in the conversation further. She already felt on edge about everything that had transpired throughout the day and realized this squabble wasn't worth getting into.

Rain pelted the glass. Storm clouds continued to move inland, thunder acting as its rallying cry. The windowpane rattled with each rumble. A nagging sensation in her gut told her that she had to find her friends as soon as possible.

"You mentioned seismic activity?"

"Correct. It's not unheard of for Deran to experience volcanic activity, but it's been occurring at a suspicious, rhythmic pattern."

Rocking her forehead against the window, Jane-Marie closed her eyes. Exhaustion set in. It would be challenging enough to traverse a foreign land, let alone doing so in the middle of a tempest. She engaged in a tug-of-war with her heart and mind.

"You need to rest."

She sighed.

"Please. You need to rest in order to recover your injuries," Lepus insisted, softening the edge in his tone. "We can talk more in the morning. I'm sure we can help each other."

"Fine." Jane-Marie turned to find a make-shift bed of straw and the blanket. Lepus stood at the edge, fluffing a bundle of hay like he would a pillow. He stepped back and bowed his head.

"Thanks," she muttered.

As soon as she lay down, Jane-Marie's eyelids grew as heavy as stone. Warmth enveloped her.

"I'll wake you at first light."

"Good night, Lepus," she replied, folding her hands against her stomach. Thoughts swirled like an infinite whirlpool.

What threat was Lepus talking about, and why would he care if he didn't live here? I'll need to ask him in the morning. Maybe we could use Kai's Sapphire together...

Eleven Days left of The Luce

Rays of light filtered through the window, piercing through Jane-Marie's eyelids. She groaned, joints cracking as she rolled onto her stomach. Incoherent thoughts swam through the fog of her mind. The earthy scent from the hay filled her nostrils.

"Lepus?" Jane-Marie rubbed her eyes.

No response.

"Lepus?"

Sitting up, Jane-Marie scanned the hut. He was gone. So was the shield.

"That little thief!" She stumbled from her makeshift bed and kicked the door open. She flinched as her elbow throbbed to life. Staring out to sea, Jane-Marie's heart sank. "That jerk could be miles away by now."

After everything that happened to her, Jane-Marie had found a glimpse of hope in that sapphire. She glanced at the sky. Adin and Deva were ghostly versions of themselves during the daytime. They were halfway transitioned from their eclipse, and she wasn't so sure she could find everyone in time.

If everyone's still alive.

Gulls took off from nearby trees in clusters, making her jump in her skin. They cawed loudly as they scattered in various directions. A sense of dread filled Jane-Marie. She dropped her gaze. The sand, still moist from the rain, broke apart in chunks. Half a second later, the earth shuddered, throwing Jane-Marie off center.

The ground beneath her feet swayed. Panic splintered through her nerves. It almost felt like the earth would flip over, and she would fall into the sky. Jane-Marie fell on her knees and shielded her head with her hands.

This must be what Lepus was talking about!

It was over as soon as it began. After waiting a few seconds, Jane-Marie sat up. Gripped with despair, tears welled in her eyes. She still had no idea how she arrived in the building beneath the sea. She was lost and alone.

As she tried to steady her breath, Jane-Marie made out warped imprints in the sand. Oblong in shape, it looked much like rabbit feet. The paw prints headed in inland.

Balling her hands into fists, Jane-Marie grappled with sadness that threatened to overwhelm her. They both wanted to borrow the artifact's powers, but she had found it first. Not that she would've minded sharing it either, and yet, he left without further discussion.

Why did he do that?

The rolling plains expanded for miles until the horizon swallowed them whole. Hills and tree lines blurred in the distance. To Jane-Marie, everything blended into a never-ending landscape, presenting her with a daunting task and no direction. Somehow, the vast emptiness put Jane-Marie on edge almost as badly as the underwater tunnels.

Almost.

Following Lepus was a start, and since he chose to travel by land, she had a chance to track him down. Perhaps she could still convince him to share the sapphire's powers. It could mean the difference between escaping the island or remain trapped in Amicita—Deran, whatever this island was called, for the rest of her life. She needed to find her friends and a way to restore her memories. There was no other way but forward.

CHAPTER

13

Eleven Days left of The Luce
Landree

Every time Landree blinked, her eyes burned as if sand
were trapped beneath her eyelids. Between the lumpy
ground and shadows that haunted her, she hardly slept since
her friend's disappearance. Ms. Clio's reaction to her encounter with the beast bothered Landree. Even though she
claimed to believe her, Ms. Clio's clipped tone and one-
word replies hinted otherwise.

They spent yesterday searching for Jane-Marie. Landree
swore they left no stone unturned, and yet they returned to
camp empty-handed. Nicholas kept to himself the entire
time.

That bothered Landree more. Ms. Clio's cynicism made
sense. Magical beings only existed in epic tales invented to
entertain young children.

But not in Nicholas' mind. No wonder he's behaving noncha-lantly.

Landree rolled over and stretched. Beyond the pile of ash, Ms. Clio lay on her back. Her chest rose and fell steadi-ly. A blanket, folded into a perfect square, lay a few feet away. The fogginess in her brain lifted.

After releasing a yawn, Landree slid from her blanket and stood. "Nicholas?" she whispered.

Craning her neck, Landree searched the sea of brambles. A fog hovered inches above the earth. The early rays of the sun extended its fingers into the swamp. It didn't appear nearly as spooky during the daytime, but she hesitated to move. If she searched for Nicholas, she might get lost again…and run into that *thing.*

"Good morning."

Smooth words cut through the humid air. Swirling around, she found Nicholas stepping from the shadows. His cheeks were flushed, and sweat glistened from his brow. His black pearl earring twinkled in the morning sun.

"Where were you?" she asked.

Nicholas held up a batch of frogs. "Breakfast."

"How do you just appear out of nowhere like that?"

Nicholas ignored her and gathered the last of the twigs in the camp area. Ms. Clio stirred. Landree didn't want to dis-turb her, so she reached for the flint.

Stopping short of the stone, she stared at Ms. Clio's out-stretched hand. Violet lines branched out like roads in a me-tropolis beneath her paper-thin skin. Landree blanched. Ms. Clio had to be in her late twenties, yet her hand appeared as frail as a seventy-year old's. Ms. Clio groaned and curled into a fetal position.

Making her way to the pile of twigs, Landree cradled the flint. She eyed Nicholas warily.

"I think Ms. Clio's getting worse," she said.

Nicholas swiped the flint from her. After two strikes, sparks gave birth to flame. "She'll be fine," he replied.

"And how do you know that?" she asked, folding her arms.

Standing so he could appear at eye level, Nicholas leaned forward. Heat washed over Landree as she shrunk back. His long, thin lips curved into a frown.

"Even if she was getting worse, what can we do about it?" he asked, voice low and slow.

Landree swallowed a hard lump in her throat. Although she knew he was right, she resented his matter-of-fact attitude.

He turned and drew his dagger. Working swiftly, he skinned the frogs and suspended them from tree branches. Helplessness taunted Landree. She scoured the camp for something to do while Ms. Clio continued to sleep.

"Let me refill our canteens," Landree said. She dug into her pack and wrapped her fingers around the cool metal tin. Liquid sloshed within as she picked it up.

"Already did that. I don't want you getting lost again."

The intense pressure of frustration bubbled from her toes to her scalp. Obstacles compounded over one another ever since she snuck out of her home, and she grew doubtful of her ability to overcome them. The shipwreck threw everyone off guard, and Nicholas' insults were salt rubbed into her wound. He never even mentioned his theory to anyone else, and even if it was true, tackling the problem alone was foolish.

What if Nicholas is right? No way!

With a sigh of resignation, Landree forced her emotions behind a mental dam. She found that blocking out every negative experience on this trip helped her cope...for now. She plopped by the fire to see what was so interesting. The orange and yellow flames flickered weakly. It continued its chaotic dance, occasionally sizzling as blood dripped from the frog corpses.

The fire reminded her of her friends on the East Team. Shuddering, Landree hugged her legs to her chest. She hoped they were safe, that shadowy creatures weren't stalking them. Landree tugged her necklace, but the thread snapped. Shells the size of thumbnails tumbled into the waterlogged earth. Some rolled into the fire.

Perhaps that represents my chances of ever returning home.

With a grunt, Nicholas fussed over breakfast. "Almost done. Best to wake Ms. Clio."

Landree grabbed his wrist. Nicholas' skin was cold as ice. She flinched. His eyes widened.

"Do you believe my story?" she asked, her voice growing brittle with each word.

Pulling away gently, Nicholas stared at the dirt. "I thought you only believe in things that could be explained by logic," he replied sarcastically.

"I need you to believe me," she pleaded. "I know you

don't like me, but something's not right on this island." She paused. "Maybe…just maybe, there's some truth to what you told me the other day."

Nicholas ran his hand through his ebony hair as he nodded.

Scooting closer, Landree fought for his gaze. "So, you do believe me."

Nicholas scratched his nose and turned away from her. "You should learn not to rely on the validation of others. Especially if you ever want to develop leadership qualities." He balled his hands into fists. "I'm going to wake her."

Throwing her head back, Landree squeezed her eyes shut and fought the sting of her tears. Joints ached, and the bruises on her calves throbbed. Physical pain was easier to endure than anything abstract like emotions. Landree failed to save her best friend, and Nicholas offered no comfort. Cracks in her emotional dam deepened.

I guess I have been dependent on others for validation. I saw what I saw.

Ms. Clio's groan snapped Landree from her trance. In the corner of her eye, Nicholas helped Ms. Clio sit up. He whispered into her ear, and she shrugged. His whispers grew more urgent until the teacher nodded. Landree wanted to ask how she was feeling, she really did, but the force of guilt held her back.

"Hey," Landree blurted awkwardly.

Ms. Clio rubbed her eyes. Her hair stuck out from all ends, looking like a lion's mane. "Good morning."

She can't hate me if she said good morning, right?

Nicholas rushed to the skewers. He knelt and offered Ms. Clio one. Her freckled nose wrinkled, but she accepted the meal. Landree cringed at their charred eyes, but her stomach still growled.

After offering Landree a skewer, Nicholas kicked dirt over the fire. He pocketed his hands and scanned the skies. The sunlight blunted the bite of the morning breeze. Landree indulged in the goosebumps that erupted up her back.

Blowing steam from her roasted frog, Landree couldn't help but notice his left leg jiggle restlessly.

"What's wrong?" she asked.

Nicholas straightened, muscles taut. "What?"

Landree flexed her fingers. It was like having a conversation with a wall.

"It's almost like you've been waiting in a line for something."

"We're on a time crunch. Of course I look like I'm on edge."

The muscles in Landree's face relaxed. She made some headway. "You can't control everything."

Scratching his ear, Nicholas turned his nose up on her. "Like how you couldn't control losing Jane-Marie?" he snapped.

The mental dam shattered. Waves of self-hatred and disappointment undulated in her body, sapping what little strength she had left. Tears cascaded down her cheeks, and her breaths grew shallow. Wiping her face with her sleeve, Landree scrambled to keep it together. His words broke her in no way she'd ever felt before.

"I'm going to shut my eyes for a few minutes," Nicholas said coldly.

"Of course. You must've been up all morning to prep this meal," Ms. Clio spoke up.

Landree turned on her seat. She sniffled and rubbed her eyes, hoping Ms. Clio didn't catch her crying.

The edges of Ms. Clio's lips twitched up. She stared past Landree at Nicholas.

Green with envy, Landree would give anything for Ms. Clio to smile at her again.

When Nicholas sat against a dying willow, Landree redirected her focus. Mouth filling with saliva, she sniffed her skewer. The opaque flesh was charred at the edges. Unable to wait any longer, she used her front teeth to rip off a sliver of meat. The piece hit her tongue as if it were still on fire, and Landree swallowed it whole.

Meanwhile, Ms. Clio rolled her skewer between the palm of her hands. Landree laughed nervously.

"Be careful. Hot," she said.

"Thank you," Ms. Clio replied.

"Listen…" She searched for the right for words. "I know what I saw. Jane-Marie and I did what we could to escape this creature. B-but if it means anything, it took her alive."

Ms. Clio ripped into a frog leg. Her deeply visible veins disappeared at her wrists, and petechiae plagued her arms like stars on a moonless night. Rings of yellow also appeared on her flesh. She grimaced when she swallowed.

"I believe you," she replied.

Landree's chest inflated.

"I just hope that if we find her, she is *still* alive."

Landree's shoulders slumped. She busied herself with the roasted frog and accepted the silence.

No sooner had she picked her meal clean, nausea took hold. When Landree stood, the world around her started to swirl. She slapped a hand to her forehead and steadied herself.

"Woah."

Perhaps I'm dehydrated and stood too fast.

"You feel it too?" Ms. Clio asked, tone spiked with urgency.

"What?"

Pebbles rattled and ash spiraled from the extinguished fire. Landree's stomach somersaulted as she waved her arms, still fighting to balance herself. A guttural rumble oozed from beneath the ground.

"It's an earthquake!" Ms. Clio gasped.

Heart in her throat, Landree pounced over the ashes and stumbled toward Nicholas, still asleep. She grasped his shoulders and shook them.

"Wake up!" she exclaimed. Landree craned her neck to face Ms. Clio. "What do we do?"

The way the earth swayed was a sensation she'd never experienced before. It felt as if the world jerked left and right, threatening to split right at her feet. This phenomenon only existed in Landree's world history scrolls, never her reality.

"Nicholas!"

His head flopped back, eyelids fluttering open and exposing nothing but a white surface. Landree gasped and nearly dropped him. Fear rattled her hands as she cradled the back of his skull. When she brushed hair from his face, her fingers grazed his piercing. The black pearl seared her fingertips. Landree howled and shook her hand.

With a shudder, the earth stilled. Doused in cold sweat, Landree froze as if a sudden breath could awaken its wrath once again.

"What. The. Hell," she said, grinding her teeth.

A gale brushed through camp, rustling the branches of the willow. Moisture clung to her every pore, heralding an oppressiveness beyond the existing humidity. An invisible energy, like charged particles from a thunderstorm, caused the hairs on the back of her neck to stand. When a shadow washed over Nicholas' face, Landree hesitated before looking up. Clouds with sharp edges materialized, twisting its spindly arms inland. It carried the darkness of a storm cloud, but it existed only as a thread against the rest of the pale blue sky.

Landree froze. Her blood curdled at the unearthly sight. Perhaps it was smoke from a fire, but only the coast lay to the west, and it certainly wasn't the white smoke from Thamni's group. No matter how hard she tried, Landree couldn't rationalize the swirling vortex.

"What's going on?" Nicholas asked as he blinked awake.

Landree dropped him and scuttled backward. She cleared her throat. "I think we just had an earthquake." Steepling her fingers, she turned to Ms. Clio. "Right?"

"Correct. There are volcanoes off Amicita's coast. It's not surprising, I suppose."

"Then there's that thing," Landree said, pointing up.

Nicholas lifted his chin and hummed. Landree stared at his earring as she waited for a reply. Rubbing her index finger against her thumb, her skin stung from the burn. The black pearl glistened indifferently.

"Let's get going. We're burning daylight," he finally replied.

"B-but, that thing in the sky—"

"Do you believe me yet?" Nicholas snapped, cutting her off.

He rocketed to his feet, huffing before jogging to Ms. Clio and gathering everyone's belongings.

Landree followed close behind, grumbling all the way.

Landree, Nicholas, and Ms. Clio cleared mile after mile, trudging through the never-ending wetlands. The air remained thick, much to the point a blade could slice clean through. Sweat soaked Landree's tunic, and she gagged at the stench of her body odor.

Time was running out, and they had to move on. Ms. Clio recommended that they continue west, and if they were lucky, they'd fine Jane-Marie as well. Nicholas confirmed a couple sites of interest on the map that could provide supplies and perhaps a vantage point to look for Jane-Marie. Because the shadow creature vanished beneath the bog,

Landree had no leads as to which direction it went. She felt idiotic when admitting this to Ms. Clio, who simply rolled up the map and shook her head. Landree insisted on exploring all possible reasons behind the vanishing act, but her teacher didn't want to hear any more.

"I'm ordering you two to remain quiet for the next few hours," Ms. Clio had said. "I have a headache, and I just want to hike in peace."

The sun traveled toward its mid-point in the sky. All the while, Landree clamped her mouth shut and her head down. She acknowledged that Ms. Clio felt unwell, but even she admitted to herself that she needed to consider all possibilities in Jane-Marie's disappearance. If there was a more sinister threat stalking them, the race against time to rebuild a vessel seemed less of a priority.

Landree stumbled over a loose object. When she glanced down, she pursed her lips and *oohed*. It was rectangular in shape. Lines etched into the corners. She scooped it up, observing its grainy features.

"Check this out," Landree said. "Some piece of architecture?"

"We have no time for distractions," Ms. Clio said curtly. She slowed to a stop, fingers twitching. "...What is it?"

When Ms. Clio turned around, Landree tossed it into her hands. Her eyes roamed over the object hungrily. Landree stared down at her boots, caked in mud. The brown color contrasted to the half-buried pearly white structure. Landree's lips parted.

"Most intriguing," Ms. Clio said breathily. She giggled

like a little girl on her birthday as she examined every angle. Even her cheeks radiated with a glow Landree hadn't witnessed the entire trip. When Ms. Clio caught Nicholas' eye, she cleared her throat and dropped it into the mud. "If only we were in better circumstances."

Landree knelt and scooped up the artifact. "I'll hold onto it. It's small enough to bring back at least."

Ms. Clio offered a half smile.

Nicholas stepped in between them. Landree seethed. He always had a knack for ruining good moments.

He thumbed toward two gigantic willow trees. "I think you guys will be able to explore more than you think."

"What?" Landree elbowed past him. She rushed past the slender branches while Ms. Clio followed close behind. At the end of an incline, she dug her heels into the ground and gasped.

Outlines of buildings stretched across the skyline. Her heart soared. This was a sign of a former civilization and an extension of the bit of granite she pocketed.

"Maybe Jane-Marie is there!" she exclaimed.

Landree took off, ignoring whatever Ms. Clio and Nicholas had to say. The waterlogged soil squelched with each step. Flecks of mud spattered against her hot cheeks. Brambles and other woody bushes thinned out, giving way to a more structured path. Even a sapling or two waved its leaves at her.

Signs of life.

Although bogs still dotted the space between Landree, they shrank in size and viscosity. The sun warmed her back and the breeze dispelled the acerbic, stale air. The possibilities of finding her friend, resources for the crew, and even items of historical significance for Ms. Clio imbued her with a sense of hope. Even redemption.

The foremost building stretched the highest. Green tendrils curled around bricks of granite all the way up its cylindrical tower. Only half the shingles remained attached to the steeple. Rectangular windows stretched twice as tall as Landree. Shattered glass sat in their frames like jagged teeth.

She stopped short of a bridge, or at least the remnants of one. Half eaten by termites, the dual wooden posts were the only parts left standing. Leaning over the edge, Landree spied another bog. Peat and other dead plant material circled around chunks of the bridge as well as a roof to a building and a waterwheel.

When she heard Ms. Clio huffing nearby, Landree beckoned her over.

Ms. Clio leaned against one of the bridge posts. "Can you not do that again? I don't want to lose you either."

"Sorry," Landree replied sheepishly. "But, look. I think that used to be a mill. See the waterwh—"

A resounding *snap* cut her off.

Ms. Clio toppled over the post and into the bog below.

Landree shrieked. She searched for Nicholas who was sprinting toward her.

"Ms. Clio, she—"

He dove, knocking Landree off her feet...and into the bog as well.

The viscous sludge sucked them under the surface.

Landree's arms burned as she swam. However, with each stroke, the muck tugged back. Landree alternated kicks with her arm strokes until she finally reached the surface. She wiped the gunk from her eyes and glared at Nicholas. As soon as she was about to scold him, he wrapped a hand around her mouth. He jerked his head upward.

Two winged creatures circled around the church-like building. Their feline features matched that of the one she faced the other night except for their coloring. The feathers on these were a cerulean blue with orange tips, contrasting to the ones from earlier—completely dark as if borne from the shadows. Regardless, Landree studied their claws, hoping to find Jane-Marie.

One clutched a deer carcass. The pursuant carried nothing. They screeched, causing the tower to shudder. Bricks toppled one by one. Some even bounced into the bog, narrowly missing her. Nicholas inched Landree backward until they reached the flooded mill where Ms. Clio hid. Her eyes were as wide as orbs.

The empty-handed creature rammed its head into the other's abdomen, but it continued to grip the deer. Although teeth grindingly sharp, Landree almost made out words in its cry.

"Give... Me—ee!"

"These are the real thing. We don't want to mess with them," Nicholas uttered.

"Real thing? Compared to what?" Landree blurted.

The creature in pursuit halted, allowing the other to escape. It pointed its beak downward in the direction of her voice. Uncurling its forked tongue, it cried once more. "Give... Me—ee!"

Nicholas scowled at Landree.

"Oops," she whispered, covering her mouth sheepishly.

The creature dove, extending its yellowed hind-claws. Nicholas climbed onto the roof and unsheathed his dagger. He waved his arms and shouted.

"Come get me!"

Just as the creature crashed into the roof, Nicholas rolled forward. It flicked its tail, knocking his blade from his hand. The metal glistened in the light as it plopped into the bog. Landree swam furiously as it sank, hilt first. As soon as Landree nabbed the dagger, she inched her way toward the mill. Nicholas dodged the creature, narrowly missing its beak.

The roof caved beneath his left leg, sending Nicholas crashing onto his seat. Wood snapped. His other leg fell through. Landree threw herself onto the waterwheel, ducking its thrashing tail. The creature reared its head, and Nicholas let go. He slipped into the mill, narrowly missing another attack.

The creature struck the roof, goring into a wooden beam with its beak. Growling fiercely, it shook its head in attempts to free itself. Landree lunged at the monster, securing herself onto its back with her knees. As she plunged the dagger into its flesh, the creature snapped the beam and screeched, sending shards of wood flying in every direction. Flapping its wings, the creature generated an updraft. Landree's hair whipped over her face, obscuring her vision. It rocketed to the skies with Landree in tow.

How am I going to get off this thing?

The high-speed winds snatched the air from her lungs. Landree's stomach somersaulted, shooting acid up her throat. With one hand, she clung to the dagger. On the other, she grabbed a handful of feathers. The creature veered left, then right, then upside-down. Landree's grip slipped. Daring to peek over her shoulder, terror gripped her soul. They were some good two-hundred feet in the air.

She had to do something. Mustering the dregs of her energy, Landree ripped the dagger out. She slipped a few inches but managed to stab it a couple of times before twisting the blade to secure its position.

"Let me down!" she screamed.

Accompanied by the sound of wailing, the creature's flying grew erratic as it thrashed. Landree flipped onto her back, now holding on with one hand. A wide building stood at the precipice of a cliff. Beyond that stretched the sea. They seemed to arrive at the western most point of Amicita.

The beating of the creature's wings slowed, and they descended.

Did I get through to this thing?

Landree's hope was fleeting. The creature hurtled toward the ocean.

"Damn it!"

Seconds ticked by. Soon they would pass the cliffs, steep and imposing. Even if Landree survived the fall, there would be little to no chance of making it to shore. The creature zoomed over decrepit homes. Landree couldn't make out their roofs. Most were caved in.

Thatched, maybe?

But she was still too high. Glancing back and forth between the cliffs and homes below, Landree needed to make a calculated decision, and time was almost up. Tightening her abdominals, she rolled onto her side and focused on the wide landmark before the divide. Larger than others, its roof was relatively in-tact. More in-tact than most.

The creature wavered, dropped a few more feet, but continued toward the sea. Landree counted down in her head. Right before they passed over the final home, she closed her eyes and let go.

CHAPTER

14

Eleven Days left of The Luce

Images of her parents flashed in her mind: from her father teaching her how to nock an arrow to de-feathering her first chicken with mother. Memories of the trip to Bleeding Heart as well as the first playdate with Jane-Marie as a child reeled through at double speed. Jane-Marie, while always petite, enjoyed her role as the boss in her circle of friends. Now she risked returning home with a failed mission and lost friend. That's if she ever made it home. Landree wished she never applied for the Amicita expedition.

Landree's legs made contact with the roof. The structure gave way, but the tufts of the straw padded her back as she collided onto the floor. Pain fired though every nerve in her spine. Landree gritted her teeth and curled her toes, swallowing a scream that bubbled at the back of her throat. Clouds of dust exploded into the air, tickling her nose.

Landree sneezed.

"Oh man," she groaned.

Landree sat up slowly, covering her nose with the crook of her elbow. When the dust settled, she stood. Her legs wobbled like jelly. Although plagued by aches, she didn't detect any broken bones. She looked up through the hole in the ceiling. She had to have fallen at least twenty-five feet. Shock dulled her pain. Landree had no idea how she was able to time it just right.

Landree scanned the dust-laden room. A bedframe covered in cobwebs occupied one corner. Across from that stood a bureau with a shattered mirror. Termites had chewed the wooden legs to the core, leaving the remnants to a colony of dark gray mold. Flecks of white paint surrounded them on the floor like snow.

The floorboards creaked as she took her first steps. Leafy growth found its way through the cracks. Every movement roused clouds of particles. Landree retched at the musty, dank aroma.

A comb and a handful of empty silver vials lay on top of the bureau. She grazed her thumb across their tarnished surface. Searing-hot pain shot through her shoulder as she tugged the drawer. Landree cursed. The drawer was empty.

Landree pulled the second drawer out more gently this time. A number of bejeweled rings rolled around, the metal bands clacking against one another pleasantly. Landree *oohed* as she fingered a diamond-encrusted ring.

"Precious gems. Amicita's secret wonder," she said bitterly as her thoughts drew to Nicholas like a lodestone.

Amicita was a mysterious frontier, and it was a common topic with guests at the inn. She'd catch bits of conversation when she served their meals and found that it always concluded with how it was blessed with more gems than one could humanly desire. Some mentioned the mythos surrounding their ties to the elements but only for entertainment purposes. No one took it seriously like Nicholas did.

She wondered if Amicita would still hold people's interest once those treasures were milked dry. Despite the thought, she pocketed a handful, hoping it would prove useful later. She still needed a peace offering for her parents.

Landree paused at a diamond ring. She peered over her shoulder before slipping it on her middle finger. Chewing on her lip, she entertained the possibility of enchanted gemstones. Nicholas' words slithered into her mind. Landree focused on her warped reflection on its glistening surface.

What if…?

Nothing happened. She didn't feel anything except for humiliation.

"What am I doing?" Landree chided herself. She tore off the ring and tossed it into her pocket with a twinge of disappointment and continued rifling through the bureau. Admittedly, supernatural powers would've come in handy.

Silk clothes lay in the bottom drawer, folded into a neat square.

"Now that's something I could use," Landree said, frowning at her soiled outfit.

Landree plucked the clothing from the drawer one by one. Most were nightgowns, but she finally discovered a tunic. There were a few loose threads at the seams and a tear on the neckline, but it was clean. Landree tugged off her top and relished in the luxurious fabric. Jane-Marie often wore silk and loved it. Now she knew why.

Landree also found cotton slacks which she happily changed into. The fit was slightly loose and much too long. While rolling up the pantlegs, Landree searched near the bedposts and spotted a weathered belt.

Perfect.

Feeling slightly refreshed, she examined the room for an exit. A curtain, riddled with holes, flickered in the breeze on the opposite wall. She stepped over the debris and crossed the room. Every time the floorboard creaked, Landree paused, listening for footsteps. When she pulled the curtain aside, one of the rings caught on a screw. Landree yanked the curtain harder, and the rod fell with a deafening crash.

"Damn it," she said, fanning herself. "I need to seriously relax."

Landree hopped over the curtain rod, entering a circular room. Suede cushions peppered the space, most of its smooth surface faded away. Crown molding connected the walls to the ceiling, and silver trim traced double doors. Child-like wonder goaded her curiosity. She rubbed her hands together.

This had to belong to someone important.

Growing up, instead of fussing over the perfect braid or exchanging beauty tips with other popular girls, Landree roamed the forest adjacent to Goldenrod with Grant, pretending to search long lost civilizations. They often drew maps and stayed out late. That is, until she entered secondary school. Rose put her foot down, emphasizing the importance of studying and developing a good work ethic instead of wasting away in a fantasy world. It only made sense that the advent of The Luce occurred during her lifetime.

As she approached the oak doors, Landree passed a desk. She paused to study the scraps of paper and a quill that covered the surface. Wine stains smudged most of the writing, but Landree continued to flip through each one, searching for any familiar words.

"Ae—." Landree chewed her check and scratched the back of her ear. "What in Adin's name is this word? Aeon—eon? Or Aeonian? I've never heard that word before. Something, something… This manor will be used as shelter. Or, was shelter?"

Landree traced her finger down the parchment. It crinkled pleasantly at the slight pressure. Beneath a tall, looped signature, it read "District of Buryan".

She clicked her tongue. "Must be the name of this town. I bet this is where its leader lived."

After shuffling through more unintelligible papers, Landree returned them to the desk. Excitement ignited sparks that boosted her mood—she discovered a lost city on her own. Its worth far exceeded the diamond ring in her pocket.

Just like in my childhood days—but for real this time!

Another item, this time behind the desk, caught Landree's eye: a longsword, mounted against a frame. An opal the size of her palm was embedded in the hilt. The stone shimmered in various shades of white, pink, and purple.

"Wow," she said breathily.

Opal was her favorite gemstone. Although rare in Camilla, Landree had been saving up chore money to buy one. She didn't care if it was in a bracelet or by itself. Jane-Marie's parents had connections in Harebell, and they had promised to keep an eye out for anything opal. The fact that this one was attached to a sword made it twice as cool. Landree grinned.

Although the casing collected dust, the longsword was in perfect condition. She circled the desk and removed the frame from the wall.

It's almost too beautiful to use.

Landree kneed the glass. After a few clumsy attempts, she freed the blade. She pursed her lips. It felt a lot lighter than she expected. Turning it over, Landree stared at the opal once more. When she traced its surface, a shock pricked her fingertips, flooding her body with sweltering heat. She took a step back as sweat beaded at her hairline.

"What in Adin's name?"

She looked around the room. Nothing else seemed to change.

Landree drew a blank. For a moment, she forgot where she was or what she was doing.

Something shattered downstairs, snapping Landree from her trance. She slid her back against the wall and held her breath. Waiting a minute in silence, Landree searched for a scabbard, which she ended up finding beneath the desk.

After equipping the sword, a renewed rush of energy numbed her injuries and bolstered her confidence. Landree snuck toward the double doors and inched it open. The oak groaned, fighting against the rusted hinges. Landree bit her lip, hoping she didn't give away her position.

As soon as she could slip through, Landree tip-toed into the hallway. The first thing she met was a life-size portrait; however, its image had been slashed multiple times. Unlike the room she previously was in, the hall lacked windows. Barren candle holders lined the corridor. Melted wax had solidified on the carpet.

Shrouded in darkness, Landree moved swiftly. She kept one hand on the hilt of her sword like a child clinging to her security blanket. The corridor led to a spiral staircase. Landree peered over the railing, scanning for any disturbances.

When it felt safe, she descended to the foyer. With a boost of confidence in her recent discoveries, her footsteps grew lighter. Who knew what else she could stumble upon in Buryan?

A chandelier lay in the middle of the first floor, buried in rubble. She stepped backward until one of her heels met the floor with a *crunch*.

Landree's tongue glued to the roof of her mouth. Her skin crawled as she rotated slowly on the spot.

"Oh my Deva!" Landree yelped, hands clutching her chest.

The shattered remains of a skeleton surrounded her boot. Only when she saw this skeleton did Landree realize the foyer was littered with bones. All her excitement vanished, leaving her steeped in a void of horror. The closest thing she ever encountered in the past were animal bones during an archaeology session with Ms. Clio last year. Those bones, however, were smaller and bleached clean. The sea of corpses in the foyer were still dressed in soiled clothes and patches of silver hair on their skulls. Some were still bound by sinew. Landree pursed her lips and nudged the body in front of her.

It appeared human. A very tall one, complete with skull, torso, and limbs.

"I've to get the hell out of here."

No book or class had prepared her for this. Landree rubbed her arms and legs as invisible bugs crawled beneath her clothes. It chilled her to the core more than her most troubling nightmares. For that many beings to perish in one spot told Landree they had dealt with something powerful... or even supernatural.

She flew to the main entrance. An iron bar was lodged through the handles and bent at each end. Flecks of rust rained onto the floor as Landree tried to pry it free. It didn't budge.

Landree pushed and pulled. Finally, one end snapped, and one of the oak doors opened. A wall of bones filled the other side. They fell one by one until they cascaded indoors like an avalanche of death. Landree turned and sprinted in the other direction. When she reached the opposite end of foyer, Landree paused at the only other exit, highlighted by an archway, and turned around. The sheer size of the pile prevented her from seeing a way outside. She dry heaved.

"Get it together." Landree, still shaken, continued through the archway. Her legs tensed, ready to sprint at a moment's notice. Thoughts collided in her mind all at once.

There were civilizations here. How did they die? Is the threat still around?

In order to harness the panic spreading like a wildfire in her consciousness, Landree inhaled deeply and exhaled through her mouth. It didn't help. She gripped the hilt of her sword and focused on locating the exit immediately.

Pots and shattered dishes littered the following room. It was a grease-stained kitchen, but it at least was void of any corpses.

The shattered remains of a porcelain cup sat at her feet. Looking up, she spotted the teacup's siblings lining to the top of a cabinet. One trembled. Gasping, Landree drew her sword.

The cup fell and broke. Landree yelped. A pair of beady eyes stared back.

A mouse crept into the light, brushing its whiskers. Landree sighed and sheathed the sword. She wasn't sure if her nerves could take anymore. The mouse squeaked and disappeared, not before pushing a third cup from the shelf.

Shaking her head, Landree stepped over the mess and discovered a back door. She swung it open, welcoming a kiss from the sun.

Frogs and dragonflies scattered as Landree rounded the building until she discovered a path. Cracked cobblestone wound past toppled gates. Cattails waved from stagnant pools of water. It wouldn't be long until the entire town transformed into an extension of the swamp.

Landree jogged down the path, testing her body's limits. Her shoulders and back ached, and her feet cried in protest, but nothing felt serious. She slowed down as she approached a cluster of buildings. Unlike the manor-like one she left, these appeared worse for wear. Each were one or two floors and crammed next to one another. Faded signs hung on one or both hinges, and their roofs had caved in.

Landree witnessed movement in her periphery. When two figures burst through the door, she drew her sword and pointed it directly at them with both hands. The blade rattled in its hilt.

"I can't believe it! You're alive!" Ms. Clio exclaimed.

Ms. Clio and Nicholas' familiar faces sent waves of relief through Landree. When she secured her weapon, Ms. Clio pulled her in an embrace.

"I don't think I could've continued on after losing two students!"

Landree squirmed in her bony arms. The sword pressed against a bruise on Landree' thigh. She winced.

"Look at you." Nicholas pocketed his hands and nodded. "You're alive. Glad to see it."

When Ms. Clio pulled away, Landree nodded in acknowledgement. "Thank you."

Nicholas's gaze traced her face then fell to her hip. Deep lines formed across his forehead as his eyes lit up. Landree shifted her weight uncomfortably.

"What's that?" Ms. Clio asked.

The longsword sung as Landree pulled it from its sheath.

"Isn't it beautiful?"

Nicholas covered his mouth but was unable to mask a wide, crooked grin. His shoulders relaxed and his knees started to buckle. When he caught her eye, he straightened and cleared his throat. "Didn't think to get me anything to replace my dagger you lost?" he asked, examining his nails.

"There's no way you're getting this." Landree cradled the blade.

He chuckled. Landree's cheeks grew hot as the tension in her body eased slightly. Perhaps after the scare with that creature, he decided to lighten up a bit.

"It's got an odd glow to it," Ms. Clio remarked.

"Sure does." Landree sheathed it. She thought of Nicholas' pearl earring, but she forced it into the back of her mind. "Is there anything for us here?"

Nicholas shrugged. "The homes in this village, or town—whatever this was, are made of stone and iron, all of which has completely rusted out. Most of the thatched roofing is gone, so most items within have been destroyed by weather and time. We could check a few intact places in this downtown area, but it's not very promising."

Landree crossed her arms. She had briefly forgotten about their much larger objective.

"Surely we can find some things here," Landree said.

"But the question is, will it be enough? We should only notify if there are enough supplies. We don't have the luxury of time to ride back and forth to grab only 'some things'," Ms. Clio said.

"Sorry. Was just trying to remain positive."

Ms. Clio clasped her shoulder. "That's alright. Sometimes positivity is the only thing that keeps us going."

With each decrepit building the three searched, the more Landree's hope dwindled. Many appeared to have been shops eons ago, and everything had been cleared out. Landree discovered some wooden chairs and tables, but nothing else.

"Why did we choose to go west, again?" Landree asked. Her stomach growled.

"Various scrolls documented an advanced civilization ran this area. The presence of the mill proved it. Given the possible history of manufacturing, I had hoped there'd be lots of left-over material or at least a forest nearby in order to assist in their production." Ms. Clio's voice grew strained. "But now it's just a rotted-out village flooded by a swamp!"

Nicholas stepped down from a ladder empty-handed. "Now, now. A lot could've happened since the last documentation of the area."

"Like their collective demise," Landree blurted.

They blinked at her, wide-eyed.

Pocketing her hands, Landree wrestled with the horrifying images in her head. "I landed in a massive manor and found some documents. It referred to this place as the District of Buryan. In the main foyer, I found..." Words clogged the back of her throat. "I found..."

Ms. Clio encased Landree's hands in hers. "You don't have to talk about it if you don't want to," she said softly.

"Death. You saw a whole lotta death, didn't you?" Nicholas asked. He leaned against a window and stared outside.

Landree sniffed and nodded. Her blood ran cold, sending shivers throughout her body.

"Come here." Ms. Clio pulled her into another hug and raked her nails through Landree's hair.

Head pressed against Ms. Clio's chest, Landree felt their hearts beat—Ms. Clio's even more rapidly than hers.

She must be terrified. I need to be brave like her, too.

Pulling away, Landree steeled her nerves. "I'll be fine."

"Are you sure?"

Nicholas coughed. "You know, if you continue to baby Landree, she's never going to develop a backbone."

Stepping in front of Ms. Clio, Landree shook her head. "She's not babying me. I'm fine. Let's go," she said, voice hard.

Landree kicked the door open and hopped onto the path. Nicholas only acted tough because he hadn't seen the monstrosities that she had. Even though he continued to discourage Landree, his words stung a little less each time. Even less so after her trip through the manor. She lifted her leg and aimed at a speckled rock.

Something feels different.

Pebbles vibrated against the ground. Dirt swirled from the crevices in the road. The quake felt ever so slight. Landree dropped to her knees and pressed her ear to the ground.

"Do you feel that?" she asked, filling with dread.

Nicholas' face clouded as he nodded.

"Not again," Ms. Clio whispered.

The tremors faded. Landree gulped.

Nicholas jogged through the path, muttering, "There's not much time."

"Hey!" Landree chased after him. "No time for what?"

They approached a formidable wall with a drop gate. It stretched for miles in either direction.

Running a hand through her hair, Landree caught several knots. She missed the simplest of luxuries, like a brush. "This must've separated the town from the rest of the country. Maybe we'll have better luck in the wild. So to speak."

"I agree. Every day is precious, so let's not waste time here." Ms. Clio gestured to the watch tower. "That may contain the mechanism to this gate."

Landree stepped forward, but Nicholas swung his arm out. "I'll take care of it."

"I'm fully capable of checking it out," she insisted.

"Stay here," he said firmly.

Nicholas took off, leaving Landree to fume. She jammed her hands against her hips. "I hope he falls and breaks a foot."

Ms. Clio snorted. "Sorry. That's not professional of me."

"I think we are way past that, Ms. Clio."

"Then, you can drop the 'Ms.'," the teacher quipped with a smile, exuding warmth.

Landree returned the smile as the weight of guilt eased from her shoulders. When they connected gazes, she no longer sensed blame, but rather understanding. "In your studies, have you ever read anything that described those creatures?" Landree continued as Nicholas vanished up the stairs to the watch tower.

"The last expedition returned with a handful of scrolls. Most of it was unreadable, but it had mentioned Amicita was home to two native species. Both lived nomadically."

Landree gestured to the ghost village behind them. "So, who created *this*?"

"Immigrants from other countries, I suppose." Clio blinked as if whacked with an idea. "A home to immigrants. This should be interesting to report back considering what the Republic wants to do."

"After all those corpses I saw…I think this is more of a warning to stay very far away from Amicita. Something horrible happened here." Landree chewed on her lip. This island so far had been a far cry from what she fantasied it to be. There was no serene valley where she could frolic, and every corner that was ripe for discovery was also filled with death.

"I was only able to translate one of the two names of the native species. Ka-Na. Or Kana? They were the more aggressive species—"

Landree threw her head back and scoffed. "Those *had* to be them." Her stomach squeezed. "Wanna know something odd? I think it was a Kana that took Jane-Marie, but it appeared different than the two that attacked us…like a shadow version of a Kana."

The gate rattled, snapping Landree's train of thought.

"That was fast," Clio commented.

She scanned the tower. "He's a know-it-all show off."

The rattling intensified, but the gate didn't rise. Landree's gaze followed the rope and pulley system. They remained still.

Cupping her mouth, Landree shouted. "Nicholas! You alright up there?"

Metal screeched as something rammed into the gate. The impact sent shockwaves down the path, upturning cobble stones and knocking Landree and Clio off their feet. She propped herself onto her elbows in time to witness swamp water ooze beneath the gate. She squinted her eyes. It was dark like the bog, anyway. Although gelatinous in consistency, the substance darted back and forth like a cobra hunting its prey. Landree scrambled backward as it drew near.

"S-stay away from that, Clio!" she shouted.

Its inky blackness reminded her of the shadowy Kana.

As if cognizant of her thoughts, it swirled from the ground. Tendrils writhed like hungry, deformed fingers. It snatched Clio's wrist and yanked her onto the ground.

"Get off me," Clio yelped as she cycled her legs.

Landree drew her new sword and drove the blade into the shadowy goop. It hissed as it writhed in place. Additional streaks branched out and lunged at Landree, wrapping itself around her forearms. Her breath hitched at its icy-cold touch. Landree tightened her core and wrestled with all her might. Her mind raced. Her fingertips tingled, then numbed as it ate its way to her elbows.

The opal attached to the longsword's hilt flashed. Rays of light pierced the shadows, restoring warmth in her limbs. As if the gemstone jumpstarted her heart, Landree poured all her strength into her weapon.

In an explosion of light, the shadow dissipated from

Landree's arms with a deafening hiss. She cringed but kept her resolve. When she pulled her sword from the dirt, a whirlwind erupted from the tip of the blade. The shadows receded from the gale.

Landree blinked, unable to utter a word. She wouldn't have believed it if she hadn't witnessed it with her own eyes. The opal radiated with its own light as a new truth sunk deep into her bones.

The gemstones of power are real!

She rode the high and pumped one fist into the air.

The force chipped away at the substance; however, it forked around the windy force field, replicating into twice as many tentacles that had been destroyed.

Once the gale died down, the shadows surrounded Landree, washing away her short-lived cheer and replaced it with terror, but Clio's screams kept her focused. The substance whacked the sword from Landree's grasp and looped back to arrest Clio's ankles.

Clio stopped kicking. Her cries muffled—the goo covered her face and swallowed her torso.

"No!" Landree yelled. The sword lay five hundred feet away.

Too far. Too late!

Landree bolted toward her friend. Just as the darkness completely enveloped Clio, she sprung forward.

The next few moments seemed to slow down. Landree extended both arms. She clenched her jaw, bracing for the freezing plunge.

But it never came.

Landree crashed onto the ground, pain lancing through her injured shoulder. The tendrils of shadow evaporated like steam. She pushed herself onto her hands and knees, patting the earth over and over. Her breath became shallow, uneven.

"No. It can't be. No. She was *just* here," she said. "Clio? Clio!" Landree pounded the ground with her fists as she released a flurry of screams.

No answer.

The area around her returned to its sleepy state. Landree glanced at the gate. Dents that didn't exist before dotted the rectangular surface. The shadowy substance rose skyward, leaving a disturbed path of overturned dirt in the ground.

Lifting her head, Landree's stomach soured as the shadows stretched into an inky cobweb across the sky. It slowly twisted like a vortex toward the center of the country.

Where's it headed? I need to find Nick!

Landree retrieved her sword and sprinted toward the watch tower. Her throat constricted, and her tongue glued to the roof of her mouth. She ducked through the archway and ascended the spiral staircase only to face a wall of rubble. Heat rose to her cheeks.

"Not you, too. Nicholas?" she whispered. "You're right about the stones! Please, answer me!"

No response. Choking on tears that welled in her eyes, Landree pulled down stones one by one. Once she got the larger ones out of the way, she clawed furiously. Her nails broke and her fingers bled, but she refused to give up.

"Nick? You better tell me off for calling you that! Nick!"

Landree pounded the mass of debris. No matter how hard she tried, Landree attempts barely made a dent.

"Please tell me you're alive!" she sobbed.

A warmth radiated from Landree's hilt. Eyes widening, she grabbed her sword. She stared at her warped reflection in the blade, but her attention fell to the opal. Even in the absence of direct sunlight, the stone shimmered, reminding her a lot of Nicholas' black pearl.

Clutching the hilt to her chest, Landree closed her eyes and recalled the moments leading up to Clio's disappearance. It all happened so fast. The opal's warmth seeped through her tunic and kissed her skin. Her memories lit up like a struck match. Each stroke of the sword elicited a gale of some sort.

Wind.

It all seemed surreal.

She peeked at the mound of debris. It made no sense to use a blade to hack away at stone, but perhaps the wind would come to her aid again. In her fight against the shadows, the opal generated the power of the wind without much thought. It felt almost…natural. Landree didn't want to overthink it, but she was curious how it worked.

I was so focused on saving Ms. Clio. Maybe that's all I needed.

Metal sang as Landree hacked at the bricks. Sparks rained over Landree, but it failed to procure a gust of wind. She continued to swing her sword, eyeing the opal; however, it ceased glowing. Her failures echoed in the winding staircase. Landree's muscles burned as the dregs of her energy dwindled. She continued to hack and slash until she could stand no more. Her legs gave way, as if her muscles turned into mush.

I look stupid. I can't control the power of wind. Maybe this is all in my head.

Landree curled into a ball and nuzzled her face into her forearms. Confusion outpaced all the other thoughts that darted through her mind. None of this made any sense, but the worst thing of all was that she was alone.

First Jane-Marie, then Clio and Nicholas. What about the others in the East Team?

The tower vibrated. Landree lifted her head, heart aching over the loss of her friends. Stone pieces loosened from the blocked stairs. Swallowing the lump in her throat, Landree sheathed her sword and trotted backwards until she reached the outside.

Groaning like a dying giant, the tower shuddered from its foundation. It collapsed, piece by piece, crushing the gate which gave way like it was made of paper. Landree shielded her eyes, and the barrier to the wilderness collapsed both ways.

She coughed as the tremors faded. When the billows of dirt cleared, she stepped gingerly toward the ruins. Her fingers twitched. No signs of the shadowy things. Rolling up her sleeves, Landree picked through the tower remains. She struggled hour after hour turning over stone.

The least she could do was recover Nicholas' body—if the shadows hadn't already claimed him. Although Nick was nowhere near her when the shadows attacked, she still felt it was all her fault.

Did he vanish as well?

Hopelessness rattled her soul as she wobbled toward the

final untouched mounds of debris. As much as Nicholas was insufferable, Landree wasn't sure if she could mentally handle losing him too. Landree crashed onto her knees. Pain radiated around her kneecaps, but it didn't deter the guilt that overwhelmed her like a mudslide: thick, heavy, and crushing. Cradling her face in the palms of her hands, Landree wept.

What would Jane-Marie's parents think? And Clio's family? Landree would be branded as a failure if she ever returned to Camilla.

"It's all my fault." Landree's voice cracked.

A nearby brick slid a couple inches. Sniffling, Landree wiped her nose with the back of her hand. She settled her breath and kicked the brick away. Another rush of heat flooded her veins. Landree checked her longsword, finding the opal pulsing to the rhythm of her racing heart.

She clawed at the opening revealed by the brick. After shoving a wooden beam to the side, Landree first noticed the black pearl. She could barely make out if the gem glowed at all.

"I got you, Nick," she said.

Reinvigorated with hope, Landree pushed and shoved chunks of metal, wood, and stone. She cradled his neck as she gently guided his body from the refuse, each breath loaded with prayer.

His pulse felt weak, fleeting. Landree brushed grime from his cheeks—there were no signs of bleeding, but his left wrist twisted upward in the most unnatural way.

A groan eased from his lips. "It's Nicholas, not Nick."

Landree shrieked and pulled him into an embrace.

"You're alive! Thank Adin!"

Nicholas gagged and clawed at this neck. "Please. Ge'r off me."

"Sorry." Landree sat back on her knees and tucked her hair behind her ears. She wrangled her fingers as he struggled to stand. "Do you...remember what happened?"

Bone cracked as Nicholas stretched his left wrist. Grimacing, he tilted his head to the side. "I recall another earthquake."

Silence stretched between the two, snuffing out Landree's short-lived joy. She avoided his gaze and scanned her surroundings until it landed back on his piercing. Landree instinctively clutched the hilt of her sword.

"Um. Did the black pearl, I don't know...Feel any different?"

"Excuse me?" Nicholas asked, both eyebrows lifting.

Landree shook her head. "I can't believe I'm admitting this, but you're right. It's real. I think this opal possesses the power to control the wind," Landree drawled as she observed Nicholas. When his features remained unchanged, Landree buttoned her mouth shut.

Still nursing his wrist, Nicholas rotated on the spot. Dirt crunched beneath his boot. "Where's Ms. Clio?"

Landree's mouth grew dry. "She's...vanished."

"What?"

Nodding, Landree fought the hot stinging behind her eyes.

Don't cry.

"After the quake, this...shadowy substance consumed her. I-I have no idea how, but it looked like the same material that spirited Jane-Marie away."

Nicholas ran his good hand through his hair, twisted and splaying out in all directions. His ice-blue eyes connected with hers, and the edges of his lips twitched downward as he listened.

Wiping her nose with her sleeve, Landree sniffed. "Do you believe the shadows and disappearances are related to whatever The Luce is warning us against?"

He opened his mouth to reply but hesitated. Landree waited with bated breath, but Nicholas crossed his arms and averted his eyes instead.

"What?" she pressed.

"These enchanted talismans became myth for a reason. The world is better off without the presence of magic. We mortals are too greedy, too cruel, too corrupt to wield them, and for some reason, their powers are returning. If humans ever re-discovered this possibility, they'd *kill* for those stones," he answered reluctantly.

Landree's hand jerked toward her sword. "Maybe the shadows were sent by someone seeking all the gemstones?"

"Em." Nicholas tugged his ear and fiddled with his black pearl stud. "Maybe."

Her palms grew slick with sweat as she tightened her grip around the hilt. "All the more reason for me to hold onto this."

"Just don't use it unless you need to."

"Because it drains you, right? I certainly felt spent after my tussle with the shadows."

Nicholas eyed her wearily. "I meant more as a precaution that you don't become...too addicted to it."

Landree released her grip and laughed nervously. "You think I'm one of your super greedy, cruel, and corruptible people that—"

A *snap* interrupted her sentence. Nicholas held a piece of wood to his bad wrist.

"Just be careful," he growled.

Landree stumbled toward him. "Let me help you."

"No," he said tersely, turning to rummage through his backpack. "I have rope somewhere here. I can do it myself."

"Fine," Landree quipped. She blew a strand of hair from her line of vision and focused beyond the gate.

Rolling hills of grass stretched as far as the eye could see. Occasional birch trees and clusters of orange flowers dotted the landscape. One path, overgrown with weeds, began at the gate and carved its way right down the middle. Above it all, the two moons, Adin and Deva began to appear in the summer sky as dusk approached. They no longer were perfectly eclipsed. A warning whispered into Landree's ear: *No one made it home safely without the guidance of The Luce.*

Blood curdled in her veins. Despite that fact, whatever spirited her friends away proved to be more dangerous. If she didn't do anything about it, there'd be no one left to sail back to Camilla.

The opal in her longsword vibrated. Landree stroked the gem gently with her thumb. People had also said there was no such thing as magic welding stones, and she used to be one of them.

Landree focused on the single image tarnishing the sky— the shadows that took Clio now existed as warped charcoal clouds that continued to wind its way toward the center of

the island. Maybe it was exhaustion, but she started to believe Clio and Jane-Marie were on the other side of the darkness.

"We need to find Clio and Jane-Marie," Landree de-
clared. "And we'll start by following that thing. I'll take
down whatever threatens our goal."

Nicholas appeared by her side, finishing his makeshift
splint. "What about Giles and finding supplies?"

Scoffing, Landree gently elbowed him. "I can't believe
I'm saying this, but there's definitely a threat that needs to
be addressed. It's just going to pick us off one by one. If I
don't do something, there'll be no one left to gather supplies."

"Good choice." Nicholas nodded as color drained from
his cheeks. "My uncle told me that this threat's only goal is
to…consume. Consume until nothing's left. If that's the
case, it's not just Amicita that's impacted. It's our homes.
The world," he said tremulously.

He opened and closed his mouth, almost as if battling
with himself. Nicholas continued to fidget—he ran a hand
over his face and tugged his ear repeatedly.

Licking her lips, Landree summoned the courage to ask
one more question.

"Does your black pearl possess any power?"

As if on cue, he cleared his throat, secured his backpack,
and started walking. "We're burning daylight."

Landree waded through the debris and followed him into
the wilderness, promising herself to never let him out of her
sight.

CHAPTER

15

Ten Days left of The Luce
Amelia

She couldn't tell if she was upside-down or right-side up.

The water churned in various directions. Whenever Amelia was flung toward the center of the basin, the waterfall would pummel her beneath the surface. She kicked her legs in vain, muscles aching and losing strength by the second. Fear wrapped its claws around her neck. It didn't take long until most of her body was numb.

Amelia gasped and gagged as arctic temperature water shoved down her throat. Images of the shipwreck flashed through her mind. Perhaps she had cheated death, and now it returned to finish the job.

If she was subjected directly to the falls one more time, Amelia feared she may not be able to resurface again.

Craning her neck, Amelia could barely make out the

speck that was Thamni's corpse. An occasional scream ricocheted in the chasm.

Grant and Brenna!

A wave slammed Amelia against the wall. She slid her arms up and down, feeling for a crevasse—anything to grip onto before she got sucked toward the center. A flame of hope lit in her chest when her right hand found a protruding root or man-made structure—it didn't matter.

Amelia fought the current and pulled herself close to the ledge. It lowered a few inches when Amelia leaned her full body weight into it. A click echoed, followed by grinding stone. She gasped and started reciting prayers, hoping she discovered a saving grace.

A solid mass pressed against her torso. Amelia carefully released the switch and clung to the now protruding step. She barely made out a series of similar steps that circled around the basin—its speckled gray surface glowing under the moons' light. Pulling herself onto her feet, Amelia fought for balance. She hopped from ledge to ledge as water sprayed in all directions.

Amelia's boot slipped on the slick stone. She crashed onto her left knee, and she cried out as pain radiated up her thigh. Her body wanted to give up. She was soaked to the bone, her clothes weighing three times more than it should. Bandana gone, wads of her hair clung to her face, and the waterfall continuously sprayed water into her eyes. All of Amelia's limbs trembled, and her lungs burned.

Regret deluged her body as violently as the waterfall. She was a quiet, studious girl who had no place in a dangerous country. Instead of listening to her parents, Amelia wished to prove that she was different than her sister.

Perhaps my parents would be better without me.

Thamni's last moments reappeared in Amelia's mind.

He sacrificed his life to try and save me.

Wiping the stream of water from her eyes, Amelia pressed back onto her feet. Using the wall for guidance, she stepped onto the next block. She drew energy from Thamni's sacrifice, refusing to let his death go in vain.

She grunted, taking one large stride after another. Each step simulated walking through sludge. Amelia stuck out her left leg, but nothing was there.

"Woah!" she exclaimed, leaning back.

I don't understand. I'm not even halfway up the basin.

Amelia could barely hear herself think. The waterfall's roar stung her eardrums to the point where everything sounded like a singular hum.

Quelling the stitch of anxiety in her belly, Amelia once again felt the walls in search for another lever. Her teeth chattered violently.

Amelia grasped onto a handle. She instinctively pulled, then pushed. The wall slid left, sending her tumbling into a room. She turned on her seat and noticed that the wall was a part of a hidden door. Water seeped onto the floor. Amelia scrambled onto her feet and pushed the sliding door closed with a satisfying click.

Gasping for air, Amelia leaned against the wall as adrenaline continued to surge through her veins. She swatted the sides of her head, emptying water from her ears. Her prayers were answered—she escaped a watery grave and discovered a secret entrance deep within the basin.

Her relief was short-lived—she wasn't sure if she had found safety or if she doomed herself to a worse fate.

The walls of the circular room muffled the raging waterfall, transforming into an unsettling and ever-present hum. Shivering, Amelia wrapped her arms around her body in a tight hug. She took one step at a time, ducking her head to accommodate the low ceiling. Torches fixed in metal casings were ignited, filling the area with a steady warmth. One that Amelia deeply appreciated.

"How is this possible?" Amelia whispered.

Behind each torch was a flint attached to a network of chains and cogs that vanished into vents in the ceiling. Amelia played various scenarios in her head, concluding that the force generated from the draining basin pushed the cogs in a clockwise fashion, which then caused the bar holding the flint to flip down, striking it against the wall. So long as the room remained dry, sparks would've landed in the oil-slicked center of each encasement. Intrigue and disbelief tickled Amelia.

The civilization that created this city must've been advanced! I thought Dr. Barnes was the first to utilize hydropowered technology. He's going to be devastated when I tell him.

Her fingers traced along the wall. Painted murals, smudged by the hands of time, decorated the space between torches. Red figures with tails held whips. Gray formations kneeled in submission. Amelia stepped back until she bumped into something. She turned to find a short pillar in the center of the room. Upon closer inspection, a gold-plated handle stuck out from the side.

She looked to the left, then the right. There was no other door than the one she entered in.

"There's got to be a way out," Amelia murmured. Oddly enough, a smattering of excitement infiltrated her skyrocketing apprehension. Instead of perceiving her situation as a trap with no way out, perhaps she could view it more like a puzzle.

She eyed the handle, spotting a faded red arrow. With a hopeful sigh, Amelia pushed against the handle. The stone groaned but moved steadily.

When the room vibrated in response, she clutched the pillar. The walls stretched higher, revealing more paintings. A tingling sensation filled her stomach as the floor dropped one level. An alarm rang in her head.

I'm only descending deeper. How will I get out of here alive?

When the room shuddered to a standstill, Amelia spotted two hallways. Fear snaked through her gut. She always struggled when she had no information to make an informed decision. Stuck at the bottom of a waterfall, Amelia had to choose blindly. The sound of dripping water felt like a ticking clock. She didn't know if it was coming from her clothes or somewhere else in the room. It didn't matter. Sucking in a rattled breath, Amelia tip-toed toward one doorway.

Amelia approached cautiously, one foot in front of the other. Something scuttled from behind. She swiveled around, but the room was still empty. Multiple drops of water echoed now, sending a shudder up her spine.

A rickety door loomed at the end of the corridor. Grabbing the steel handle, Amelia pressed it open and found a simple room. It, too, housed four lanterns with an active flame. A desk hugged one corner. Books were splayed all over the floor. She flipped through each one, disappointed to find waterlogged or moldy pages.

Amelia scanned the otherwise vacant space. Kneeling on the ground, she traced her fingers against the wall, taking note of multiple water stains.

"This room's clearly been flooded," Amelia said, standing back up. "A lot." The four walls seemed to close in on her as she imagined the water filling the room from floor to ceiling.

She tried to shut out the nightmare and made for the door to her left.

Dread crawled beneath her skin. The following room was pitch black. The tip of her boot tapped against an object on the ground. Amelia picked up a torch and flinched. A splinter lodged into her thumb.

Amelia retreated to the previous room and lit it with one of the lanterns. Steeling her nerves, she returned, lifting the ball of fire high. Its orange glow revealed a much larger area, the opposite wall nowhere in sight.

"I wonder if I'll ever find a way out of here."

As she crept forward, Amelia held her breath, listening for any unusual sounds. The rhythmic *plip plip* of water droplets echoed between the walls. The floor creaked beneath her feet, and the air was thick with humidity. Her soaked clothes seemed to grow heavier with each step.

Amelia followed the wall until she bumped into a wooden beam. Jumping back, she realized that it wasn't just a beam; it was a statue. As Amelia she craned her neck, her heart raced.

Thousands of lines etched features of a fox—or a wolf—looking down from its upturned snout. There was no shortage of inch-long fangs that protruded from its jaw. Running her hand over the calcified wood, Amelia admired the attention to detail. Fur was depicted by smooth strokes while hard edges outlined a sash that draped across its chest. It certainly appeared humanoid in nature and nothing like the animals she'd dealt with on the surface.

Looks like another statue of the Foti.

When Amelia came full circle, she examined the chains dangled from its hollowed-out center. Bones lay at its feet. Blood drained from her face. She tripped over another pile of bones as she stumbled away. Chains had been strewn everywhere. The stench of death settled deeply into her lungs. This room didn't honor history and culture, it honored torture and dismemberment.

Amelia broke into a sprint, desperate to exit the room. She spotted a door and rattled the knob. It didn't budge. Amelia's breath grew shallow, and she began to kick the door. Her eyes stung with tears as she then tried to ram into it with her shoulder.

What have I uncovered?

The hinges snapped, and Amelia toppled forward. The sounds of dripping water now felt like an incessant hammer to her head. Barely able to hear her own thoughts, she continued to make for the nearest doorway she could find. Tunnel vision set in. Panic had finally taken hold.

When she had progressed through another corridor, she found herself entering another circular room. Bending over, Amelia rested her hands on her knees. She gasped for breath, trying with all her might to stop hyperventilating.

"Keep it together," she said. "Don't give up. You'll find a way out."

Her boots splashed with each step as she ventured into the waterlogged area. In the center stood a golden statue of an ape. It cradled a shroud in one hand, and a ruby pendant in the other. The gemstone sat alone, tethered by a thin, gold chain.

"At least it's just one corpse and not a boneyard," she said bitterly.

She avoided the shroud and stared at the ruby. The gem radiated heat and pulsed with its own light. Amelia dropped her torch, the flames fizzing out when it landed in a puddle. Its rhythm mesmerized her.

She drew closer as if it were calling her. Amelia paused, inches away from it. Glancing at the shroud, she gulped. Could swiping this gem cause some nightmarish awakening of the dead? And yet, the ruby's life-force winked at her seductively.

The Amicitian Lore.

She'd always fantasized about wielding supernatural powers. When she was much younger, she'd ask her friends and family, "If you had a magic power, what would it be?". The replies were more or less the same: "What a ridiculous question."

Amelia always fantasized over of the power of telepathy. Ever since age six, she imagined opening the doors of communication to her parents, sister, and friends. She always found conversing with others a challenge, and it led to some of the most isolating feelings she had ever experienced. If she was able to read minds and exchange thoughts—which flowed more naturally than speech—perhaps her life would've unfolded differently.

She shivered.

A quake swelled beneath Amelia's feet and shook the walls. Dust rained from cracks in the ceiling as she fought to maintain balance. Once the room returned to stillness, Amelia noticed a burning sensation against her thigh. Jamming her hand into her pocket, Amelia pulled out the bloodstone fragment. It flashed in warning, burning her fingers. Amelia tossed it from hand to hand, cursing. She finally flung it into the air.

The stone seemed to defy logic as it floated gently onto the ape's opposite hand...and onto the shroud. Amelia gulped. Her saliva scratched her throat like sandpaper. She stepped toward the bloodstone in trepidation. Extending her arm, Amelia swore she felt the same draw as the ruby.

The edges of the shroud fluttered in the nonexistent breeze. Once the gem stopped glowing, everything stilled.

But only for a second.

The figure beneath the shroud shot upright. A bony paw slid from beneath the shroud and dragged the stained cloth off. Amelia opened her mouth wide, but her vocal cords froze. It hopped from the golden ape's hand and landed clumsily. Its joints cracked as it straightened, standing a foot taller than her.

She cringed at bone grinding against bone as it turned its skull in her direction. Amelia stared into its sockets, its blank gaze curdling her blood.

The creature was not of human origin. A snout protruded from its skull. Although not a trace of fur remained, its tail—a string of cartilage and tiny bone fragments confirmed her theory. It had semblance to the wolf-like statue in the torture chamber.

Could I be face to face with a real Foti?

Its skull tilted ever so slightly as if looking at the ruby, then back at Amelia.

Lifting her hands, she fought for words. "I-I mean no harm. I j-just want to get out of here."

Opening its jaws to expose its fangs, the skeleton lunged. Unable to nock an arrow in time, Amelia crossed her forearms and braced for impact. Her previous injuries ignited, sending pain firing through her nerves.

The room quaked more violently than before.

Amelia dodged a sluggish punch, wrapped her legs around the skeleton, and wrestled her way on top. Its jagged claws dug into her skin, refusing to let go. Sucking in a breath, Amelia rolled over again, using the momentum to throw her assailant against the base of the golden ape. The statue teetered as the earth continued to come to life.

A crimson glow appeared in her periphery. The ruby landed in a puddle to her left. She scrambled toward it, but the skeleton whipped its tail, smacking her hand and sending the ruby flying across the room.

Amelia broke into a sprint, gathering her bow and quiver in one fell swoop. The skeleton thrashed once more, but she leapt into the air, avoiding its tail. She pumped her legs harder. Each step was uncertain as the floor shook with increasing intensity.

The skeleton dogged her steps, gaining up on her with ease. In a last-ditch effort, Amelia dove. She tucked her chin into her chest, rolling forward.

As soon as she enclosed the ruby in her hand, a flash of bright red sent shockwaves behind her. Amelia propped herself onto one knee and glanced over her shoulder.

The skeleton lay in a twisted pile a hundred feet away. Burnt, smoldering. Panting heavily, Amelia pocketed the ruby and nocked an arrow.

"Why do you want this so much, huh?" she said through gritted teeth. Amelia spat blood. Fighting through the haze of her muddy glasses, she took aim.

With a crunch, the skeletal wolf crept on all fours. Its lower jaw had completely dislodged and lay on the ground. Amelia's fingers twitched. The monster paused, its tail flicking back and forth. Amelia wasn't sure if she was hallucinating, but it rotated its head back and forth as if shaking its head at her.

"Come on!" she exclaimed, fury coursing through her veins. "Try and finish what you started!"

It pawed the ground and bent forward. When it pounced, Amelia shouted. An intense heat flushed down her arms.

The tip of her arrow ignited as she released the arrow. It pieced the skull, shattering it completely in a ball of flames.

The Fotian skeleton collapsed. Amelia dropped her weapon and stared at her hands. Her fingertips tingled as she flexed them. Her eyes widened. She then fished for the ruby. Hot to the touch, the gem's glow faded.

"Did I just…?"

Amelia waited a few beats, staring at the pile of bones. No movement. She stepped gingerly past the creature and made for the other gemstone. It, too, stopped glowing. Both at this point had cooled significantly.

She knitted her brows, uncertain she had witnessed everything correctly. Amelia hadn't even realized the earth ceased quaking.

"Impossible. That'd mean the legend must be true," she muttered in awe.

Amelia's hands trembled as they fell to her sides. Her thoughts circled endlessly, unable to decipher a rational explanation behind the combustion. The more she tried to figure it out, the more of a headache she developed. Sucking in a deep breath, Amelia recognized her inner child—celebrating the idea of magic as reality, but the other half of her cautioned that its existence doomed the world of logic.

The ruby pulsed in her hand, mimicking her heartbeat. Seized by fear and curiosity, Amelia brought it close to her face.

"I can't wait to tell everybody! But first, I need to get out of here."

With a brilliant *zing*, a beacon of light emitted from the

center cut of the ruby. Amelia squealed with delight. It seemed to react to her thoughts and desires, but she told herself that she had a lot more to learn on how to control it. This stone could be the key to her survival, but…at the same time, she worried over the consequences.

Shaking her head, Amelia made up her mind. She put the ruby pendant around her neck and swiped the blood-orange stone as well, wishing not leaving it in an underground tomb. After gathering her bearings, Amelia focused her attention back through the door.

Minutes passed painfully. After venturing back through the torture chamber, Amelia chose the door to the right. She made her way through the dank corridor. All the torches had since been extinguished, so she used the ruby to ignite a flame that hovered a few feet in front of her. Using cautious steps, she traced her hand against the mossy wall as the corridor continued to twist without end.

"I wish I had a compass on me," she said to herself.

When she rounded a massive bend, the ceiling stretched into a gilded arch. Glyphs were carved across its length in shapes that Amelia didn't recognize. She grumbled and rapped her fingers on her hips.

"I *also* wish I had my copy of 'Myths and Legends Across the World'."

Chewing on her cheek, Amelia commanded her flame to expand as she studied for anything familiar. She stopped short of another Fotian statue at the center of the room, dividing the tunnel into two paths. It stood approximately seven feet tall and resembled the one in the torture chamber, complete with sash and braided mane. Kneeling, Amelia brushed off dust that coated the base.

"Wait. I think I can make something out...F. That's definitely an F." Amelia breathed hot air on her glasses and wiped it against her tunic. It only smudged the grime further. "Come on," she said, sticking her tongue out. She grazed her fingers against the markings, feeling a rounded circle, then two lines meeting perpendicularly.

"The Foti of Ogonia? That's it! They must have colonized and built this city. Awesome!"

A crash sent her stomach flying up her throat, and she choked on her spit. She swung her bow around and retrieved an arrow. Breathing heavily, she turned toward the source of the noise.

In the tunnel to her left, a silhouette stood, cloaked in darkness.

"Who are you?"

The figure didn't reply. Snorting impatiently, Amelia commanded the ruby to direct the flames in its direction. As soon as it illuminated its features, the fire snuffed out.

Mustering all the courage she could, Amelia nocked the arrow. "If you don't show yourself, I'll shoot."

"Amelia..."

Her eyebrows rose. "Nicholas?"

"Amelia." A hollowness resonated in his voice.

"Nice try," she snarled and released the arrow.

It struck a surface with a *thud*. She rushed forward and snapped her fingers to summon another flame. The arrow lodged against the clay wall, but she didn't find the source of the voice. Amelia plucked the arrow and returned it to her quiver. Goosebumps spread all over her body as she circled in place. She strained her ears. Her breath wavered.

"Amelia!" the voice taunted from further down the left tunnel. Footsteps padded the floor. "If you ever want to return home, you gotta catch me!"

Securing her bow, Amelia huffed and charged down the corridor. She illuminated a second flame, positioning one in front and one beside her. Multiple theories threaded in her mind—perhaps she was hallucinating, but given the fact it never happened before, she dismissed the thought quickly.

Could something be mimicking Nicholas, and if so, why Nicholas?

She was never close to him. If this person or thing wanted to strike a chord with her, it would've chosen her mother…Ms. Clio, or even Landree or Brenna. This led her to believe it was Nicholas, but even that hypothesis still had no solid ground. Amelia pumped her arms, pursing the echoing steps as fast as she could. Whatever it was, Amelia didn't want to lose her pursuant. She was determined to find answers.

INTERLUDE

II

The woman stared at the sky, her bed of stone immensely uncomfortable. Folding her hands on her lap, she said, *You can't force them like pawns in a game.*

It's not a game, the boy replied, receding into the shadows. *These girls would be running in circles accomplishing nothing if I hadn't pushed them along.*

They will misunderstand the mission, the woman said. Her foot twitched. She wished she could walk again.

It doesn't matter, the boy said. *It has to be this way, or we all die.*

CHAPTER

16

Six Days left of The Luce
Brenna

Brenna concluded that she just discovered the most barren corner in the world. She expected more after passing larger-than-life wooden walls.

With a barricade at least twenty-feet high, they must've been trying to keep someone or something out...or in.

Instead of a jungle, Brenna arrived at a wasteland. One without an ounce of green and a plethora of sand. She leaned against a boulder and wiped her brow. After the fiasco at the abandoned city of iron and rust, the mission seemed like a lost cause from the get-go.

She barely knew Amelia and Thamni but losing them dealt a blow to her morale. It was as if she had been cursed. Brenna always ended up alone one way or another. She couldn't even defend them. For the past few nights, she wondered why she bothered to continue searching for supplies.

Am I just doing it so their deaths wouldn't have been in vain?

"Don't you ever get tired? Wait up!"

Grant's voice grated her ears.

Traveling alone with Grant taught her that the concept of loneliness wasn't such a bad thing after all. Even the intermittent earthquakes and the inky, black streaks in the sky bothered her less.

Waving her index finger in his direction, she snorted. "I'd do anything to create a distance between us."

Grant huffed. Minimal shade had left him burnt in the face, neck, and arms. She wasn't any better off. Even the slightest movement, like frowning, caused her skin to sting. Norlenders weren't made for this kind of weather.

Wiping his nose with the back of his hand, Grant flipped his hair and eyed her up and down. "Why you gotta be so hateful all the damn time?" he whined.

"Because you're an annoying, petulant boy," she snapped.

Grant shrugged. "Or maybe you're a snot-nosed brat with no people skills."

Brenna plucked her staff that was strapped to her pack and twirled it around, smacking the back of his knees. Grant fell back and shouted.

"What the hell?"

"What did I tell you from the beginning? No small talk. We need to find these resources then get out of this forsaken island." Brenna zipped her lips shut, unable to contain her anxiety.

Isn't this what you secretly wanted? To run away to a secluded island?

Sitting up, Grant exaggerated a pout. "You'll never land a boyfriend if you continue to be so violent."

Brenna crossed her arms, ignoring Grant. Something was inherently wrong. From the shipwreck to the creatures that stalked them. No matter what, she couldn't fathom living a life of peace if she ignored all that. Ignored her friends.

Grant glared at Brenna. His emerald eyes contrasted his lobster-red cheeks, nose, and forehead. "You've been extra grouchy since we buried Thamni—"

Brenna snatched his tunic and yanked his face toward hers. "And you've been extra insensitive since we lost both Thamni *and* Amelia. Have you ever felt the consequences of death?"

When Grant opened his mouth, she let go.

"Don't bother answering."

"Woah, now. Don't go on assuming that I don't care that two of our team mates just died. Have you ever thought that people grieve in different ways?"

Brenna secured her staff and waved him off. It had been a mistake to engage in conversation just because he pushed some emotional buttons. She scanned the eastern horizon, barely making out where the sands begun. Dirt and sand patches blanketed the land, speckled with dead grass and rocks. Fissures infiltrated the ground, like human veins.

Had they always been there or were they the result of those earthquakes?

She kneeled and inspected the parched soil.

"This almost seems like desertification. Drylands that were once fertile. Doesn't look like there are nutrients to sustain much plant life."

Grant feigned surprise. "No way!"

Brenna growled and cracked her knuckles.

"Anyway, I gotta tell ya. This doesn't look good. Amelia told us that the east should have a lush jungle. There's not a damn green thing as far as the eye can see," he exclaimed. He snapped off a twig from the skeletal remains of a bush.

"It was supposed to be a jungle. Not anymore," Brenna said, monotone.

Scratching the tip of his nose, Grant shifted his weight back and forth between his feet. "I think we need to turn back."

Brenna's shoulders tensed. "Excuse me?"

Grant's eyes widened. He lifted his hands. "I'm being serious. There's nothing for us here. We've traveled for weeks, and we need to head back to Giles. Not to mention the increasing earth tremors and eerie clouds. Want me to keep going?"

Brenna cocked a brow. "What's so scary about clouds? Are you afraid of a little storm?"

Ignoring her insult, Grant pointed up. "How have you not noticed? These black swirly things were present before, during, and after the storm the other night, which I was *not* afraid of at all. Those things don't belong in a sunny landscape!"

Ominous wisps inched west. The coloring did seem off-putting, but Brenna shrugged. "They're just clouds."

Grant adjusted the straps on his back. "We need to turn around."

Heat erupted the back of Brenna's neck. "No."

"Uh, yes."

She got in his face, and Grant flinched. "We need to keep searching. If we return with nothing, we'll still be stuck with nowhere to go."

"But there's nothing here!" He flung both arms wide, voice rising.

Matching her tone with his, Brenna squared her shoulders. She stood almost as tall as him. "If we find supplies, we can build a ship. Even if The Luce vanishes, we have a vessel and can risk navigating our way. Even Ms. Clio mentioned she may have figured it out."

"That's not a guarantee. Her map went down with the ship. Do you expect her to remember everything?" Grant jammed his thumb against his chest. "We already lost two people. One of them was the leader of this expedition!"

"Oh, so you do care!"

"Brenna. You need to learn when to turn in." He reached out, but Brenna jerked her hand away.

"I'm not returning empty handed!" she exploded, spit flying from her lips.

In the corner of her eye, Brenna noticed Grant reaching for his belt—or rather an item holstered to his hip. His tunic hung loosely from his emaciated frame, but Brenna could still make out the outline of his dagger. She drew her staff once more and thrust forward, stopping an inch short of his chest. Brenna's nostrils flared as she steadied her breath. Sweat dripped from her hairline.

"Don't move," she seethed.

"I-I didn't mean any harm. Just trying to convince you to come back with me," Grant pleaded.

Tilting her head toward the path they had been traveling, Brenna said, "Go if you want, but I won't give up until I find what we need."

Grant swallowed visibly. He moved his hand away from his dagger.

"Good. Now give me the signal powder."

He pulled his pack around and produced a sack, roughly the size of a coconut.

"Drop it," she commanded.

He obliged.

"You're free to go now." Ice coated her words.

"Brenna…"

"Not another word."

Grant slipped his pack back on and backed away slowly. Brenna continued to clutch her staff, refusing to take her eyes off him. A tiny voice in the back of her mind implored her to reconsider, but it was too late to change her mind now.

I'd look like an utter fool in front of this sorry excuse for a man.

Grant walked backward on their path. The giant barrier loomed a few miles behind him. The wooden walls almost appeared to be dancing in the heat waves reflecting from the ground. Brenna blinked but couldn't shake the visual. Soon, Grant's form also became visually distorted, a speck of color in a wall of brown.

When he was out of ear shot, Brenna released a wavering sigh. She continued to breathe heavily, doing her best to maintain her composure. She couldn't give up.

"I don't need help. I'm perfectly capable on my own." Brenna swooped down and grabbed the signal powder. "Even if he's a Norlender like me."

Turning toward the east, she chuckled. Of the entire expedition, anyone would've bet Grant and her to be the tightest of allies given their shared roots, but it couldn't be farther from the truth.

When she lived in Norlend, Brenna noticed how proud its citizens were, and any that moved to Camella tended to stick together. The culture and food were familiar. She didn't expect anyone else to enjoy pickled onions with salted fish gizzards. Regardless, she never felt a pull toward one group or another. Even if that were part of the reason Grant gravitated toward her, that was his problem.

After emptying her canteen of water, Brenna resumed her journey. The day was half over, which meant a few more hours before she had to worry about finding shelter…and food…and water.

Brenna pushed forward, using a scarf to shield her from the sun and curtains of sand that rolled through. Mile after mile, she discovered nothing but rock and dirt. The wind picked up, scattering sand and dust into the air and cutting visibility in half. Despite the desolate horizon, she focused on keeping a steady course.

Brenna soon stumbled upon large, flat slates arranged in

a path that wound around a dune. Brenna's eyes stung. She picked up the pace and rounded the corner. Brenna reached a large boulder and couched down, taking brief shelter from the sandstorm. She shook her head violently, trying to dispel Grant's voice that haunted her.

While she waited, Brenna studied the ridges in the formation. A mix of sharp and smooth edges told her it was more than just a rock. The top had been chiseled down to the shape of a reptile's head; but between the sandstorm and the statue's weathered features, she couldn't tease out any further details. For all she knew, it could represent a deity or a simple good luck charm, and she was too exhausted to rack her brain for anything Amelia might have mentioned.

She would be all over this statue.

Bowing her head, Brenna closed her eyes and mourned her friend.

After a brief respite, the winds calmed. Her tongue clung to the roof of her mouth, and every time she swallowed, she cringed at the sandpaper-like sensation that scratched her throat. An alarm rang in the back of her mind. Time was running out. Brenna massaged her legs before picking back up where she left off.

Pillars and archways hinted at another civilization, one more primitive than those that dwelled in the city of iron. She wished she had Amelia by her side.

Brenna ventured through the central archway and toward a ravine. Hope flickered in her chest like a lone candle. She picked up the pace, ignoring the chaffing between her thighs. Brenna didn't pray much, but she found herself hoping, speaking to some invisible force, that water was nearby.

Peeking over, Brenna's breath hitched.

Mounds of bones lay hundreds of feet below. Massive femurs and triangular skulls with rows of fangs piled on top of one another. The claws alone were the size of a human head. Scratch marks plagued the walls of the trench. Brenna wondered if these creatures caused the civilization to vanish, or if they were the civilization.

To the left of the divide stood a chasm, connected by a narrow, natural bridge. To the right stretched a blanket of sand. A strip of navy lined the horizon: the eastern border to the island.

Curiosity struck Brenna, so she followed the ravine's edge toward the natural bridge. Her head spun as she crossed the narrow path. It was a steep drop with nothing to cushion her except more sand, tumbleweeds, and bones. As the wind whistled in her ears, Brenna ordered herself not to look down. When she reached the end, she faced the mountain that dropped into the chasm.

Shriveled trees extended their fruitless arms into the sky. Large columns were carved from the rocky surface, and the vines that once wrapped around them broke off into the wind. More statues sat atop each column with blank eyes. Such detail had been carved into the side of this mountain. Brenna wondered if this was a place of worship.

Brenna examined the entrance. Wooden beams and rock formed a pile at the center. She tried to kick around some of the debris, but nothing budged. Chewing on her cheek, Brenna circled the face of the mountain, searching for additional entrances. No luck.

When she reached the very edge that dropped into the chasm, Brenna sighed. She had wandered until her feet blistered only to come up empty-handed. This colony was just as deserted as the previous destination. She really believed her team could've found resources by now. If her calculations were correct, she had traversed at least one third of Amicita.

Pulling off her boots, Brenna zoned out. "Living here in Amicita was a terrible idea."

The final rays of the sun melted into the horizon. An evening chill dropped the temperature steadily. Sweat dried on her skin, and the breeze sent shivers throughout her body.

Brenna sat at the steps between the two statues and hugged her knees. She rocked back and forth, straining to hear a sound. Any sound. The silence screamed loudly, and it told Brenna that she was all alone. Maybe sending Grant away was a mistake.

No way...Maybe.

She drew a blanket from her pack and rested her head on the ground. Brenna had finally gotten used to sleeping outdoors, but at least she got to rest on spongey soil for most of the trip. She placed her bo staff by her side in case those wolves or anything worse showed up. Brenna closed her eyes. In the morning, she promised to start fresh and give this area another thorough search. Unless the West Team lit their smoke signal, giving up was not an option.

CHAPTER

17

Six days left of The Luce
Landree

Sitting against a lone oak free, Landree struggled with dark, intruding thoughts. Her eyes burned. She had been keeping watch over Nicholas for the last hour. The whites of his eyes shined from the otherwise green landscape. Nicholas lay on the ground, the rise and fall of his chest the only sign that he was alive. Since they departed Buryan, he had fallen into this catatonic state a handful of times, and usually, it came without warning.

The first time Nicholas' eyes rolled to the back of his head and collapsed, Landree nearly had a heart attack. It was a few days back after the two had finished dinner. He had spent the afternoon encouraging her to practice with her longsword, and in a perfect accident, she knocked some birds from the sky when the opal flickered to life and cast a gale in their direction. When they finished their meal, he teetered toward his pack and unfurled a thin blanket. It was odd—Landree remembered that he kept glancing at the sky, ticking numbers off with his fingers, and mumbled beneath his breath. The sun had set, and she went to see if he'd like her to extinguish the campfire. As soon as she touched his shoulder, Nicholas' knees buckled. Landree tried to sit him up, but he was completely dead weight. She panicked for hours, shouting his name and splashing water over his face. The only notion that he was alive was his pulse.

Oddly enough, his black pearl earring shimmered to the same rhythm.

Each episode left Landree mulling over Amicita's threat for hours, and each time, she became more suspicious of Nicholas. He never answered whether his black pearl wielded powers. She also realized she'd been blindly following him toward some unknown danger, and the thought often left her feeling foolish.

Crickets chirped nearby. Landree exhaled and rubbed a hand over her face. At that time, she figured she was just seeing things. Pearls were inanimate objects, and yet, she continued to notice the same pattern every time he passed out. Including this one. Nicholas was still as a log as the final bits of daylight vanished. The ear with the piercing faced her direction, winking as if it held a secret.

Her dark thoughts returned, coming full circle once again. Landree would've thought nothing of the black pearl if she hadn't discovered the Buryan longsword. The opal on its hilt possessed incredible powers, one she still knew little about. She tried practicing with it daily—once in the morning before packing up, and once at night before bedtime. If she willed it, the opal granted her a gust of wind, and it came with a price each time. It sapped her of much needed energy, so Landree limited her use. She was far from mastering the mysterious force, but she developed a knowledge of the basics—at least compared to the day she accidentally killed those birds. By now, she could direct wind in the direction of her blade and even utilize it to enhance the height of her jumps. Landree smiled inwardly. She probably could leap across a wide river with it…if she had the courage.

If Nicholas' lineage stems from Amicita, it's not impossible to believe that black pearl wields power like this opal does. Not to mention…he wasn't around during both Jane-Marie and Clio's abduction. And now that's they're gone…does this mean I'm his next target?

Landree stretched out her legs while her sword lay beside her, opal emitting a feeble glow. She groaned, raking her scalp with her fingertips. It was a hunch, but she didn't have proof. After tying her hair back into a ponytail, she stared up at the night sky. Adin and Deva now barely touched. The month-long eclipse could conclude any day now.

They've been side-tracked one too many times: first the fire, then the disappearances. Thamni's team never used their smoke signal, which proved they hadn't found anything either.

Hopeless or not, Landree still had to find Jane-Marie and Clio. Not only were they her friends, but Ms. Clio was everyone's only hope navigating home without the guiding light. Being stuck on the island was a likely death sentence, but they should have a chance if they worked together. No one deserved to be alone. Priorities had to be realigned, and Landree's was to unite her friends.

If everyone's still alive.

The inky streak across the sky still stood out at night. Landree noticed yesterday that they stretched from three other points on the island—and they all converged at one spot. The unnatural blackness twisted their way toward the center of Amicita, unwavering and ever-present since the shadows consumed Clio.

That's when her gaze returned to Nicholas. The longer she stared, the more turbulent her emotions thundered within.

He warned me not to fall for the seduction of power, but who's to say he hasn't?

Balling her hands into fists, Landree stood and stomped toward him. Nicholas' ebony hair cascaded past his forehead and spilled over the grass. His high-neck tunic was nearly spotless, as were his black slacks. The only signs of travel were indicated on his muddy boots.

Landree nudged him with her foot. After no response, she kicked harder.

"Wake up," she seethed.

His ear piercing caught her eye. Glowing in the same rhythmic manner as her opal, the black pearl, once again, mimicked his heartbeat. She drew closer, holding her breath as if the slightest disturbance could awaken something powerful. Landree's thumb grazed the pearl, studying the setting that kept it hostage.

I wonder...

Landree pinched her fingers around black pearl and yanked.

The earring popped off, and the pearl's heat and light vanished instantly. Nicholas seized and gasped, crystal blue irises rolling back to normal. After looking around wildly, Nicholas glowered at her.

"What the hell were you thinking?" he snarled. "Give that back to me!"

Nicholas lunged, but Landree side-stepped the boy. He crashed onto the dirt, swaying as if he still hadn't completely awoken from his stupor. She dangled the earing above her head.

"Tell me the truth," she demanded. Her heart hammered so intensely, she thought it would burst. She hated confrontation of any kind, but she steeled her nerves. Her gut told her Nicholas withheld information, and enough was enough.

His lip curled as he raised both hands in the air. "I've told you the truth."

"I need more than that this time. Don't think I haven't wondered about your little episodes. You know more than you let on." Landree inched to the left, mirroring his movements. She refused to show her back to him. "Let's review, shall we? The fire. The shipwreck. The shadows and the earthquakes. This all seems too planned. Nicholas, what do *you* want?"

Nicholas' nostrils flared. He punched a fist into the palm of his other hand. "What do I want? It's not what *I* want. You'd never understand because you're nothing but a simple girl!"

"You're the one controlling the shadows, aren't you?" Landree thundered. The pearl vibrated in her hand, feeding off the fury that ran rampant in her veins. Her thoughts careened out of control.

It has to be him. I can't believe it. Snake. This whole time, he's the one who wanted the stones of power for himself. I—I should teach him a lesson!

Opening her fist, Landree stared hungrily at the pearl.

"No!" Nicholas wrapped his fingers around her wrist and twisted. A pins and needles sensation pricked her hand, and the pearl dropped from her weakened grip. In a flash, he caught the pearl and swung his leg around, knocking Landree off her feet.

When her head connected with the ground, stars exploded behind her eyes. A cold sweat doused her body. She blinked a few times, trying to gather her bearings.

"W-wha?" she stuttered. For a moment, she forgot what she was doing.

Nicholas fastening his earring. The shimmering of his pearl pieced her thoughts together. She stood slowly, watching his every move. Her breath rattled. Before she could draw her sword, he snapped his fingers.

Every muscle fiber in Landree's body froze as if gripped by an invisible vice. Her vocal cords refused to obey. Only her breathing was spared, as she watched in horror as Nicholas stalked toward her like a tiger closing in on its prey.

As he inched his face close to hers, his lips thinned into a long, crooked frown. His eyes traced the outline of her face, causing the hairs on the back of her neck to stand. Smokey tendrils expanded from the black pearl, climbing up his arm and spreading across his torso. He cocked his head.

"Look at yourself. You almost unleashed powers you didn't understand because you couldn't control your temper," he mocked in a low whisper. "Now imagine if these were in the hands of every human? Even those with the best intentions could cause major destruction. This is why I believe these powers were intentionally banished. Humans can't handle this much power."

Landree's brain was foggy, but despite the tirade of thoughts entangled her mind, her soul shuddered. She almost lost control, but wouldn't anyone in her situation?

He's playing games with you!

She squirmed, fighting with all her might, but Landree couldn't budge. All she wanted was to break free and unleash all her pent-up anger. He controlled the shadows, and that meant he was behind Jane-Marie and Clio's disappearance. There was no doubt in her mind that he messed with Thamni's team as well.

"I know what you're thinking," he said, voice staccato as the darkness spread across his limbs. "You're wrong. I'm not the bad guy here." Nicholas paused. "Remember what I told you the day Clio disappeared?"

After a brief respite, Landree strained her arms and legs again. Her foot twitched. Her mouth cracked open slightly.

"Oh, I'm sorry. You had something to say?"

A dark tendril brushed across her lips, restoring movement in her neck, jaw, and tongue.

"You mean the day you kidnapped her?" Landree fired back, skin crawling in disgust.

"The lore passed down to me spoke of this threat and its

single goal: consume, and *its name is Telos*. A symbol of greed, an invisible disease in the form of a creature, threatens us. If it fully regenerates and takes on its corporeal form, it won't stop at Amicita. It will spread across the seas with its insatiable appetite."

"The Republic has a navy, while Norlend and Irelle have strong armies." The three countries never collaborated to that extent, but Landree hoped this would be the perfect reason to.

"It's an insidious evil. No military can defeat it. Yes, I was a seeking a stone of power, but not for personal gain. An emerald fragment—a sister shard to what is powering this *thing*—could shut down its revival, but it's gone missing," he said bitterly.

"If this is really true, why won't you let us help you?" she pleaded.

"Well, that was the backup plan. I toyed with the applications in order to gather a team and use other existing gems to silence Telos once and for all—"

My opal!

"But of course, you were all a bumbling mess. With limited time left, I choose to take matters in my own hands."

Landree struggled with her binds again. The viscous shadow gave way a few inches. She wriggled her fingers and flexed her wrists.

"What did you do to my friends?" she screamed.

Nicholas jeered. "How else could I expedite the process? Telos is coming, and I had to move you guys around to find Amicita's talismans."

"We aren't your pawns in this game of yours. You

could've just told us what to do!" she spat, loosening up her entire left arm. "You know what I think? I think you're full of shit. You sent us out to find the stones alright—to keep for yourself."

Shadow consumed Nicholas' body, save his eyes. All his other features appeared warped, much like the shadowy Kana.

"I knew talking was a waste of time. You've proved my point. If you'll excuse me, Ms. Clio needs my attention. If you really don't believe what I'm telling you, it's best that your hurry and follow me..." Nicholas' voice diminished.

Anguish expanded in her chest, crying out for answers. Joints popped and bones cracked as Landree clashed against his powers. She bit through the searing pain and pressure, stretching and reaching for her sword.

As soon as her fingers grazed the hilt, the opal answered her call in a wave of warmth. It flowed through her system, invigorating what has already been exhausted. In a burst of energy, she cried out, expelling a gale that ripped the binds away. It dispelled the wisps of shadow, Nicholas along with it.

Landree collapsed onto all fours, breathing hard. Her blood boiled as she watched the traces of darkness rise to the sky, joining the inky tendrils that swirled inland.

"He took them. I won't let that stand!" she shouted.

Every second counted. After securing her sword by her hip, Landree tore through the path, leaving nothing but a trail of dust behind.

CHAPTER

18

Six Days left of The Luce
Brenna

Norlend was infamously known for its frigid climate, and Brenna's night in the desert reminded her of home. Not that she had many memories. Drawing the blanket closer, Brenna shivered. The twin moons appeared to be in its final days of the eclipse, resembling a sideways figure eight. She never thought much of Adin and Deva until now. In the past, the twin moons were just glowing orbs in the night sky. How was it possible that celestials located millions of miles away could have a significant impact in the world, and more importantly, this tiny island?

Turning on her back, Brenna faced the statues that protected the fallen shrine. Their features were just as weathered as the giant one she'd taken shelter behind the day before. Unease settled deep in her bones. She wasn't sure if she wanted to live where entire civilizations up and vanished without a trace or even a legacy.

Brenna wasn't sure how long she'd been awake, but dawn arrived in no time. She was grateful to be relieved of her thoughts. As she packed her blanket, Brenna prioritized water above all things. Then, she'd resume her quest for resources.

Why bother? Grant's right. The odds are slim as it is. Why risk your neck for a bunch of people that treat you like an outsider?

Brenna lowered her head in unfamiliar shame. Not everyone was cold to her, like Landree and Thamni. But the nasty looks and frosty words from a few spoiled it for the many.

Pebbles rattled at her feet. A familiar vibration rose in intensity, sending a rush of terror and frustration careening through her body. These earthquakes have come and gone more frequently, but its occurrences were unpredictable.

Her thoughts shattered when a loud snap resounded from above. Chunks of rock broke from the mountainside and bombarded her. She dove to the side as one boulder crashed nearby. Tucking into a roll, Brenna sprung back onto her feet and made for the stairs.

After another guttural rumble, as if coming from the bowels of hell itself, a fissure etched into the ground. Brenna skidded to a stop as it split wide open. She wobbled violently, fighting with every ounce of her life to not topple into the abyss. She whipped around. Now pinned between a fissure and the mountainside, Brenna searched desperately for cover. Boulders tumbled and bowled into the abyss, and although she managed to dodge each one, each subsequent boulder seemed to miss by a fraction of an inch.

One of the columns chiseled into the mountainside split and collided into one of the statues. The tremors continued with no end in sight, displacing every loose object. Brenna noticed the debris that had blocked the shrine's entrance had begun to collapse. It still didn't open up the door completely, but Brenna bolted for it. She side-stepped the rain of stone and climbed up a statue.

Holding her breath, Brenna balanced herself on the fallen column. Stepping lightly, she scooted along the length of the object, taking her toward the top arch of the shrine entrance. Brenna hopped onto the rubble. By now, the opening was barely large enough for a human to squeeze in through. She swallowed the enormous lump in her throat. Her breath was quick and shallow, and her brain no longer operated with complete thoughts. It was time to pick: risk getting knocked into the abyss or risk shelter in the belly of a collapsing mountain.

Brenna shoved rocks aside, further opening up the hole. Dirt filled her nostrils, sending her into a sneezing fit. When she managed to shift a sizeable wooden beam, Brenna crept through the opening, but the straps from her backpack held her back. She pushed and kicked, but her pack wouldn't fit.

Shoot!

A deafening roar sounded from above. Gritting her teeth, Brenna removed the pack. Taking only her staff and signaling powder, she tossed her weapon in first, then made one final push.

She toppled forward and the world around her shook. Brenna curled into a ball and covered her head with her hands. Closing her eyes, she prayed for it to end. The room she took shelter in groaned, its support beams seeming to snap beneath the pressure.

This is it.

Silence swept around her like a curtain. Dust settled on the ground, and light feebly filtered through trace cracks from the shrine entrance. Brenna's lips trembled as she looked up. The opening had been filled up once more with large stone slates and wood. Instead of relief, all she felt was—

Trapped.

In order for Brenna to explore the ruins for another way out, she had to lower to her knees and crawl on her elbows. Even after lowering her head, her hair still grazed the collapsed ceiling. The wood paneled floor splintered her forearms as she inched along. Her ears filled with the sounds of scraping and her labored breathing.

Brenna paused where the floor dropped off into a massive hole. Given the jagged edges and uneven shape, something huge had to have crashed through. She felt around for her staff. When she wrapped her fingers around her weapon, Brenna tossed it down the hole and strained her ears. It plopped into a body of water, seemingly not too far below. Mustering as much courage as she could, she pulled herself over the ledge and dropped down.

Landing with a splash, Brenna celebrated such a joyous sound. Her parched tongue cried for a taste. She dropped to her knees and scooped her hands into the water and splashed her face. The cool liquid calmed her burnt skin, and she shivered with delight. Brenna licked her lips. Although her gut warned her about the unknowns, Brenna's instinct overrode the words of caution. She scooped again and took a small sip. The water tasted sweet, free of any bitter or sour notes.

Brenna slurped greedily, diving into the pool for more. After several more gulps, she dunked her entire head in and rinsed her hair. She rose slowly, wringing her strands dry. When she tied it into a bun, Brenna giggled. Her voice bounced off the walls. No one could hear it, so Brenna broke into laughter. She rested her hands on her knees, still in shock with her luck.

"What are the odds?" she asked herself out loud.

A few minutes passed as Brenna stretched, allowing the effect of the water to take hold. Clarity pieced together in her mind one by one, and finally, she had the strength to keep fighting.

Brenna picked up her staff and waded through the cavern. With minimal light, she could barely make out a thing. Extending her arms, Brenna felt for a wall. The cool slate was a welcome change to the blistering heat, rocks, and sand. She followed this wall slowly, relying only on her sense of touch to progress forward.

Wings flapped in the distance. Squeaks echoed close by. She ducked instinctively as bats swooped above. They flew up the gap Brenna had entered the cavern and circled back.

"Shake it off," she told herself, trying to fend off the insidious feelings of hopelessness and despair that threatened to return. The slate wall led her to a narrow tunnel. She paused at the entrance, taking a moment to commit her path to memory. With no map, Brenna knew it was unwise to wander aimlessly. Psyching herself up with a forceful breath in, Brenna proceeded to crawl through, contorting her body to the impossible twists and bends. When she came through the other side, she noticed a soft glow in the far corner.

As she neared, the light expanded. It washed over an opening seven feet high where a steady stream of water poured from. A pillar stood as tall as Brenna's bust, and sitting on top was an open trinket box. A chunk of amber rested on top of a silk pillow. The amber radiated a burnt-orange and tan aura.

That's bizarre.

Its warmth beckoned her.

She plucked the amber, realizing it sat on a silver casing: a ring. Although not one to wear jewelry, Brenna slid it up her middle finger. It fit snugly as she waggled her fingers. She paused, gaze darting around the cavern. Brenna half expected a monster to leap from the shadows to guard the amber or another earthquake to rise; however, nothing happened.

"How anticlimactic," she said, shaking her head.

After the brief moment of amusement ended, Brenna tried to take the ring off.

The ring didn't budge.

Brenna tugged, but the ring refused to slide down her finger. Her skin burned as she tried twisting it. The more she struggled, the more the amber shined. A sudden jolt zapped her fingers that tried to pry the ring free.

"Yeowch!" she exclaimed, shaking her other hand then sucking on the fingers.

Brenna examined the stone. Its glow pulsed like a heartbeat. She huffed, blowing wet strands of hair from her face.

"I've been in the dark too long," Brenna growled. "Fine. Stay there."

She shifted her focus back to the trickle of water. An idea struck Brenna. Clutching her staff, she waded back until she reached the opposite end of the cavern. She wiped the sweat from her hands and took a few deep breaths.

Brenna charged. She hoisted the staff over her shoulder, then struck the bottom against the ground, propelling herself into the air. Brenna kicked her legs as she shouted. The momentum slammed her against the wall, but she was able to reach the source of the water. As she pulled herself up, jagged rocks scraped her skin and tugged at the frayed ends of her tunic. Cool water drenched her abdomen.

Damn it. This is even more claustrophobic than the main entrance.

Brenna's lower half dangled from the opening as she continued to squeeze her way through the hole. She only managed to climb through to her hips before she couldn't travel further. Brenna panted, wanting to rest her head, but water took up half the crawlspace. A little voice in the back of Brenna's mind told her to climb back down and find another way through the cavern, but she refused to give up. She didn't see another way out, and if water found its way into the room, there was an exit on the other side.

Brenna extended her left hand. The narrow tunnel, bathed in the warm glow of the amber, seem to stretch into eternity. If only she had the strength to stretch these walls. Brenna's stomach soured; she had enough of rock, dirt, and sand.

The amber buzzed. Visible waves of golden light throbbed from its center. When it brushed the tunnel walls, the rocks seemed to expand. Brenna blinked her eyes repeatedly. The earth groaned obediently as the path before her stretched larger and larger. The downstream flow of water increased. When the amber's light faded, everything stilled, leaving Brenna lightheaded.

"Oof," she slurred, holding a hand to her head. After shaking the lights from her eyes, Brenna inspected the tunnel. Once barely able to fit her body, it now doubled in size.

Is this a mirage?

She slid her hand against the surface, bending forward as she verified the vast difference in space. Brenna took no chances.

Move now, think later!

She hustled through the jagged corridor on her hands and knees. The patch bent directly upward, and when Brenna squeezed through, she craned her neck to peer through the other side.

Sunlight warmed her face. She breathed in the dry heat as she heaved herself out of the gap. A vast pool of water stretched before her like a hidden oasis. Throwing her head back, Brenna giggled incredulously. She hugged her waist as she fell to the side.

"I can't believe it! I just can't believe it made it!" She rolled into the pool, splashing around playfully. Sweat and grime washed away as Brenna celebrated her escape.

Extending her hands into the air, Brenna waggled her fingers. The sun's rays filtered through the amber ring as it shined, brighter than ever. The sight pulled her head out of the clouds and grounded her. All she could think of was Amelia.

"I'll be damned. She may be right about the mythical gems," Brenna said out loud. Curiosity and melancholy interwove a complex web in her mind, trapping all her other thoughts in place except for one: regret. Regret for not believing in Amelia. Regret for not saving her. Clutching a fist to her chest, Brenna vowed to honor her friend. She would keep the amber, study it, master it, and use it for good.

Once she cleaned up and let her clothes dry off in the sun, Brenna suited up. The amber ring caught her eye.

"Not sure what you are, but I'm glad I found you."

The amber ring buzzed back, startling Brenna. She had no clue how a fancy rock was able to generate supernatural powers, but she concluded there was plenty of time to figure that out. Beyond the pool of water looked more or less like the same sandy blanket she walked into yesterday. Dryland. Lots and lots of dryland.

The sun was almost at its mid-point. As much as Brenna wanted to huddle by the pool until the cool shoulders of the afternoon, she had to make up for lost time. Her positioning led her to believe that she stood on the other side of the mountain. Knowing that the face of the other side had collapsed, Brenna would explore this stretch of land.

The earthquake left deep scars in the dryland, but Brenna trekked her way around each one. She followed dunes and inspected dried up shrubs. The parched lands of the east seemed endless, perhaps right up until the coastline. Brenna wasn't sure how far that blue strip was—if only she jotted down notes from Amelia.

Her chest tightened. Amelia was one of the smartest people she'd ever met. She didn't deserve to die. Brenna massaged the space between her eyes. The Republic of Camilla didn't seem to care about the dangers their "brave little volunteers" could possibly endure. The hype of honor, adventure, and a pass to escape their average life free of parents and homework did all the advertising for them.

And for what?

If the expedition managed to arrive home safely, Camilla would be blessed with countless jewels and a map to Amicita. If the expedition failed, well, they didn't lose contributing members of society.

Camilla wouldn't send a rescue party. Why would they, especially after The Luce vanishes?

She scoped the immediate area for a way down. Most only revealed a steep drop-off; however, one side had step-like engravings etched along its face. Engravings that seemed a little too neat to be natural.

Rubbing her eyes, Brenna smiled. "I don't know how I missed this!"

She stretched out her left leg and proceeded to descend

the precipice. The journey took an hour, sapping what little energy she had left. Brenna focused on her breathing to distract her from the fiery burn of blisters that formed and ruptured on her palms.

A rock loosened. Brenna's right hand lost its grip. Tightening her core, she swung forward and grasped another edge of the cliff. Brenna's eyes widened at the sound of ripping. Somehow a rogue twig caught onto a pocket zipper.

She wiggled her right leg but was unable to free herself. When she swung back to re-secure her grip, the twig snapped, but not before pulling the zipper down, sending its only content into the wind: the signaling powder.

"No!" The hot breeze brushed past, Brenna's red locks covering her face. She spat out her loose strands and tried to blow them away from her eyes. Frustration mounted on her shoulders as she tapped her forehead against the rock. "Idiot!"

Brenna had to keep going. Looking down, she noticed the ground was temptingly close, but she couldn't jump just yet. After descending another few feet, her right foot sought an opening and found none. Straining over her shoulder, Brenna tried to find a secure spot. In a cascade of cracking, Brenna lost her footing completely. Gravity sent her stomach somersaulting. She cycled her arms and legs.

Twisting her body, Brenna clawed anything she could reach. She missed one branch. Then another. On her third attempt, she snatched onto a meager root jutting out from the cliff. It bent from Brenna's weight, sending puffs of dirt into the air. The root snapped, sending her tumbling down.

A sharp pain pierced through Brenna's ribcage when she slammed into a pile of bones. Her chest rose and fell rapidly, each cycle of breathing caused her side to throb. She stared at the chunk of root that remained in her grip.

"Thank you, poor little root for breaking my fall."

With a groan, Brenna rose steadily. Vertigo overwhelmed her, causing her to stumble against the cliff wall. Her vision grew in and out of focus.

"Steady, girl."

She stepped gingerly off the mound of bones. Dread crept up her spine. Even with the desolate fields before her, Brenna had hope...until she lost the signaling powder. Even if by some miracle she found resources, there was nothing she could do about it.

Brenna fell to her knees, whimpering. She pounded the ground with her fists. Frustration bubbled up her throat, exploding into a scream.

"It's hopeless!"

Shoulders trembling, all she could think about was that she let her friends down. And that she should've turned around with Grant.

Footsteps echoed in the chasm. Brenna lifted her head and bit her lip. Wiping tears and snot from her face, she zipped around the bone pile and crouched. The crunching grew louder, picking up in speed. Wrapping her fingers around her staff, Brenna whispered a prayer of thanks to the wind.

A twig snapped.

She sucked in a breath and twirled her bo staff around.

"Hey!"

The bo staff halted an inch from Grant's head. Brenna heaved. "Oh…oh my Deva."

He lifted his callused hands in the air, locking gazes with his blood-shot eyes. Covered in dirt and tunic torn to shreds, Grant was barely recognizable. Instead of irritation, nothing but gratitude flushed through Brenna's cheeks.

"I was worried," he said. "But looks like you got everything under control." Sporting a wry smile, Grant rose both hands in mock surrender.

"What are you doing here?" Brenna uttered.

"I know you're gunna kick my ass for this, but it didn't feel right to leave you. Yes, you're capable, but sometimes you just can't accomplish everything alone—no matter how strong a person you are."

Brenna's lips twitched upward. She dropped her staff and leapt in for a hug. She squeezed as hard as she could. He winced but then relaxed his arms around hers. Hot tears spilled down Brenna's face.

"It's been such a weird day," she said, burrowing her face into his shoulder.

"Can't wait to hear all about it," Grant replied.

After unwrapping from their embrace, she cleared her throat. "No time for that."

Grant tilted his head, patiently waiting for more.

Lower lip trembling, Brenna fiddled with her hands. "I-I dropped the signaling powder. I m-mean, there's nothing here anyway. I was so stupid—"

"Hey, now." He grabbed her hands and fought to meet

her gaze. "All the more reason for me to be here by your side. We'll figure this out."

His deep green irises bore into hers, and for once, coated her with a newfound sense of calm and control.

Nodding, Brenna replied. "Okay."

A pregnant pause spread between them. As Brenna traced her gaze around Grant's face, she couldn't help but notice that the whites of his eyes yellowed and his cheeks had sunken in. She slid her hands over his and noticed a persistent tremor. When he pulled away, the tremor vanished. Brenna bit her tongue, shocked over a genuine concern taking over.

"You've been declining for a while. I'm sorry for never asking before, but...has something happened?"

He folded his hands behind his back. She leaned forward, but Grant flinched. Brenna sighed.

"I should've been nicer to you."

Grant traced a circle in the ground with his boot.

"I wasn't gunna smack you," Brenna insisted. "Something in your backpack?"

His lips parted, exposing swollen, bleeding gums. His voice croaked in reply. "Ah, I—"

The air filled with static, concentrating in the space between them. When Brenna touched Grant, multiple shocks lit her nerves on fire, surging from her hands and up through her arms. Before she could react, the sphere of energy erupted and bowled the two over onto their backs. The scent of scorched skin made Brenna gag. Her reflexes continued to make her heave until she emptied the contents of her belly.

"What the hell," she spate. "Grant! Are you okay?"

He moaned in reply and curled into a ball while one of his legs jerked forward and backward. Brenna crawled toward him, blinking through the sand that assaulted her eyes. Her hair fluttered about, obscuring her vision. When she finally reached him, Brenna pinned his legs with her knees. She patted his cheek.

"Was that you or something else?"

Pupils dilated to the point where his green irises seemed nonexistent, Grant's head lolled side to side.

"This isn't a joke. I'm not a doctor!" she shouted.

A whirring sound generated overhead, and a shadow cast over them. Brenna tumbled to the side and snatched her bo staff. She aimed it at an obsidian orb that danced over Grant. Without hesitation, she flung the staff in its direction, but it simply passed through the mysterious substance.

"Get away from him," she growled.

The outline of the black object blurred as it vibrated. Tendrils shot out and snatched one of her wrists. The amber ring immediately flashed. A ring of sand swirled around Brenna, cutting off the bind, and covered her like a protective curtain. Fighting the urge to hyperventilate, Brenna focused on the amber.

If it weren't for this thing…I've got to save Grant!

Brenna had no clue how the amber functioned, but it seemed to feed off her instinct and desires. She snapped her fingers, and the barrier dropped. However, the orb was no longer there. Instead, a shadowy figure of Nicholas stood a few feet behind Grant. His arm hooked around another shadowy figure about his height. Her hair was tied in a bun, and a distinct shell necklace draped across her neck.

Landree!

She shook her head, but the vision still remained.

"Grant?" her voice rose to a shrill. "Please tell me you're seeing what I'm seeing!"

"Ugh…" he babbled.

"You're next," Nicholas' voice oozed from the figure's unmoving lips. His blank eyes lowered until his gaze was fixated on Grant, who continued to writhe on the ground.

Brenna swung her arm. "No!"

She flung herself on top of Grant.

Shadow Nick exploded into a flurry of dark particles and rained on her. Each drop was ice-cold as they covered the two. Brenna refused to let go. She squeezed her eyes shut and braced for death.

CHAPTER
19

Two days left of The Luce
Landree

Landree traversed miles upon miles of rolling plains, ignoring curious stares from deer and rabbits. Over time, the trail had become less clear, overrun with wild grass and saplings. Fear lurked in the back of her mind, and it grew stronger each time she glanced at the shadow-streaked sky. Its inky tendrils swirled in its vortex-like fashion from four main directions: north, east, south, and west and converged somewhere in the middle. That is where Landree headed. She could only hope that her friends were following the same thing, and that they weren't harmed.

The journey grew increasingly difficult. She lived off wild berries and a vole. She quenched her thirst with morning drew and a passing rain storm. Blisters formed and popped on the soles of her feet, forcing her to rest frequently.

After spending most of the previous night lying down and rinsing her wounds, she carefully wrapped her feet with cotton strips she tore from her slacks. Landree cringed as she wiped the crusts of blood away. She slipped her boots on and wiggled her toes. Everything still burned, but the pain was tolerable. When the sun rose, Landree ran.

I'm so close.

Wind weaved through her walnut-colored locks. Massive green hills towered to her left, spilling into grassy plains—where the shadows connected and funneled downward. The wind picked up. If Landree didn't know any better, she would've thought she'd be headed straight toward a twister.

She'd been completely focused on finding her friends and returning home, but as she approached the final few miles, Landree couldn't stop analyzing her last interaction with Nicholas. On one hand, her gut feeling had been right—his behavior always seemed off-putting, but on the other hand, she didn't have proof that he was lying about Telos, either. A headache throbbed between Landree's ears as her internal thoughts became a shouting match in her mind.

If Nicholas controlled the shadows, it didn't exactly explain the earthquakes.

Up ahead, a river carved through the land. The water churned and gurgled as if furiously trying to rush to its destination. The current seemed too strong to swim across safely. Landree reached for her sword and directed it skyward. Her confidence wavered, still unfamiliar with her new power. However, the thought of her friends in danger overrode her doubts and fears.

"Lend me your power!" she exclaimed.

The opal gleamed overhead, expelling a gale that wrapped its arms around her legs and lifting her with relative grace. She cycled her legs as she glided over the turbulent river. Landree's stomach leapt and fell, and blood rushed loudly in ear ears loudly.

Her boots slammed into the muddy shore—the collision rattling her knees and all the way up to her teeth. She wiped her brow as she glanced over her shoulder. Landree was lucky the river wasn't any wider in case she didn't have enough energy to offer the stone. After shaking off the jarring impact, Landree sheathed her sword and continued chase.

"Yearg!" a voice shrieked. An aquamarine furball slammed into her stomach.

Landree tumbled backward, wheezing and gasping for breath. The critter landed a few feet to her left, accompanied by the rattling of metal.

It immediately cowered beneath an oval shield like a turtle hiding within its shell. Pearls and a single sapphire adorned its scratch-free surface. Even as a decorative piece, the shield was much too large for the creature. Its two long ears and tail poked through both ends.

"What in Adin's name?"

The creature inched from its hiding place. It exposed its muzzle, twitching its whiskers while sniffing the air. The lone sapphire that sat at the center of the shield sparkled seductively at Landree.

"Are you alright?" she asked.

"S-stay away! I hold Kai's Sapphire! Leave me be, and I'll spare your life!"

Its high-pitched voice grated against her ears. "The *what* sapphire?"

The creature unfurled, revealing a rabbit-like creature with a fish tail. His eyes rounded. "Another human? What in Deva's fury is going on?"

Landree's heart leapt. "Another human? What does he or she look like?"

He turned his wet nose up into the air. "I don't have time for the likes of your kind."

"What's that supposed to mean, *my kind*?"

The Kai's fur bristled as he hopped around her. "The world has long lived in peace until human ambition stirred up all sorts of trouble!"

A bush rustled to Landree's right. In a blur of gray and brown, a figure jumped into the air.

"I got you now!"

Landree's head whipped toward the source of noise. "Jane-Marie?"

Her best friend dug her heels into the dirt and gasped.

"You're alive!" Landree exclaimed.

"*You're* alive!"

Jane-Marie was barely recognizable—her ebony hair had formed a nest of knots on top of her head. Scrapes and bruises plagued her face and arms.

The two clasped hands and jumped up and down. Waves of relief coursed through Landree as she barely contained tears from spilling down her cheeks.

Landree sniffed. "What happened to you?"

"Long story, but I've been chasing Lepus over there—"

Landree followed the direction of her finger but saw a circular indent in the grass.

Jane-Marie shoved her, shouting at the top of her lungs—her green eyes wide and feral. "Stop that Kai!"

"Why?"

Jane-Marie gripped her collar. "No time to talk. We need to catch him!"

Nodding, Landree pursued the waggling tallgrass that gave away Lepus' position. As the two gave chase, Landree realized she was losing steam quickly. Her well of stamina had already been depleted. She panted heavily, and her lungs burned. Sharp pain lanced the soles of her feet, and her legs felt like jelly. Landree considered using the opal to mow Lepus down, but she barely had the energy to keep running.

When they reached the top of a hill, Jane-Marie tucked and rolled, gaining speed and bowling into Lepus at the bottom. The Kai pressed hind legs against Jane-Marie's jaw, but she had him locked in place by his ears. Jane-Marie gagged, face growing paler by the second. Her blood-shot gaze met Landree's.

"Get…shield," she choked out.

Landree continued to huff as she waddled down the hill. "Hold…on. I'm coming," she said, gulping air desperately.

When she neared Lepus, the sapphire glowed. The opal on her sword pulsed with familiarity. Curiosity distracted her from the nagging fatigue and discomfort.

"Hurry up!" her friend hissed.

Snapping from her reverie, Landree lunged and wrestled the shield from Lepus. As soon as her fingers clasped the metal, a familiar warmth surged up her fingers. She crashed onto her back, shield snuggly tucked in her arms.

"Give it back!" He twisted and landed a kick in Jane-Marie's ribs.

Landree's eyes narrowed as she drew her sword. The opal flashed in warning. Lepus' eyes fixated on the gem, He leaned in slowly and sniffed.

I'm too tired, but this Kai doesn't need to know that!

Jane-Marie stood and dusted herself off. She shuddered in disgust. "I need a bath."

"Yeah, I can smell you from over here," Landree replied with a snort. She directed her focus back to Lepus. "So judging from what I heard and witnessed in the last few minutes, you must be…a Kai? Never heard of your kind before."

Flicking his tail back and forth, Lepus nodded. He pressed his front paws together. "I beg you. Give me back Kai's Sapphire."

Landree looked down. "What would you need this for? This shield is too big for you."

His tail twitched faster. "It's not the shield I need. All I care about is the sapphire."

"It possesses incredible power," Jane-Marie blurted.

"Yeah. I can tell," she murmured, thinking of Nicholas. "Tell me what you need it for."

"I believe an ancient threat has resurfaced…many refer to it as *Telos*. With no guardians left in Amicita, I've taken it upon myself to put a stop to it."

The name struck Landree like static shock. Nicholas' voice taunted the back of her mind. "Telos...So, it's real."

Tugging at his ears, Lepus whimpered. "Time is precious! Have you not felt the earthquakes worsening as the eclipse passes? That's the abomination, clawing its way from deep within Chailara Hills."

"Are the Chailara Hills anywhere near that dark vortex?" she asked.

Lepus nodded wildly, causing his coral earrings to clack against one another. "It certainly appears it's at least in the same direction."

Landree squeezed her eyes shut then re-opened them. She wished this was a nightmare, but Lepus still stood before her.

"Are you okay?" Jane-Marie asked, touching Landree's elbow.

"It's Nicholas. He's the one that spirited you and Clio away," she replied as she rubbed the space between her eyes.

"You're saying he's behind all this?" she asked in an alarmed tone.

Pacing back and forth, Landree clutched the shield and stared at the sapphire. Lepus thumped his foot impatiently.

"He mentioned a Telos as well, but who's to say he's not controlling that thing? Jane-Marie, he rigged the applications for this expedition. He knew about these stones of power. I think he's using us to do the dirty work and collect it all for himself!"

Her friend frowned. "He's rough around the edges, but

you'd really think so?"

"I don't know what you two are squabbling about, but Telos is not human. Or at least, not anymore."

Landree offered the shield to Jane-Marie. Lepus swiped at it, but the girls lifted it above his head.

After securing the shield, Jane-Marie gestured to the Kai. "I don't know about Telos—or what Nicholas has to do for that matter, but we'll soon find out. I can make a safe bet that we're all headed in the same direction."

Turning to Landree, Lepus pointed one claw at her sword. "Is that why you have Tuuli's Opal?"

"Who?" All the new terminology swam around Landree's mind. Her skull throbbed, ready to explode.

"Let me rephrase: does that opal contain the powers of the wind?"

Jane-Marie's head jerked up, eyes lit in curiosity.

Stroking the opal, Landree nodded. "I found it in an abandoned home to the west. Buryan was the name of its settlement, I believe. I'm still getting used to it, for sure."

"Peculiar," he replied.

Jane-Marie rolled her eyes. "Don't tell me. There's some secret prophesy that humans would discover this forbidden island and save its dwellers from an ancient evil?"

The two girls snickered.

"No!" Lepus exclaimed, stomping a hind paw on Jane-Marie's foot. "Ladies, this is serious! I'm not just worried about the Kai, this threat extends to all of us."

"Ouch! What's that for!?" Jane-Marie hopped on her good foot.

Stifling her laughter, Landree waved a hand in the air. "Okay, enough joking around."

Lepus growled. "You're the ones joking around!"

"Then why is this peculiar?" Landree asked with a shrug.

He lifted his gaze toward the sky. "I've explained this to your companion already. None of these gems are meant to carry powers anymore. A wise and just queen eons ago banished them from this world as it was poisoning the minds of the living with a thirst for power."

"Even though the four tribes that lived here are gone, the queen's talismans—the most powerful of the legendary stones—were secured in hidden spots for safekeeping...and to ensure no one would stumble upon them just in case their powers ever were to return."

Landree sighed. "How does this sound? Let's all head toward that swirling vortex of death. We can fight over these gems afterward, because, clearly, they belong to neither of us."

"I still think I'm better suited for the sapphire!" Lepus blurted.

Jamming her hands on her hips, Landree glared at him. "Weren't you the one who said we don't have any time? Let's just agree to head to our destination and figure it out from there. Right?"

Jane-Marie stared back, stone-faced.

"Right?" Landree pressed.

"Yeah, yeah," she finally replied, jutting out her lower lip.

Landree jerked her thumb in the direction of the shadows. "Let's go, then."

The two girls forged ahead as Lepus hopped along, keeping pace.

Grazing shoulders, Landree whispered, "I thought I'd never see you again."

"Me neither," she said, misty-eyed.

"What happened to you?"

Jane-Marie sucked in a breath and pursed her lips.

"What's the matter? Are you hurt?"

The two hiked in silence, landscape twisting into a blur of yellow, green, and brown. The fields of tall grass that once tickled their arms thinned out into sporadic patches. Lepus coughed as they traversed the parched earth.

Jane-Marie shuddered. "You won't believe me."

Landree scoffed. "Try me."

"I woke up in a temple of sorts beneath the sea."

"What?" Landree exclaimed. "That's pretty cool, actually."

Lepus threw them a side-eye.

"That's not even the weirdest part," Jane-Marie said, crestfallen. "I...can't remember."

Landree chewed on her cheek. "What don't you remember? I mean, you clearly remember me."

"I woke up remembering nothing of the expedition. The last memory I have was going to sleep the night before leaving Camilla."

Landree hummed. "It makes just as much sense as everything else going on. I'm sure..." she paused. "Maybe you hit your head. I'm sure you'll regain your memory once this nightmare is over."

The opal buzzed. Looking up in alarm, Landree's tongue clung to the roof of her mouth. The looming vortex expanded larger as they drew closer.

"Do you feel the sapphire's energy?" Landree asked.

"I do."

She reached for Jane-Marie's hand. "Everything's going to be okay. Besides you didn't forget any memory that was important."

"But it's terribly jarring waking up in another world," she bemoaned.

Fissures stretched their jagged fingers around them. Warped, decayed trees straddled the gaps. The farther inland she had traveled, the more desolate it became. Even the dirt they kicked up…

Is this ash?

"Another world, indeed."

INTERLUDE

III

Do you think they're ready? the woman asked, voice hoarse.

The boy frowned when her rattled breath filled his ears.
Don't waste your energy worrying.

Are they ready, she pressed.

They've used their powers a little, the boy replied.

Are the ready? the woman asked a third time.

The boy's chest tightened. He never displayed his fear, his anxieties; however, each day dealt a fresh crack in his façade.

The woman broke into spastic coughs.

They are, the boy lied.

CHAPTER

20

Two days left of The Luce
Amelia

Amelia stumbled, catching her balance against the wall. She pounded her fist against the cool stone, fighting the urge to hyperventilate.

I think it's been days.

After chasing the specter for what seemed like an eternity through various forks in the tunnel, the footsteps had vanished, and the voice never returned. It left her with no choice but to continue down the path instead of turning around; however, it wasn't long before her legs gave out, forcing her to take frequent breaks.

Although she'd utilized the ruby to light her way, the flames often extinguished until she rested. Sometimes, Amelia would blackout and wake up completely disoriented. Whenever Amelia summoned fire, the ruby left her weaker than before.

She had to sleep on the ground, drink water that leaked from corners of the ceiling, and eat any insect she came across. Amelia hung her head at the memories.

It was Thamni's death that provided her with the will to live. She knew him only for a brief while, but when he opened up about his daughter, she witnessed a vulnerability that few people ever exposed. Her heart ached for his child.

Nayana. That was the last thing he said. Maybe that's her name! I need to return so I can tell her how brave her father was.

She had to fight through the exhaustion. Not for the glory of Irelle or even for her parent's praise, but rather for her new friends and Nayana. She traveled for days, but there had to be an exit at some point.

"I can't give up. It's not like I want to turn back now."

Forcing herself to straighten, she took a few wobbly steps forward.

One step in front of another.

She repeated the mantra until she noticed another Fotian statue five-hundred feet away. Two door handles replaced what would've been paws. Amelia would've spilled tears of joy, if she had the hydration to spare.

She tugged on the handles. Amelia tried pushing instead. The door didn't budge. Frustration mounted her shoulders as she rattled them.

"You've got to be kidding me! I didn't travel all this way just to turn back around!" Amelia's voice ricocheted against the narrow walls.

The ruby vibrated against her neck. Temptation beckoned her to call upon its powers once more. Grappled with hesitancy, Amelia wasn't confident she had much energy left.

Will I pass out? Will this gem overtake me?

She tugged the handle again. "I need to get out of here before I go insane."

Gripping the metal, Amelia forced all her thoughts and worries from her mind. Bending her knees, she balanced herself and let the ruby's powers leech into her own. She grimaced as sweat beaded across her forehead and down the back of her neck. Her body lit up with sweltering heat.

Amelia cried out as a hiss erupted. She gripped tighter as the steel melted in her hand. Amelia pressed into the lock. A metallic scent stung her nostrils and filled the back of her tongue with its acrid taste. Her entire body trembled until her legs collapsed.

Crashing onto the ground, Amelia clutched the hand that melted the lock. Her breath rattled as her body cooled. Tears soaked her lashes. The pain overwhelmed her, and despite the fantastical assistance from the ruby, she wasn't sure if she was making a deal with the devil.

"I must..." she said between labored breaths. "...must save my team."

Blood rushed from Amelia's head as she fought to stand. When she took one step, the room seemed to spin, and she crashed into the door, shoulder first. Wood splintered. Amelia cried out in pain.

The door groaned and gave way. Amelia stumbled out into the open, greeted by the bright rays of the sun. She tensed her legs and rubbed her eyes until the vertigo let up.

"I'm finally out!" Amelia exclaimed joyously. She lifted her arms as she fell to her knees. Hot tears spilled down her cheeks. The air never smelled so fresh, and the daylight warmed her like a maternal hug. It took a few minutes for her eyes to readjust, but Amelia relished every second outside the damned tunnel.

When she finally observed her surroundings, her mouth grew slack.

Gold bricks lay by her feet. Beyond the mounds of bricks, Amelia found herself standing in the walls of a naked foundation. The wooden beams splintered in half, hollowed out by termites, or other insects of the like. Stepping gingerly over the rubble, Amelia made her way outside the dilapidated structure. Broken tables and chairs stripped of its upholstery peppered the first floor. Amelia pinched her nose at the whiff of mold and mildew, but she was used to it by now.

Marble staircases wound up toward a non-existent second floor. A tarnished chandelier lay in a pool of chipped tile.

Am I in central Amicita?

The nagging voice in her head demanded that she find her way back to the city of rust, or even base camp with Giles and wait until everyone returned. Amelia ground her teeth, torn with indecision. It her guess was correct, she was at the castle she read about in "Myths and Legends Across the World". A monarchy once ruled from a palace in the middle of Amicita, ruling over four tribes. This was history.

Perhaps she could spare a few minutes to look around.

Amelia circled the area. The roofing had collapsed, exposing the interior to the elements. Entire towers vanished into the fissures from past earthquakes. She paused. If the tremors continued to worsen, it could potentially swallow the entire palace. Then, it would be as if it never existed. To Amelia, that was sacrilege. Scores of historical artifacts waiting to be discovered could vanish, if they hadn't already.

Hobbling through the rubble, Amelia craned her neck around nooks and crannies. A desire to find just one item to bring home pulled her forward. She studied faded tapestries and discovered piles of weapons ranging from axes and spears. Amelia stumbled over a shield.

She nudged it over with her boot. The surfaced was scratched and faded, but she made out an outline of an avian creature. Specks of red paint clung to the edges. Amelia frowned when she discovered the straps had disintegrated. She moved on, wading through a sea of rot and rust.

As Amelia debated to leave, an ivory door caught her eye. She scurried through it to find a well-preserved rectangular room. Shattered stained glass covered the carpet. Rows of pews faced a granite altar.

"Wow." Amelia wiped her glasses against her tunic.

Scurrying over to the alter, she examined its surrounding area for clues. Amelia found a handful of brass candle holders, the shattered remains of a glass case, and moth-eaten scrolls. She knelt down to unfurl them one by one. Although much of the parchment had been soaked through, Amelia made out letters used in the common language.

"If only I can bring these all back with me."

A family of mice darted past her feet and vanished through cracks in the foundation. Her blood curdled as a familiar rumble returned. Window frames rattled. Hinges to the ivory door snapped one by one. Amelia's movements grew frantic.

"No, no, no..."

The wall facing the altar shuddered and swayed. One brick fell loose, then another. Dust fell in layers and the quakes ratcheted up in all-too-familiar intensity. Amelia's hand rested on a scroll tied with a satin ribbon. She shoved it underneath her arm and rolled backward. The wall toppled, covering the altar.

Breathing heavily, Amelia told herself it was time to go. The ivory door had fallen, blocking the entrance. She made for one of the windows, biting through the pain as she brushed against glass fragments. Amelia's chest ached at the sound of history collapsing. When she finally squeezed through, she dove into the dead grass.

It was a skeleton of a courtyard. Barren fruit trees and dried-up fountains lined a network of cobblestone pathways. Each one circled into a dead-end.

A hairline fracture raced between Amelia's legs. She swallowed a lump in her throat. The crack widened. Steam hissed as the earth parted. She yelped and bolted down a stairwell and through a maze of dead shrubs.

The earth by then had split wider than Amelia could jump. She veered away from the widening gap. Thorns scraped her body as she raced through an old courtyard.

When Amelia managed to run far from the reaches of collapsing architecture or fissures, she turned around. Her own heart shattered into pieces to see the remnants of this castle sink into the bowels on the earth.

She gripped the sides of her head and moaned. Her stomach sank. History vanished in a blip. "And just like that..."

A strong gale nearly tore the scroll from her grip. Amelia glanced skyward, noticing rows of dark swirls that streaked across its canvas like a hellish cobweb. In the distance, they funneled into a singular vortex. It traveled like no other cloud formation she'd studied. She wrapped her arms around herself as goosebumps pricked her skin.

"What is that?"

Before Amelia could take a step, another microburst of wind stole her breath away. She hugged the scroll tighter as a pool of darkness expanded a few feet in front of her, appearing to be of the same substance as the tendrils in the sky. Ripples formed in rhythmic fashion.

Amelia tucked the scroll between her legs and whipped out her bow. She knocked an arrow and aimed at the shadowy cocoon. It expanded steadily. Amelia inhaled deeply as she took aim. Humanoid features hallowed out, causing her stomach to sour.

Steady.

In a pulse of energy, the plumes of shadow vanished. Amelia coughed through the haze. The two figures screamed.

"Stop! Who's there?" she ordered in a shaky voice.

"Amelia?" replied a frenzied voice.

"What's going on?" the second voice, baritone in contrast, followed.

The fog parted, revealing Brenna and Grant tangled up on one another.

"What...how...*Where*?" Amelia rushed to their side. She pulled Brenna away from Grant, who rolled onto his back as if paralyzed.

"Are you okay?" she asked.

He nodded.

"You're alive?" Brenna cried out, half-laughing and half-crying.

Before she could answer, Brenna embraced her friend. A wave of sweat and dirt washed over Amelia.

"B-but how?" Brenna's voice quivered as she released her grip. She spotted her bo staff on the ground beside them and cradled it like a lost child. "Thank goodness this came along!"

Amelia exaggerated a shrug. "There was a hidden chamber beneath that waterfall. I was lucky enough to escape through there instead of drowning."

"I'm relieved." Brenna's eyes glistened.

"As am I," Amelia said, cracking a tiny smile. "Glad to see you're both safe."

Brenna wiped a tear from her eye and sniffed. "Where are we?"

"I believe we're in the center of Amicita," she said matter-of-factly as she bent over Grant. His pupils were dilated, and his cheeks were flushed.

"You believe?"

Amelia propped him up, trying to avoid her most recent memories. "Brenna, I just emerged from an underground passage, and I hadn't seen the sun in days. I'm just as confused as you."

Brenna sat down and rested her head against her knees while Grant continued to stare ahead. Amelia's thoughts cycled over and over, trying to connect the dots. The ruby purred against her neck. When she took it off, it ceased glowing.

"Did you…pick something like this up along the way?" Amelia asked, holding up the ruby. She brushed her thumb against its smooth surface, and it pulsed to her heartbeat.

Nodding eagerly, Brenna waggled her fingers. A chunk of amber rested on a ring. It came to life on cue. The two girls turned to Grant.

"You?" Amelia asked softly.

Brenna clicked her tongue. "Nah."

Grant swayed in place. Huffing impatiently, Brenna waved her hand over his eyes.

"Hello?"

Sucking in his lips, Grant shook his head.

"At least I don't think so, anyway," Brenna concluded.

"This is all too much of a coincidence," Amelia said, mind already racing for a deduction.

Brenna exaggerated a nod. "Sure is." She unzipped Grant's pack, half of which had been torn open. After rummaging around the only in-tact pocket, she produced a vial. "Salve," she said. "It's not much, but we need to patch up some wounds before we even consider moving forward.

While I look at injuries, Amelia, tell me more about Amicita legend. It's now become an interest of mine," she said with a snort.

"What? Why?" Amelia rolled up one sleeve and checked her elbow.

"I once thought the concept of supernatural powers was complete idiocy. Obviously, I'm the idiot."

"It's hard to have faith in the things that can't be proven by someone or something tangible."

Brenna gestured toward Amelia with the vial. She shook her head.

"Grant appears to be in bad shape. He looks like he suffered a head injury."

"Then this thing ain't gunna do a damn thing," Brenna growled.

Amelia shot her a knowing look before reaching for her scroll. "I know a little, but maybe this'll tell us more." She undid the ribbon and unfurled it with bated breath. Most of the words were indiscernible, but a few sentences dotted throughout the parchment filled her with excitement. She ran her fingers across the rough surface until she landed on the first sentence. "Four tribes united under law had shed blood through years of civil war. The first queen and her daughter sowed seeds of peace. Blah blah."

"I don't need you to read me a fairy tale," Brenna quipped. She rummaged through her sack. "Damn, nothing to soak up blood. Never mind."

A prolonged ripping sound interrupted Amelia as she searched for the next readable line.

"Stones of power granted to the royal family. No wait, just the women."

"Cool," Brenna added.

Amelia smirked.

"Wind, water, earth, fire." Amelia glanced up. "Do you know what your amber does?"

"Haven't used it much, but it seems to impact the way the dirt moves."

"Earth," Amelia corrected.

"Sure."

"My ruby controls fire," Amelia said excitedly. "Grant, what about you?"

"Ugn…" He flopped forward. Drool dripped from his lips.

Brenna sat him back up. "Gross," she said.

"This is tough to read," Amelia said as she slammed a fist against her thigh in frustration. Her eyes burned as she tried to make sense of the warped ink. "Something about *Aeonian*. No idea what that means. Blood. War. More blood. Typical history."

Amelia clenched her jaw. She fumbled down the scroll as Brenna started working on her elbow. Brenna tried to appear busy, but Amelia felt her staring over her shoulder.

"A Healer was raised from the dead. Something about a queen's last wish to banish the powers away with an emerald."

"Because of a Healer? Doesn't sound terribly dangerous." Brenna smeared the tonic onto Amelia's wound.

She recoiled as pain forked up her arm. Brenna fussed

and applied one more layer. She sighed and tossed the scroll aside. "That was useless."

Sitting on her ankles, Brenna offered her the salve. "Can you help me out? My side hurts when I take deep breaths."

Amelia nodded as Brenna lifted her tunic. She peered past Brenna, checking to see if Grant would make a crude comment. He continued to stare into space. As inappropriate as the boy was, his behavior seemed deeply troubling.

Amelia got to work on a melon-sized bruise on Brenna's ribcage.

"It only just adds a touch of context behind what I know. Once upon a time, the earth granted this island gems with the ability to control various aspects of nature. Soon, many nations immigrated here, and blame was placed on some renegade man who slayed half the country before he vanished by the power of shadow."

"Through one of the stones?"

"Good question." Amelia emptied the contents of the vial onto her hand and massaged it gently onto Brenna's skin. "Ultimately, multiple countries got involved with this thirst for supernatural powers, and the queen put an end to it."

"And the meaning behind The Luce?" asked Brenna through clenched teeth.

"No clue; however, if these gemstones were meant to be deactivated, I don't need historical documents telling me something's wrong. The balance this kingdom tried to achieve has been disrupted." She rolled down Brenna's tunic. "All set."

"Although I think this expedition turned into an utter mess, perhaps it's a good thing that we're here," Brenna uttered. She pointed at the funnel of shadows touched down in a field of dead grass.

Figures a few miles back approached the funnel.

"Hey, look!" Amelia exclaimed. Her stomach jumped up her throat.

Brenna looked over her shadow and gasped. "Could it be them?"

Straining her eyes, Amelia shook her head. "I can't tell for sure. They're too far away. Two humans and... something blue," she trailed off.

"What? I hope everyone's okay."

After gulping water from Brenna's canteen, Amelia scrambled to gather what little items she had: her bow and a quiver of four arrows. Her heart raced faster than her mind could process what she saw. "We need to hurry!"

Brenna emptied the contents of Grant's pack. Other than the now empty canteen, all that was left was a few articles of clothing and some rope. She rubbed her chin. "I'm not even sure it's worth carrying around anymore."

"I'll carry it. You never know."

The two girls turned to Grant.

"Are you going to be alright?" Amelia asked.

"I'll be fine," he replied, monotone.

Brenna cast Amelia a side glance, and she shrugged.

"We haven't a moment to spare!"

CHAPTER

21

Two days left of The Luce
Landree

Landree lifted her tunic over her nose. The wall of ash stung her eyes and nostrils as she neared the dark vortex. The path ahead was near impossible to see. Jane-Marie hacked non-stop, so she slowed down. Not that she minded a break. Lepus was lost in the sea of ash nearby.

Nerves firing out of control, Landree drew her sword and called forth the opal's powers. She cautioned herself not to overuse the gem at the risk of passing out, but the idea of facing Nicholas provided her with a sliver of fuel. It flickered to life as she prayed for an opposing gale to protect them. A circle of light expanded, blowing away the particles and wrestling for dominance against the tornado-like force. Landree's arm shook as she tried to channel as much strength as she could into the stone.

An explosion straight ahead propelled her off her feet and knocked the sword from her hand.

"Damn it," she exclaimed.

Lepus hopped into her peripheral vision. "Are you girls okay?"

The wind settled. Stillness expanded into the air, and yet the darkness continued to funnel at the bottom of the final hill directly ahead. Ice-cold horror burrowed up her spine, and fear froze her from the inside out.

A sea of ash and debris filled a massive crater in the field. Clio lay at the center on a slab of granite while the tail end of the vortex drilled into her torso. Bruises covered her arms and neck, and her clothes hung loosely from her frail body. Nicholas stood to the side, hands clasped behind his back with a bored expression.

A burst of white-hot fury shattered the steel cage of fear, and without further thought, Landree picked up her sword and charged.

"Leave her alone!" she screamed.

Nicholas glanced up. His smirk sent rage careening through her veins. The opal flashed in warning. When Landree sliced her sword horizontally, a blast of wind rushed toward him.

He lifted his hand nonchalantly, dispelling the gust. Plumes of ash erupted from the aftermath. Landree lifted her arms to shield her eyes.

"What are you doing to her?" she exclaimed.

Nicholas bent over Clio and whispered something into her ear. Clio's eyes snapped open.

Landree pumped her legs, fighting knee-deep ash that slowed her pace. Jane-Marie huffed not too far behind. Lepus, on the other hand, struggled to keep his head above the ash.

With a snap of his fingers, Nicholas summoned the vortex to branch out and form a barrier around him and Clio.

Landree slashed and pierced, but the darkness absorbed her blows like sludge.

"She's not ready!" Nicholas exclaimed. "I'm trying to help her, and you need to stop interfering."

"Liar!"

The shadow splintered further and latched itself around Landree. She wrestled against its sticky surface but couldn't break free. Its consistency was like paste, and the more she resisted, the more it clung to her. Jane-Marie tried to hack away with the pointed end of her shield but to no avail.

"The more you resist, the harder it's going to be," Nicholas warned. "You've left me no choice. You're acting upon instinct and not your mind."

Confusion and denial rattled her bones as she replayed all her interactions with him since Mayor Erebus read their names.

Why us? What if he is telling the truth? If he is, why is he doing this?

She clung desperately to a thread of hope that perhaps she was wrong, and that Nicholas was simply a stick in the mud, a humorless grouch, and not some power-hungry villain.

The goop spread up her neck and over her mouth.

Landree crimped her lips shut as it consumed her face.

Please, Nick! Stop this!

Landree couldn't breathe. The shadowy substance absorbed her tears and filled her with despair. She didn't want her life to end like this, especially at the hand of another classmate—or even a potential friend.

An arrow zipped past Landree. Once it connected with the shadows, it exploded in a ball of fire. Sweltering heat washed over her and melted the substance away. When she fell onto her knees, Landree whipped her head in the direction of the source.

At the top of the hill stood Amelia, bow in hand and a fierce scowl on her face. She nocked another arrow, set the tip ablaze, and released. Landree dove out of the away as fire rained over the field. The shadowy cage hissed as it evaporated. Landree pumped her fist in the air, and Amelia nodded in her direction. Brenna appeared beside her, supporting Grant around her shoulders.

Brenna's hair whipped about like a raging fire. Grime and blood covered her skin and clothing, but she stood tall and proud like a warrior. She waved an arm and shouted Landree's name while Amelia's eyes were still trained on Nicholas.

Hope swelled in her chest. She turned to him, taking pleasure in his dumbfounded expression.

"What now?" she barked.

Nicholas' nostrils flared. "I told you already. I'm performing a necessary enchantment on Clio." He pointed a dagger at Amelia. "Don't waste your arrows on me."

A shriek rattled the air as Lepus tackled him from behind. The Kai thrashed his tail, fighting to secure his grip. Nicholas clawed at his neck, finally throwing Lepus over his shoulder.

"Do not interfere! Do you know who I am?" he spat.

Taking advantage of the diversion, Landree directed a gust of wind from the tip of her longsword. When it bowled him over, Jane-Marie pounced and pinned his legs down with her own. She smashed the edge of her shield into his face. Blood spattered into the air.

All at once, the shadow vortex dissipated. Clio's screams erupted in the air, and her limbs seized. Landree sprinted in her direction as Jane-Marie kept Nicholas pinned down.

"You imbeciles—" he gagged. "—don't know what you're doing!"

Grasping Clio's shoulders, Landree tried to stabilize her teacher. Clio's arms and legs continued to jerk, and drool leaked from her lips. She looked around desperately. Nicholas knocked Jane-Marie off and sprinted toward her. Landree tensed. Her sword was on the ground, but she didn't want to let go of Clio.

"Stay back!" Brenna shouted. She moved her hands as if conducting an orchestra while a burnt-orange glow radiated from one of her fingers. When the light intensified, her muscles bulged through her tunic, and her face grew purple. A strained grunt echoed across the field.

The soil shifted beneath Landree's feet. Unlike the jerky movement of earthquakes, the movement felt smooth, rolling. It surged from Brenna, beneath Landree, and toward

Nicholas. A pillar of dirt and ash erupted beneath him, casting him aside like a rag-doll.

Brenna, Amelia, and Grant arrived by Landree's side. Jane-Marie followed. Landree squeezed them into a side-hug.

"I'm so glad you're here," she said.

Everyone smiled back at her except Grant, who nodded slowly. Her friends intertwined their arms with one another while Landree continued to hold Clio down.

"I've had enough of this nonsense. You're harming her!" Nicholas shouted in a rich timber.

Landree's stomach lurched. A pins and needles sensation crept up her legs as she and her friends levitated off the ground. No matter how hard she fought, Landree couldn't free herself. She flinched, anticipating another wave of darkness to attack, but Nicholas ignored them and trudged toward Clio.

What does he mean that we are harming her?

Clio's eyes rolled to the back of her head. Sweat soaked through her clothes. Her movements grew more extreme as her head lolled back and forth. Nicholas extended a hand and placed it over her eyes. Mumbling incoherently, his black pearl shimmered. When he finished, Nicholas pointed at Amelia with his free hand. His chilling blue eyes sparkled with glee.

"Ah. You have it, good." When he snapped his fingers again, an inky swirl shot from his pointer finger and circled Amelia.

The tendril produced a blood-orange stone. Landree

gaped in amazement.

"Hey!" she exclaimed, wrestling in her invisible prison.

In a flash, the bloodstone popped into Nicholas' possession. He inspected it for a beat before securing it between his palm and Clio's forehead.

Clio ceased moving. Landree stared, heart sinking.

"Come on," Nicholas muttered to himself.

She studied him with biting curiosity. He could've ended her and her friends' lives already, but all he did was push them away while he tended to Clio. This whole time, she was blinded with anger and suspicion, and now, she started to doubt herself.

Nicholas' features were pinched, almost worried.

If he isn't after the gemstones of power for himself, then all this talk about Telos is real. But what does it have to do with Clio?

"You need to explain what's going on here" she begged.

"Shut up," Nicholas shouted. He now pressed both hands against the stone.

Clio arched her back, releasing a wretched scream and swiping at the air. Landree's heart tore to pieces. She never felt so helpless in her life.

Darkness washed over the area. Clouds had rolled in, covering the sun. When her shadow vanished, so did the pins-and-needles sensation. Landree sprung onto her feet. She had but only minutes before the clouds passed.

Although she didn't fully understand what was going on, she knew Clio was in pain. Her cries tortured her, and Landree had to find a way to stop it. Pumping her legs, she sped as fast as she could and tackled Nicholas to the ground.

A blinding flash of red, orange, and yellow expanded from the stone slab.

"Hey!" he shouted.

As the light vanished, so did Clio's screams. Nicholas rolled away, nursing his shoulder. Ignoring him, Landree scuttled toward Clio. Her mouth ran dry. The gemstone lay embedded in her forehead.

Clio snatched Landree's hand. "Don't. Touch. It," she croaked. Her entire body trembled. Veins popped in her neck and forehead.

"Are you okay?" she asked, voice shaky.

"I think so," Clio answered, struggling to steady her breath.

Landree heard Nicholas' footsteps. She picked up her sword and spun around. Everything about him pissed her off. "Stay back. I'll command the winds to keep the clouds in place if I have to. Then, you'll be powerless!"

He lifted his hands in surrender. "She's alive," he murmured.

"Yeah, no thanks to you!" Jane-Marie added as she helped Amelia to her feet.

Sighing, Nicholas steepled his fingers. Looking past Landree, he said, "Clio. I've delivered what was promised. Now, I'm going to need your help convincing these idiots that I'm telling the truth."

Landree's head whipped back and forth. "Wh-what?"

Clio sat up, grimacing along the way. The gemstone glowed softly, filling her flesh with color. "Girls. Grant, too. Nicholas isn't the enemy."

"How was I supposed to believe that?" Landree uttered. "You've been impaled by his weird shadow powers, then he lodged a stone in your head!"

By then, Brenna, Amelia, Jane-Marie, and Grant surrounded Clio who swayed in her seat. Lepus remained at a distance, attending to his matted fur.

The whites of her eyes had completed yellowed. Within a month, Clio looked like she aged years. After tucking a tuft of greasy hair behind her ear, she swallowed audibly. "I was dying..." Her chin quivered. "...and this is the Healer's Bloodstone."

Her words landed on Landree like bricks. All she could do was exchange glances with her friends. However, Landree refused to lower her sword.

"From what I've seen, you guys are now personally familiar with stones of power," Nicholas quipped. His eyes narrowed at the opal.

"Lower that sword, for Adin's sake," Clio scolded.

Landree blinked in shock but obeyed. She gestured to her friends. "I found this weapon embedded with an opal. It seems to grant me the power of wind. Well, if I have enough energy in exchange."

"This is nuts," Brenna said.

Amelia nodded. "Wind, fire, earth..." She faced Jane-Marie. "That shield has a sapphire, so it wouldn't be a stretch to say that controls all things water. It makes sense. The four primary elements of Amicita."

"We need as much firepower as possible before the coming storm," Clio added somberly.

Jane-Marie crossed one hand over another. "Woah. Woah. Let's pause for a second. Have you known all this hocus-pocus from the beginning?"

Shaking her head, Clio's eyes grew wet with tears. "Only the myth. That's all I thought it was, just as much as you knew. Then, Nicholas visited me the night before our trip. He knew I had a terminal disease—"

Landree covered her mouth. Nicholas' lips pursed as if saying 'I told you so', which only infuriated her more.

"He said he could prove to me that the myth was real— that if we found the Healer's Bloodstone, I could live a full life. In exchange, I would dedicate my efforts in stopping the upcoming storm. Telos."

Landree gulped. Blood drained from Jane-Marie's face.

Nicholas was telling the truth all along.

"You said it again. The storm. I see no storm fronts coming. And even if one did come to pass, what is so life-altering about it?" asked Brenna as she scanned the skies. "In fact, the only 'clouds' I've noticed were actually from Nicholas."

Amelia rubbed her chin. "Wasn't there a war that took place here called The Storm?"

"Correct."

Lepus hopped up to the group. He sniffed Nicholas and eyed him up and down. "You know a lot about this place."

Pressing a hand to his chest, Nicholas bowed his head. "Now that we're all calmed down here, let me explain. I'm one of the last known descendants from this country."

"B-but that's impossible. I thought they all perished

here!" he squeaked.

Nicholas tapped his black pearl stud. "This was passed down from my ancestor, a war criminal that once led the Aeonian army. He allegedly fled this country with the blessing from the queen with whom they built a friendship with."

"Aeonian! I read that somewhere," Amelia piped up.

"Me too," Landree gasped.

Lepus' whiskers drooped, and he sniffed. "I'll leave the battle to you then, Nicholas. To you and the party you choose." He turned to Jane-Marie slowly. Sadness filled his dark eyes. "Please take care of the sapphire," he said in a forlorn voice.

Jane-Marie fell to her knees and hugged the little Kai.

"What will you do?" Nicholas asked.

Pulling away from Jane-Marie's embrace, he squared his furry blue shoulders. "I'll alert my people. I trust you'll stop Telos from spreading its malice, but we'll keep watch. We will be the eyes in the ocean."

Nicholas knelt, took his paw and shook it. After a beat, Lepus stole a glance at each person, making eye contact with Landree last.

"Best of luck," he said. "You have the support of the Kai."

With a flick of his tail, he bounded south, leaving a cloudy trail behind.

The world spun around Landree as she soaked in the various emotions and blocks of information. She sat down. Rolling her eyes, Landree growled in frustration. "So, you're saying we're going to war?"

"Not exactly," Nicholas said slowly as if cherry picking his words. "There's so much to this, but time is short. Telos is an external threat that must be vanquished."

"Same thing, isn't it?" Jane-Marie asked as she hoisted her shield onto her back.

Frustration filled Jane-Marie's and Brenna's features while Amelia's eyebrows were scrunched in thought. The only person who seemed indifferent was Grant. He regarded Landree with hooded eyes.

She opened her mouth, but Nicholas cut her off.

"We must head toward Chailara Hills, which is west of here. There, we'll find the source of the earthquakes."

"I didn't sign up for this!" Jane-Marie shouted. Tugging at Clio, she said, "Come on. We need to get back to Giles."

Clio brushed her off, turning her attention to Landree. "You're the one to lead us."

Breaking into spastic coughs, Landree fumbled for words.

"What?" Jane-Marie, Amelia, and Brenna exclaimed all at once.

Pressure rose in her chest. Even when trying to force deep breaths, she couldn't remain calm. Landree gripped the sides of her head and trembled. "Lead what? You can't just dump this on me all at once!"

Nicholas rested the tip of his dagger beneath her chin and tilted her head up. "Do you think you'd believe me on day one that we needed to collect stones with magical powers to defeat the grotesque representation of greed? You didn't believe me halfway into this expedition."

The blade dug into her skin. Landree swallowed.

"I meant no one harm, but I had to arrange this trip in such a way you'd all discover the stones on your own." He withdrew the dagger. "Even if it had to be compressed within weeks. Knowing the lot of you, were doomed no matter what."

"Screw you, man," Brenna sneered.

The sun emerged from the clouds, and the black pearl in Nicholas' ear shimmered once more. Light filled the basin of ash. Silence draped over everyone. Not a single insect or bird could be heard.

The earth came to life once more. Another earthquake shook the ground. Landree looked to Brenna in desperation, but she shook her head and said, "It wasn't me".

Landree was sick to her stomach.

Extending his hand, Nicholas forced a smile. "Come. I'll tell you more along the way. But we must hurry."

CHAPTER

22

Final Hours of The Luce

The earthquake kicked up plumes of ash as the group trudged up the hill. Landree looked behind her. The view was chilling, as if they were escaping a crater of death. She wondered how many lives had been lost here. By the time the land leveled out, the ground stopped shaking.

Landree's muscles relaxed. Each experience of an earthquake was no less jarring than the last.

Clio and Nicholas walked shoulder to shoulder while Landree and Jane-Marie followed next. Amelia trailed close behind, and Brenna hung back with Grant.

Tilting her head, Landree whispered to Jane-Marie. "I thought Brenna hated that kid."

Jane-Marie shrugged. "We aren't exactly in normal circumstances, either."

Landree nodded in embarrassment. It was a silly question, but she couldn't help but want to talk about anything except the upcoming mission. She traced her fingers against her shell naked neckline. Landree hadn't been able to fix her shell necklace. She prayed she'd see her parents again.

"Ask Nicholas about your memory," she added.

"I don't think that's important right now," Jane-Marie replied mechanically.

Landree cleared her throat. "Amelia, so...uh, you control fire?"

Pushing up her glasses, Amelia grunted. "Yup. Thanks to this ruby pendant, and Brenna has an amber ring that helps her manipulate the earth."

"What about...um." She pointed at Grant. His wide green eyes glowed past his grungy hair.

Amelia shuddered. "He hasn't said or done much since I saw him."

A line of pine and fir trees greeted the troop.

"Through here," Nicholas said. Exhaustion weighed heavily on his words.

Landree couldn't comprehend his long strides and perfect posture. She jogged up and wedged herself between him and Clio.

"You look pretty confident walking into battle with a bunch of teenagers. You've even gone so far to insult me on a regular basis. If you manipulated the application process, why did you chose us?"

Nicholas clicked his tongue. Angling his face toward hers, he said, "This fight isn't about brute strength. It's about the pure of heart and the incorruptibility of one's soul."

Slapping a palm against her forehead, Landree huffed. "Is this a joke? Whatever we're up against isn't going to fold just because we're nice, or whatever you said." She elbowed Clio. "You're the adult of the group. Please talk some sense into him."

Clio trained her doleful eyes on her. "We need to trust in Nicholas' judgement."

Landree pulled her hair and groaned. She wasn't sure if what bothered her more—the fact she didn't truly deserve to be selected for The Luce expedition or that Nicholas gamed the system because of her 'pureness of heart'. Either way, Landree felt she was marching to her early demise. "What are we up against if strength isn't so important?"

"Remember when I said I believed The Luce served as a warning? It makes sense now. It's a beacon to call on saviors to stop Telos from spreading its corruptive nature. Why at a cadence of every hundred years, I'm not sure myself."

"Why does it last only a month?" Amelia piped.

Smirking, Landree bet she had a scroll and quill at the ready to take notes. There was something so endearing about that.

"And how do you know all this stuff anyway?" Brenna added.

Crossing her arms, Landree's smirk grew wider. "I bet you wish you kept us in the loop all this time instead of trying to play us like chess pieces."

Clio wrapped her fingers around Landree's arm and squeezed. She shook her head.

Leaves crunched beneath Nicholas' heavy steps. "My

uncle gifted the black pearl to me right before he died—like I said to Lepus, it originated here."

"Ever since I was little, he'd tell me the story of the island with unlimited potential that must remain undiscovered by man. *At all costs.* At first, I was just like you guys; I didn't believe him. Why would I? Stones that granted powers beyond your wildest dreams?" Nicholas paused. He drew his dagger and hacked away at a wall of brambles.

Landree and the others hung onto this every word with bated breath.

"My uncle was really the one that should've gone on this expedition. He was only forty when he died." His voice faltered. "It was unexpected. I don't blame him, but as the replacement, I felt unprepared for this task."

As Nicholas kicked at some branches, Landree reached out, but he inched away.

I guess he isn't Mr. Perfect after all.

"When you're done narrating that novel of yours, I could use your help with Grant. I swear he's getting even slower," Brenna said.

Jane-Marie waved half-heartedly. "I'll help."

While the two girls supported Grant from both sides, Amelia, Clio, and Landree stepped through the thorny patch. Nicholas went last, repeatedly looking behind him. When he stepped toward the front of the group, Nicholas gripped his dagger more tightly. A muscle in his jaw twitched.

"Are we in danger?" Landree asked. Her hand flew to her sword.

He rose a finger to his lips. Nicholas scanned the tree line. Her breath grew shallow as she tried to follow his line of vision. *What's he seeing that I'm not?*

Doves and swallows took flight from their nests and swirled in a circular pattern before scattering in all directions. Deep orange and violet hues blended into the sky, signaling the sun's descent. Nicholas knelt and pressed his ear to the ground. All Landree could do was look to Clio, seeking reassurance, but her teacher's brows knitted in concern. She turned to Jane-Marie with an addled expression.

Standing back up, Nicholas sheathed his weapon. He shook the dirt from his hair. "I-I...don't know."

"What do you mean you don't know?" Landree squawked. Acid sloshed around her stomach.

The expression of a lost child washed over his face. His square jaw trembled. "We still have another few miles to go, but my gut is telling me we need to retreat."

Lowering her parchment that had been glued to her face, Amelia's nostrils flared. "Retreat *where*?"

Brenna rested Grant against a tree stump, as Landree and the rest circled around Nicholas. The more the precious daylight trickled away, the harder Landree's heart slammed in her ribcage.

"Is this another one of your tests or tricks? No more of this," Landree pleaded.

"It's not, I swear!"

She grabbed a fistful of his tunic. "Tell me the truth!"

Clio shouted, and Jane-Marie held her back. Landree only gripped tighter.

"I truly don't know. My uncle said that if I couldn't find the emerald shard to shut Telos down by myself, I had to guide the chosen group to the Chailara Hills once everyone had an elemental stone to aid him or her. That's where Telos rests. I feel that we're already too close and in danger."

Releasing her hold, Landree inhaled sharply. "Guide away, then."

Heat rushed to his cheeks. "I don't think it's safe for us to proceed further."

Soil shifted beneath their feet. Landree tripped over a gnarled root and collided into Nicholas. The earth rumbled and groaned as fissures split open, swallowing rocks and shrubs whole. Rabbits and squirrels darted from their homes and vanished into the darkness. Supporting herself against a pine, Landree rose to her feet and tried to steady her balance.

This earthquakes' intensity had already surpassed its predecessors.

"Brenna! Can you tell where the source is coming from?" Landree asked.

"I'll try," she replied. Brenna's amber ring illuminated as she drove her bo staff into the ground. An old fir tree snapped in half and fell a few feet behind her, but she remained laser-focused.

In the corner of her eye, Landree spotted a fissure zigzagging in her direction. A moss-colored haze hissed from the depths. The air surrounding them grew stagnant. Its oppressive nature made it seem like everything moved in slow motion.

"Watch out!" she blurted.

In a blur of maroon, Jane-Marie launched herself over the widening crevasse and collided into Brenna. The two rolled off to the side, narrowly avoiding falling into the abyss.

Along with Clio and Grant, Jane-Marie and Brenna stood on the opposite side of the gap. Landree waved to them and Brenna gave a thumbs up.

"We need to join them and retreat back to the valley," Nicholas said.

"Understood." There was no time to think, and Landree certainly couldn't afford to panic any further. Stroking the opal that sat on her sword's hilt, she said, "Let's go."

She gripped hands with Nicholas and Amelia and jogged toward the hellish vapor. With each step, she picked up speed. Nicholas and Amelia matched her pace until they reached the fissure's edge.

"Jump!" Landree cried.

In a snowy blaze, a tempest born from Landree's sword cushioned their feet and carried them over the expanding gap. It guided them into a soft landing on the other side then dissipated. Releasing her grip, Landree wiped the sweat from her brow.

Amelia whooped. "That was quite the rush!"

"If you want a rush, you got more coming," Nicholas said as he gestured everyone back east.

Landree clambered her way back through the brambles and between trees that swayed dangerously. The sun had completely set, arresting the area in darkness, with only the noxious green gas outlining any silhouettes. Her lungs burned as she moved purely by instinct. Nicholas and Jane-Marie pulled ahead where the pine and fir trees thinned. They were almost there.

"Landree!"

Turning her neck, she spotted Brenna and Clio struggling with Grant. He continuously stumbled over every object in the trail. Landree cursed. She wanted to conserve her energy, but they wouldn't make it without help.

Fissures multiplied exponentially. One crack produced five more, each longer and deeper than the last. Landree snapped her fingers, and sparks flew from her hand and toward Grant. He levitated a few inches off the ground, just enough to avoid roots and rocks.

"Come on!" she exclaimed.

Clio and Brenna charged and caught up. The three sprinted, the gaps threatening to swallow them whole. They kicked up ash as they fumbled their way down a slope.

"We're not going to make it," Clio cried.

Landree began to lose footing. She clenched her jaw.

Not now. Not like this.

She shoved the three until they all tumbled down the final hill. As they picked up momentum, Landree could feel the distance between them and the fissures widening. She tucked her knees into her chest and held her breath. Objects scratched and whacked her body, but she remained steadfast.

When they reached the bottom, Landree hopped onto her feet. She scuttled to Grant and looked to Clio and Brenna. "You guys okay?" she asked, panting between her words.

Brenna nodded. The Luce flickered against the northern horizon. The sheen was noticeably dimmer than when they first arrived.

Training her sight at the cancerous earthquake, she asked, "Did you sense its source?"

"It's generating from Chailara Hills. The place we were traveling to."

"So…it's not a true earthquake."

Brenna shook her head. "It's coming from a separate entity below the surface."

"Telos," they said simultaneously.

The rumbling slowed to a crawl at the mid-point down the hill. A mournful cry echoed in the chasms as the fog reached the skies. Landree's hairs stood on end as the line of trees where they had escaped rose and fell as if a giant snored beneath them.

Pillars of dirt rocketed in a crisscross fashion, uprooting everything in its path. The core of the planet seemed to heave as a winged claw rose from the depths in a steam of sulfur and scraped the ledge. Scrambling backward in horror, Landree's jaw hung open.

"It's real." Her head swam in denial, but her heart realized Nicholas had been right.

The being pulled itself to the surface, crushing everything in its path. Its labored breath rolled over the field like a windstorm, filling Landree's lungs with sulfur and mildew. She and her friends gagged.

When it stood on its hind legs, Telos stretched its bat-like wings in a serenade of cracking bones. Landree's neck strained as she calculated its size. It was easily twelve-hundred feet in height and width. Its beady red eyes scanned the landscape before lifting its gaze toward the moon.

Adin and Deva hovered in their rounded forms next to one another, completing the month-long eclipse. As if on cue, The Luce flickered again, then faded.

Landree knew that The Luce had vanished for good.

CHAPTER

23

Standing independently in the sky, Adin and Deva shined down on Landree and her friends like two judges, patiently observing them undergo their final test. Landree gripped her sword with both hands, her palms slick with sweat. Adrenaline readied her muscles, but fear rooted her heels to the dirt. She had never experienced or heard of an abomination like Telos. Even the mountain lion she had previously encountered paled in comparison—both in size and threat.

It sat back on its haunches and released an unearthly screech. Spittle flew from its jaws, splashing and forming puddles around her. Landree turned to Jane-Marie first on her right. Tears streamed down her cheeks as she clutched the shield in front of her. The metal oval rattled in tandem with her lithe body. Every inch of exposed skin, whether it was her face or legs through torn slacks, was pale as snow.

Through her cracked lips, two words slipped out: "I'm

scared."

Landree wanted so badly to run to her and cry, too, but a voice inside begged her to hold fast. She was no more prepared to take on Telos than her friend was. She had no idea why Nicholas chose them over others in Camilla who were more versed in combat. What did the pure of heart have to do with destroying a monster the size of a mountain?

Turning to her left, Amelia and Brenna readied their weapons. Amelia's features were framed in shock, but Brenna scowled at Telos in defiance. Even then, her hands trembled as she held the bo staff close to her chest. Amelia muttered beneath her breath, "I don't want to die."

Nicholas appeared by her side, dagger in hand. The black pearl earring illuminated and generated wisps of shadow that snaked down his arm and infused into his blade. "We got this," he said.

"But I still don't fully understand my powers. Nor do my friends," Landree pleaded as if he had the ability to make it all stop by just asking. "Please."

Nicholas tilted his head. His wolfish features captured her gaze; however, it wasn't a look of disapproval or disappointment. "*Our* friends."

Nodding, Landree steeled her nerves. "Our friends."

"I've secured Grant and Clio behind us. Let's rally."

Landree turned back to Jane-Marie. "We're going to be okay." Her voice continued to rise. Landree's heart pounding so loudly, she could barely hear her own thoughts. "Telos is a threat to us and to our friends and family. We can't sit back and let this thing move another step forward."

Jane-Marie narrowed her eyes. Even though she continued to shake, her voice grew firm. "You're right. We can do this."

Another ear-piercing cry rattled the earth, forcing Landree's attention forward. Its red eyes glowed beneath its exposed skull. A blend of flesh and scales formed its snout and wrapped down its neck. Scales gave way to feathers at its shoulders, much like a decorated general.

The claws at the end of its wings swiped menacingly at Landree. Her lip peeled back in disgust. She couldn't make out what type of creature it was. The ribcage poking through its gray skin presented like humanoid torso, and yet its legs resembled that of a dragon's. Golden fur filled the spaces between its scales, and silver hair cascaded in a tight braid from the top of its head to the base of its skull. When Landree squinted her eyes, she noticed its ears were pierced by silver and gold studs—and one emerald.

Landree shouted at the top of her lungs and charged. The opal on her sword's hilt flashed, flooding the immediate area with light. Nicholas raced alongside her, smiling as their shadows stretched behind them. Telos leaned forward and gnashed its jaws, expelling more of its rotten breath. Pinching her nose, Landree slashed her sword in a downward stroke, expelling a whirlwind that slammed into its snout and forced dirt into its face.

As Telos clawed at its eyes, Nicholas waved at her. "I'm going to boost us up!"

"Gotcha!"

Landree's shadow broke free from her steps and seeped

through the grass and ash in front of her. Both their shadows bolted forward and rose to create two dark platforms.

"Jump! he shouted.

Landree sprung off her feet and landed onto her shadow. It catapulted her into the air. Landree cycled her arms and legs as she neared Telos. She landed at the top of its skull and latched onto one of its silvered braids. Telos reared its head back and shook its head. Nicholas crashed against its face and immediately started slipping. He managed to cling to one of its slit nostrils, but it wrapped its claws around him and tugged.

"Nicholas!" she exclaimed. She rammed the hilt of the sword against its skull repeatedly.

Telos released its grip on Nicholas and scratched at Landree. She dove from braid to braid, narrowly missing its sharp nails by inches. Panting heavily, she scrambled toward the back of its head, desperate to escape his reach. She should've had a plan, and now she was crawling along the beast like a flea on a dog. Nicholas' voice echoed in the chaos, but she couldn't make out his words.

When its talons got tangled up in its hair, Landree swung her legs forward and slid down its neck. When she reached its spiked back, Landree turned and drove her sword into a patch of flesh. Telos arched its back and thrashed its winged arms, ripping its locks from its skull. Landree's soul froze as she looked up. Eyeless sockets stared back. Folds of skin formed false eyelids, and a slit at the base of its neck formed a mouth.

Acid surged up her throat as the toothless mouth moved

each time Telos' head turned.

Is this one whole monster or has it absorbed other creatures?

Her thoughts swept away as Telos launched into the sky. Digging her feet into its back, Landree held on for dear life. Amelia, Brenna, and the rest shrunk into ant-sized dots below. She cursed.

Now what?

Telos turned and dove toward her friends.

A fire arrow zipped by, nearly missing one of its wings. The second one was too low. Landree wanted to cry out to Amelia and Brenna, but the dizzying speed stole her breath away.

Telos grazed the ground, talons on its feet extended. Screams pierced through the billowing clouds of destruction. Landree's grip slipped as she seized in a coughing fit. When Telos climbed back into the sky, Landree's neck whiplashed. Pain streaked down her spine and lights exploded in her eyes. Before she could register another thought, the leather-bound hilt slipped from her grasp, sending Landree tumbling backward.

The world swirled before her in black and gold. Telo's scales ripped her tunic and dug into her skin as she continued falling down the length of its back. Landree blindly reached out. She missed a tuft of fur, then another. The scales were too slippery...

Landree screamed. As Telos gained altitude, it bucked her off. Freefalling, all she could do was watch its silhouette shrink—her sword still lodged in its flesh. A body dangled from its tail. Another person flailed in its one of its claws.

Squeezing her eyes shut, Landree braced for impact.

A force slammed into her from the side, cool and wet. Bubbles rushed from her mouth as she tried to gasp.

Her lungs burned, but she held her breath as a pillar of water slowed her fall. When she landed, the entity burst in an explosion of rain. Gasping, Landree rolled onto her stomach and shook the hair from her eyes.

"Are you okay?" Jane-Marie shouted.

In the distance, Kai's Sapphire radiated from her shield. Landree barked in laughter, amazed she survived. Wobbling on her feet, she ran to Jane-Marie and jumped in for a hug.

"Thank you," Landree sobbed.

"Don't thank me yet," Jane-Marie replied.

Telos dove once more. Its mouth opened abnormally wide, as if completely unhinging its jaw. Its emerald piercing pulsed like a beacon, and a green haze formed in the back of its forked tongue.

"What is that?" Jane-Marie asked.

"I doubt it's fire, but I'd rather not find out either," Landree exclaimed. She reached to her side only to realize her sword was still in its back. "Shoot! Run!"

They split in different directions. Pumping her legs as fast as she could, Landree charged out of range. A sweltering heat dogged her steps as Telos released a beam of energy. Landree cringed as her skin blistered beneath her tunic. Her legs wanted to give out, but she knew if she stopped, Telos' attack would consume her entirely.

Spotting a boulder, Landree veered in its direction. She dove and rolled behind the rock as the green substance washed over it. Landree panted and whimpered. It felt like someone dumped acid on her back. Sharp pain warped into a dull ache that sunk deep into her joints. Every move caused her agony. Falling to her side, Landree used her elbows to drag herself to the corner. She peeked out, spotting Telos once again swooping up for another attack. Landree's eyes watered.

"This is impossible," she croaked. Even her throat felt raw. "I'm going to die here. In the middle of nowhere. Never to see my parents and home again."

Landree savored the fleeting memories of her family, and her peaceful life in Camilla. She left it behind to experience adventure, only to be dragged into a supernatural fight to the death. It was one thing to die alone, but alongside six friends—it was just too much to bear.

Landree's memories warped into nightmares of Telos crossing the sea and laying her village to waste.

"No," she said, clenching her jaw.

Crawling with every ounce of her strength, Landree pulled herself into the open. Footsteps padded her way.

"Oy!"

Brenna skidded to a stop and knelt. Placing a hand on her back, she asked, "You alright?"

Landree flinched. "I better be. How confident are you with that amber ring?"

"Not too confident."

Raising an arm, Landree shouted. "Telos! Come get me!"

Eyes widening into orbs, Brenna straightened. Sweat

dripped from her nose. "Are you crazy?"

"You're the strongest one of the bunch. Knock 'em dead." Although clouded with doubt, Landree winked.

Brenna groaned as Telos veered toward them in one seamless movement. It, again, unhinged its jaw and opened wide.

"I need you to knock it from the air. Ground it," Landree said. "Steady."

Sweeping her bo staff in front of her, Brenna sucked in a breath. Strands of her red hair fluttered free from her elastic band as the wind picked up.

Once again, Telos' emerald glowed.

"Steady."

The sickly green fog formed on its tongue. Telos' winged stopped flapping as it took aim.

"Now!" Landree exclaimed.

Brenna twirled her staff, activating the amber that shined on her finger. When she connected her weapon to the ground, the earth shuddered and pillars of dirt and rock shot vertically toward Telos. As Brenna's battle cry magnified, so did the intensity of each eruption.

Telos released its toxic breath as the ground loosened directly below. It freed a naked oak tree, which hurtled up and at its throat. The monster screeched, and its green vapor dissipated. Brenna continued to swipe her staff, eyes ablaze with rage. The earth mimicked her every move, striking Telos' right wing, head, and chest.

"Keep it distracted!" Landree shouted. The window of opportunity granted her a second wind, flooding her with the strength to break into a sprint. Her knees cracked and threatened to buckle, but she refused to give up.

Telos swiped with its left claw. Landree darted right and rolled forward. A grittiness saturated her tongue as pebbles rained on her. Narrowly missing a blast of dirt, Landree jumped and landed on Telos' opposite wing.

She tumbled uncontrollably along the ridged membrane, unable to slow down.

Shoot. I'm going to roll right off it!

A hand snatched Landree's wrist. She craned her neck, spotting Nicholas hanging on to his dagger with his other hand.

"I'm going to use the shadows to catapult you to your sword. Don't lose it this time," he said, sharing a rare smile.

Landree nodded, tightening her core in anticipation of defying gravity once more. The viscous, dark mass globbed around her waist and flipped her up and over him, plopping her on its back. She immediately ducked to avoid the haunting gaze from its second face behind its neck. Honing her focus on her sword, Landree plucked it from Telos' flesh. Silver blood oozed from its wound.

Calling on the power of wind, Landree channeled the dregs of her energy through her veins and into the opal. The gemstone flickered to life in swirls of pastel pink and purple. Heat flowed from her core as she fought to remain standing. Panic played with the fringes of Landree's mind, threating to lose her focus. True, she hadn't the slightest clue how to best direct her powers, but she did know she wanted to blast Telos into oblivion.

Thunder rumbled. Droplets sizzled as it made contact on her skin.

When Telos took to the skies, Landree noticed isolated clouds directly above them, surrounded by a deep blue hue.

Jane-Marie!

Landree directed her thoughts to join her powers with Jane-Marie's. The wind picked up and sprinkles turned into a downpour. Blinking away the rain, she stared into the clouds, praying for more. The edges of the clouds began to blur and twist, forming a funnel. Confidence rising, Landree lifted her sword skyward before digging it into Telo's spine. The rain clouds transformed into a tornado and struck its face. It pressed into the monster until it was in a full blown downward spiral.

Telos crashed into the ground. Landree fought the shock that rattled her bones as she slashed it with her longsword.

"Great work!" Nicholas cried somewhere to her left.

Telos thrashed, its agonizing cries bringing joy to Landree's crazed mind. All she could focus on was drawing blood. More and more blood. Flashes of red, blue, and amber lit up the night from all directions.

The whistling from the tornado faded, and the wind died down. Landree heaved as she lifted her sword over her head, but suddenly the sword felt heavier. She lumbered backward, stumbling over one of Telos' protruding scales. Landree landed on her seat, almost completely drained of energy. In the distance, Brenna and Nicholas faced Telos head on.

"W-what's happening to its eyes?" Brenna shouted.

Telos moaned then hissed as it rotated its head ninety degrees. Bone snapped one after the other. Landree struggled to get on her knees, legs weighing like lead. Before she could stand, she locked gazes with the haunted face on the back of its neck. Its empty sockets were now occupied with its fire-red irises and slit pupils. Telos stared directly at Landree—she swore the slit in its flesh twisted upwards in a sick smile.

"Lend me your power, little one," it said, words slick as oil. "And I will grant whatever your heart desires."

Landree gasped in horror as the slit widened into a rounded hole. In a pitch much like grinding metal with stone, it began sucking her in. Landree scuttled backwards on her hands and feet, losing grip on her sword.

Telos intensified its inhalation.

"No!" Landree cried as her blade tumbled away from her.

She dove for the hilt, missing it by mere centimeters.

"Head's up!"

A fire arrow zipped past Landree and lodged in its left eye. The orange and yellow flames licked it hungrily. Landree cupped her ears as Telos howled. Another arrow grazed her shoulder as it hit a scale below its right eye.

"Damn!" Amelia shouted.

"Keep trying!" Landree exclaimed. Hands on her thighs, she pushed herself up and staggered toward her sword.

Arrows flew above and below, failing to connect with the other eye.

"Its tail is attacking me!"

A thud followed Amelia's voice, silencing her words.

When Landree whipped her head around to make sure she was okay, the hungry force of Telos' inhalation resumed. It yanked Landree off her feet, swallowing her whole. She opened her mouth but couldn't scream.

Complete darkness enveloped Landree. Viscera wrapped its wet arms around her body and pulled in all directions. Her joints burned once more, straining to keep her body in one piece. Sour liquid forced its way up her nostrils and her ears. Landree forced her eyes and mouth shut as Telos consumed her.

CHAPTER
24

A familiar scent tickled Landree's nose, warm and inviting. It was cinnamon, wasn't it?

Camilla Viewpoint Inn appeared in front of her as if a curtain swept away the darkness. Patrons munched on their turkey legs and downed their ale. Looking down, Landree found herself in a stained apron, pitcher in hand.

"Wait. My parents don't let me serve ale," she said to herself.

"Refill please!" barked a man in the corner.

"B-but." Landree fumbled for words.

Her mother shuffled past Landree and collected soiled dishes. Cradling them gently, Rose shot her an impatient glare. "You wanted more responsibility. Hurry up or you'll be on housekeeping instead."

Landree snorted. "This is a joke. A dream or hallucination, right?"

"Now!" Rose shrilled.

Stumbling over her own feet, Landree booked it for the man sitting in front of the bay windows.

"What's going on?" she asked herself.

An intrusive, gravelly voice oozed from the ceiling. *You don't want to live the rest of your life like this, do you?*

"W-who's that?"

No response.

Scanning the dining hall, she searched for clues. Everything appeared normal, from the candles melted down to their holders to the initials carved into the tables from past patrons. Even the mystery stain at the base of the fireplace. To this day, Landree and her mother couldn't wash it from the slate. Its maroon shade reminded her of blood. Her mother always told her it was wine—but she's cleaned wine stains since she was old enough to walk. This one didn't wash away like the others.

"It's about time," the man by the bay windows spat. His nasally voice jarred Landree's thoughts.

She blinked down at Dr. Barnes.

"I've never seen you eat here before," she blurted.

Dr. Barnes' eyes narrowed, which only elongated his already huge nose. "And you weren't supposed to go on The Luce expedition, but off you went."

Breaking into a cold sweat, Landree stuttered. "The expedition…but how did you—"

Dr. Barnes slammed his mug against the table. "I asked for a refill."

She observed his flushed face. His normally pressed tunic was stained and wrinkled. Untucked from his trousers, even.

His suspenders slid down his shoulders. The ale sloshed around in her pitcher, betraying her neutral face. She'd been through so much—how come she was paralyzed by the likes of Dr. Barnes?

He swatted the air around his face. "And for heaven's sake, can you stop that shouting?"

Whipping her head left and right, Landree couldn't identify any noise beyond the general chatter from the crowd.

"Miss? Another round!" called another patron at a table by the front door.

"Um. Be right there," Landree replied, as something in her ear tickled. She brushed her hair aside, but the tickling persisted. When she traced her finger around her earlobe, she was met with a wet warmth.

Blood covered her hand. Gasping, Landree dropped her pitcher. The glass shattered in all directions, spraying ale everywhere. Dr. Barnes shrunk back, lifting his boots to avoid soiling the expensive leather.

Rose threw a towel on the floor. "Can't you do anything, right? And can you do something about that shouting?"

"The shouting!" Dr. Barnes mimicked, shaking his head.

Anxiety overwhelmed Landree. She took a step back, then another until she turned and fled to the kitchen. She gripped the sides of the sink and heaved.

"W-what's going on?"

Blood tricked from her ear. It fell into the sink with a steady *plip, plip*.

"Get a hold of yourself, girl."

The double-doors swung open, and Landree straightened. When she turned around, she spotted her mother entering the kitchen.

"Mother. I-I'm sorry I spilled the ale. Something's wrong. I'm bleeding, and I feel dizzy. Can I go to my room?"

Darkness washed across Rose's face as she broke into a sneer. "You can't handle a simple task, can you, daughter?"

Landree shook her head wildly, but the room continued to spin after she stopped. "It's not that..." her voice slurred.

Clicking her tongue, Rose stepped slowly toward her. She traced her painted nails against the porcelain counter. The oil lanterns washed the room in orange. With no help from the smoke seeping from the pots, it created the illusion of the room being on fire.

"Mom..."

Rose stopped in front of Landree. She scoffed. "I'll let it slide. It's your first day back."

Landree sighed, releasing the tension that built up in her shoulders.

"Besides..." Rose dug into her pocket. "How can I really get upset when you brought this home and gifted it to me?"

She produced a naked emerald in her palm.

Landree blanched. Her stomach plummeted. "Where did you get that?"

"You brought it home from Amicita," Rose replied impatiently.

"There's no way... Mother, you need to get rid of that." She lifted both hands to her cheeks. Her hands were clammy.

Rose ignored her and lifted the emerald up to her eyes. A Cheshire grin spread across her face as the emerald consumed her attention. "So pretty."

Landree lunged and shook her mother's shoulders. "Mom!"

"This is going to change our lives forever." Rose's voice deepened.

"Mom!"

Rose closed her hand into a fist while grabbing Landree by the collar with her other hand. She lifted Landree off her feet. "Stop the shouting now!"

Swinging her legs, Landree failed to pry herself free.

"Stop the shouting!"

Rays of green emanated from Rose's fists, blinding Landree. Rose's voice warped into a howling wind assaulting her ears. Other voices cried out, muffled. Squelching. Crunching. The kitchen dissolved into darkness with a sizzle.

Mother!

Opening her eyes, Landree found herself face to face with a weak, white light. Her mind was hazy, unable to fully process her thoughts. Was she in limbo? Reaching for the light, Landree hoped for answers.

Maybe this really is the end.

When she touched the source, the blood and mucus that adhered to the orb melted away. Landree blinked rapidly, realizing she sat face to face with her longsword. The opal glowed feebly but warmed at her touch. Shouting pierced through Telos' organs above, in front, and behind Landree.

No. I'm alive. I can't…I can't let Telos leave this island.

Landree grasped the hilt and tugged. She fought against the tendons and ligaments that latched onto the blade until they snapped. Drawing from her heart, Landree wished her mother safety—the entire world safety, safety from the all-consuming Telos that drew from human greed.

In a flash, the orb of light expanded, wiping Landree free from Telos' viscera. Her muscles stretched and contracted, filling with vigor. She released a gruff cry, pressing the sword up. When she met flesh, Landree thrusted.

Crisp, night air grazed her nostrils. She then sliced length-wise until she was able to pop her head from Telos' insides. The pitch of the abomination's screams rose and fell until it succumbed to gurgling on its own bile. When it rolled onto its side, Landree slid out onto the grass. Coughing out silver blood, she gasped for air. The muffled shouting from her friends sharpened. She looked up weakly and smiled.

Jane-Marie was the first to arrive. She fell onto her knees, ebony hair tangled in all directions. Eyes wild, she jabbered on about Landree's health, but she fell in and out of focus.

"I need Clio!"

Landree collapsed into the viscous puddle.

"Pull her here," commanded another voice.

"Get Grant to help," Jane-Marie pleaded.

"He's useless," Brenna barked.

Someone hooked their hands beneath her armpits and pulled. Landree stared at the hole she had cut open. Ribbed intestines and bulbous purple sacks splayed from its under-belly. The opaque interstitial fluid saturated the ground and bubbled. Its skull was plagued with dents and split down the middle while its red eyes had returned to its original sockets in the front, glazed over.

Brenna and Amelia rushed to Landree's left while Jane-Marie kneeled to her right. That left Nicholas, who rested her against the same boulder she previously hid behind.

"Ugn..." Landree's tongue clung to the roof of her mouth. She extended her arm, and Nicholas clasped her hand promptly.

His ice-blue eyes shined through his grime-smeared face. "You have no idea how happy I am that you're alive," his voice wavered.

Massaging her neck, Jane-Marie nodded. "Clio is on her way."

The two fell out of focus as a glint caught her eye. Pushing Jane-Marie away, she leaned forward and squinted. It was small, and yet, it gleamed brighter than the moons.

And green.

"Guys!" Landree yelped. She pulled Nicholas close and scratched at his tunic. "T-Telos. Th-the stone—"

"We need you to calm down," Brenna commanded.

Releasing his grip, Nicholas frowned. "No need to fret. The way you tore it up, there's no way it can come back from it."

On cue, Telos growled.

Everyone's heads snapped up, blood draining from their faces. Landree stood and pushed herself to the front. Dread trickled down her body, threatening to drag her deep underground. Her blood curdled as the emerald sliver in its ear flashed. Telos lifted its head, and half its skull fell to the ground with a thud. Opalescent threads of fungi wrapped around its exposed brain. Mucus dripped readily from every crevasse. Its sour stench expanded and choked Landree. Covering her nose with the crook of her elbow, she gasped for air.

"We must obliterate that emerald. It's the source of everything!" Nicholas shouted. "I thought killing the creature would kill off the effects, but it appears the other way around. We'll need everything we got. Do as I do!"

He extended an open palm at Telos. Landree exchanged glances with Jane-Marie. This time, determination filled her friend's eyes instead of tears. They nodded in unison. Both raised their hands, then Brenna, Amelia, and Clio followed suit.

"We must will the destruction of its magic with all your might!" A black sphere generated in Nicholas' palm.

The membranes in Telos' skull contracted and expanded. With labored breaths, it growled again. "If you destroy me, you lose your powers."

Nicholas lifted his head high and shook it. "You can't tempt us."

…You lose your powers…

Landree paused. She would never be able to wield the might of the winds again, or use it to fly.

Why does it have to be like this? I could do so much with it.

"Landree!" Nicholas voice cut through her like a machete.

"Huh?"

Telos staggered toward them. It leapt into the air but failed to take flight. Holes were burned into its wings.

Landree forced her thoughts into the back of her mind. It proved more challenging than she anticipated. Temptation beckoned them back, questioning why she had to sacrifice her newfound powers.

"Focus, Landree!" he pleaded.

Knitting her brows, she shed her doubts like a snake does its old skin. By doing so, she felt lighter, almost to the point of levitating. A pearly-white light burst in her hand. Landree puffed her chest in pride, accepting the purifying rays that washed over her body.

A blood-red burst from the corner of her eye told Landree Amelia had become successful as well. Then Brenna.

Almost there.

The ground quaked as Telos consumed five-hundred feet in another step. Her orb flickered. Her faith faltered.

"Jane-Marie?" Landree asked, barely moving her lips.

No answer.

Landree turned her head to spy on her best friend.

Terror seized Jane-Marie's face. "I don't wanna give this up."

"Are you kidding me? Do you see this thing in front of you?" Brenna shouted.

"Shut up, Norlender!" Jane-Marie spat.

Swallowing a lump that formed in her throat, Landree steeled her nerves. "Listen to me. We're so close to defeating Telos. We need you. I need you. You don't need Kai's sapphire."

Jane-Marie's fingers twitched and her eyes glazed over.

Telos' staccato laughter resonated around everyone as it lumbered another step.

"Jane-Marie!"

A brilliant blue blinded Landree.

When Telos reared its head, the orbs of light expelled from everyone's hand, colliding at a center point in front of the abomination. The beam exploded on contact and ruptured the emerald. Waves of energy knocked Landree backward. The sound of glass shattering magnified while diminishing Telos' hellish screams.

It crashed onto its knees, all color sapped from its body until it resembled a stone statue. In one final flash of light, the ripple of energy fractured Telos into smithereens. Ash and dust billowed in all directions as far as the eye could see.

The valley fell silent. With bated breath, Landree sat up and rubbed her eyes. She ignored the pain that radiated from every inch of her body.

Trees, waves of long grass, and a river were all she could see. Water gurgled. The breeze whistled, and the grass danced. Raking her fingers against the earth, Landree savored the soil. For the first time, Landree realized her fantasy in person. She and her friends made it.

CHAPTER

25

There was something peaceful about a sunrise. Landree rarely woke up early enough to witness one. She swayed back and forth, her gaze glued to the pastel skies. Slipping in and out of consciousness, Landree had lost track of time. Warped voices, most of them female, overpowered her thoughts. The tones were hushed, urgent, prompting Landree to comb through her headache-ridden mind for memories. She remembered a strange land and a sudden twist.

A bump jolted Landree from her prone position. She squeezed her eyes shut as pain radiated from her torso.

"Watch it, idiot!" a voice hissed.

"Well, don't walk too fast."

Sets of hands guided her back down. Landree focused on the voices to distract her from the pain. The baritone reply had to be Grant, arguing with Brenna...

My friends.

Gripping her sides, Landree clenched her jaw and groaned. She'd never been this sore in her life.

A fight.

The image of it—the beast—lit up behind her eyelids like a vision, fractured and uneven. It gnashed its jaws, tearing at its own skull with its yellowed claws in agony. The most memorable part; however, was its smell: decayed flesh emitting from its tough, hairy hide. Landree retched.

"Telos!" she gasped, eyes ripping open.

"Woah, you're alright!" Jane-Marie rushed to her side and grasped one of her hands.

Panic slammed into her like a tsunami. Landree sat up once more, causing the make-shift gurney to rock dangerously. She began to hyperventilate.

"Put her down," Clio ordered. The sunlight reflected from her bare head.

Grant released his side, sending her crashing onto the ground, bottom-first.

"Idiot!" Brenna barked.

Lifting her hand weakly, Landree shook her head. "I'm fine guys. Please, stop."

Brenna pursed her lips as her brows dipped up in concern. She lowered her end and dusted her slacks. "Sorry."

The group surrounded Landree, all kneeling by her side. Between their blood-stained clothes and muddy faces, everyone looked like the living dead. Jane-Marie, still holding Landree's hand, leaned in to rub her back. Tears spilled down her cheeks.

"You're going to be alright. We're almost there. Just

354 • J.E. KLIMOV

around the bend, really."

Landree's entire body felt like a massive pulse. Heat rushed to her core, leaving her fingertips and toes cold. "But you...Did you recover your memories?"

Jane-Marie blanched. "I hate to point fingers, but I think that was the doing of Nicholas, not Telos."

Heads turned to Nicholas. His eyes clouded as he stood.

"I tried to restore them."

"Tried?" Landree hung her head, sighed, then glared back at him. She fought the weak tingling in her legs to match his eye line. She prodded her finger against his chest. "What in the hell do you mean, tried? You can't tamper with someone's mind like that and not fix it!"

Nicholas froze and swallowed audibly.

"This is all your fault! You didn't need to screw up Jane-Marie's memories to help us defeat Telos! Am I right?" Landree swung her arms around to face Amelia, then Brenna, but her knees buckled.

Jane-Marie and Clio caught Landree and lowered her back on the ground. Although running on fumes, she wanted to throw her entire body weight onto Nicholas and pummel him with all she had.

"Hey, look at me," Clio pressed, voice steady and calm. She brushed strands of hair from Landree's eyes, her fingers lingering an extra beat. "You're injured. On top of that, you've overexerted yourself using your powers, limiting your body's ability to heal. I'm already working overtime here to expedite the process, so please relax."

Landree nodded, staring at the bloodstone lodged into

her forehead. Its orange and red hues glowed steadily. Clio cleared her throat, averted her eyes, and covered the stone with her hand.

"Ms. Clio, I didn't mean to—"

"It's quite alright. Just takes some getting used to," she replied.

"I know!" Amelia pipped up. She shuffled between Nicholas and Landree, giving him a shove before settling on her knees. "Landree, you'd say that tunic is much too large on you, right?"

"Yes?"

"May I?" Amelia asked, motioning scissors with her fingers.

"Of course."

Everyone watched as Amelia tore the hem of her tunic. After folding it over and across so it formed a triangular shape, Amelia wrapped it gingerly around Clio's head.

Clio sat back and traced her fingertips along the fabric. A smile crept up the corner of her lips. The silver wrap covered the bloodstone and draped over her head, the tip grazing the nape of her neck.

"Thank you," she whispered.

"I wear wraps all the time to manage this mess," Amelia replied, pointing at her bird's nest of a hair-do.

The girls broke into a chuckle, even Grant snorted. Landree was grateful. The brief levity was perhaps what she needed the most.

"Do you think you could walk the rest of the way?" Brenna asked.

"I'll definitely give it a shot."

Amelia and Clio helped Landree up, each hooking their arms around hers until she was steady on her feet. Jane-Marie offered a flask of water. Slurping it without abandon, Landree relished in the liquid cooling her insides. Pain continued to ebb and flow, but she felt it was at least easier to manage. All she needed to do now was focus on taking one step at a time. Nicholas positioned himself at the front of the group, but he stopped and looked back.

"Look. I'm really sorry. The burden of succeeding perhaps blurred my judgment. I didn't want to fail." His voice broke. "We *couldn't* fail. And with such little time, I needed to conjure a means to accelerate the process—to motivate. I-I promise I won't give up recovering Jane-Marie's memories."

Landree opened her mouth, but Jane-Marie waved her off.

"Thankfully you didn't wipe it all away! While I would like to remember the first part of my trip, the latter was certainly memorable enough. If...you can, that'll be great. If not, I forgive you."

Nicholas tilted his head in a slight nod. "Thank you."

Uncertainly swirled in Landree's chest.

How could she forgive him so quickly?

Patting her shoulder, Jane-Marie winked. "Hey. It's not up to you. It's up to me. After all we been through, I can live with it. And as much as a stick in the mud Nicholas can be, I know he didn't mean any harm."

Landree shot him a side-eye. "Fine," she grumbled.

"It's best we move on and out of this hellhole," Brenna added.

A collective agreement rose from the group. They trudged ahead, following a curvy trail of tallgrass and stone. Wildflowers waved to Landree in the breeze, their colorful petals reminding her of Goldenrod Village. She didn't know what to ultimately make of Amicita, home to an unbridled wilderness that took back its home from civilization. Once associated with fun and adventure, Landree didn't consider the dangers that came along with it. The insidious history of death and greed left a stain on this island, and she believed no one should trod on its shores anymore—even after destroying Telos.

Landree compulsively gripped the hilt of her sword. The opal warmed at her touch. Even after Telos had been destroyed, her gemstone still radiated with energy. She craned her neck and found the same glow emitting from Jane-Marie's sapphire. The ocean-blue stone seemed to illuminate the entire shield like a mirror facing the sun. Chewing up her lip, Landree picked up the pace until she caught up with Nicholas. The crunching beneath their boots filled the silence.

"If we destroyed Telos and its emerald, how come these gemstones seem like they're still...active?" asked Landree.

Nicholas shot her a pained look.

"What?"

"Remember when I told you the emerald existed in shards, and my initial plan was to find the other piece? It's still out there somewhere, and it seems like that needs to be destroyed too. I was wrong to hope destroying just Telos' shard was enough. That what the emerald represents—pure energy."

"Oh," Landree trailed off. "What does this mean?" She caught Grant eavesdropping from the corner of her eye.

His voice lowered. "I couldn't locate that shard. So, we just need make sure no one returns here. With Telos gone, The Luce shouldn't appear ever again."

Landree's eyes widened. "Are you kidding me? If we're lucky enough to make it home, there's no way the Republic isn't going to want every last detail."

Nicholas balled his hands into fists. "Then, we will lie."

His terse words astonished Landree. Her neck burned as she tugged on her collar. Fumbling for words, Landree was grateful when Brenna appeared at Nicholas' other shoulder.

"She has a point. The current Luce has faded. If we somehow make it back, Queen Baneberry will know it's possible to navigate to Amicita without its guidance. Even if they never know about the gemstones, her and possibly the leaders of the other countries will rush to mine them for their monetary value." She waggled her ring finger, and the amber washed her skin in orange light.

"Can your powers do anything?" Amelia quipped from behind. Her labored breath matched Landree's as they ascended a hill.

"I fear not. My powers control shadow, or interact with lighting somehow…It can't touch an energy source." Nicholas slouched. "I only know so much, and I'm afraid I'm out of answers."

Grant's voice rumbled to life. "Well, what if—"

"We don't need your sass right now," Brenna shot back.

Turning her neck, Landree observed Grant. He never crumbled under the weight of a snide comment, especially from Brenna. Although he kept up with the group, his listless eyes worried her.

"Are you okay—"

"Look!" Jane-Marie exclaimed.

Landree halted in her tracks. Amelia and Clio bumped into her. After issuing an apologetic smile, Landree glanced at Jane-Marie, who was jumping in place and clapping her hands in glee.

"Come!" she said, beckoning Landree to follow.

She tore after her friend to the crest of the hill, inhaling the salt-laden air. Hope filled her lungs, numbing her pain. Light pierced through puffy, white clouds and highlighted a pebbled-beach five-hundred feet on the other side. Landree pressed her hands to her cheeks and squeaked. "We've made it back."

"I never thought I'd be so happy to see our shipwreck," Amelia said, catching up to them. She lifted a hand to shield the sun. "Where are Giles and his crew?"

"Who knows? I'm sure they're around somewhere!" Jane-Marie shouted. "Come on!" She sprinted down the other side of the hill, nearly tripping over her laces that had come loose.

Amelia ran after her, shouting warnings in her wake. Resting her hands on her hips, Landree shook her head while Clio and Brenna helped Grant down the path.

That left her with Nicholas. He stood beside Landree, silent. The two observed the group cheering their way toward the beach. While the crow's nest poked from the sea, unchanged since the wreck, most of the ship fragments had migrated into a single open-air encampment. Navy tunics and slacks that had long since dried, swayed on a rope from one end to the other. An empty pot sat over a circle of ash. Landree even spotted the makings of a raft nearby made from crates and banana leaves.

Well, half a raft.

Jane-Marie cupped her hands around her mouth. "Hello?"

Landree's hope fizzled and stalled. She leaned over until her shoulder touched his. Nicholas jumped.

"Sorry," she muttered. "But, is it me, or should there be at least one person at camp at all times?"

He grunted.

"I dunno. Just seems odd," Landree added as Amelia and Brenna joined in on the shouting. The more they ran around, the more her stomach sank. "You didn't have anything to do with this, did you? Another stupid challenge?"

Nicholas lifted a brow and shook his head. "No, I swear. I didn't do anything. I'm sure they left early to search for supplies since they never heard from us."

Landree's heart skipped a beat. "And if not?"

Nicholas clasped her forearm. Landree detected a tremor in his grip. After releasing a long, audible breath, he shared a tight smile.

"We'll just find another way home," he replied, gesturing

to the opal on Landree's sword.

By now, Landree's nerves fired alarms all over her body. Her tongue clung to the roof of her mouth as she broke into a cold sweat. Gripping him harder, she leaned forward until she was inches away from his face.

"Is everything okay?" she asked, voice low and slow. Landree stared deep into his eyes, searching for an answer before he could even reply.

Nicholas blinked rapidly and cleared his throat. "Of course. We're going to be all right."

ABOUT THE AUTHOR

J.E. Klimov grew up in a small suburb in Massachusetts. After graduating from Massachusetts College of Pharmacy and Health Sciences, she obtained her PharmD and became a pharmacist; however, her true passion was writing and illustration.

Ever since J.E. Klimov was little, she dreamed of sharing her stories with the world. From scribbling plotlines instead of taking notes in school, to bringing her characters to life through sketches, Klimov's ideas ranged from fantasy to thriller fiction. She had most recently completed a fantasy trilogy, "The Aeonians," with Silver Leaf Books.

You can follow J.E. Klimov and stay in tune for news on her sequel among other things on her blog: http://jelliotklimov.weebly.com/, Twitter: @klimov_author, and Facebook page: @klimovauthor.